THE SOUND OF YOU

ALSO BY SIMON DOYLE

Snow Boys
This is Not a Vampire Story

THE SOUND OF YOU

SIMON DOYLE

SDPRESS
LONGFORD

First published in 2025 by
SD Press
Unit 1A Heatherview Business Park, Athlone Road SSC8117
Longford, Co Longford N39KD82, Ireland

ISBN 978 1 917539 01 2

Cover illustration © Peter Gillespie
Design by SD Press

A CIP catalogue record of this book
is available from the British Library and the
Library of Trinity College Dublin

Typeset in Anko by SD Press

For Grandad Tommy.

And for everyone who listens with their heart.

CHAPTER 1

Tommy McDaid had been standing up. And then he wasn't. That's how quickly his death came.

There was life, and then there was nothing. And it didn't matter how you tried to explain it—he was old, it was inevitable—it didn't make a difference. Not to me. He was gone, and that was all that mattered. Mum would tell you I was the one to find him, but that's not strictly true. I didn't find him dead, I watched him die. That's a huge distinction.

We'd been standing in the kitchen, a stack of my half-finished pencil sketches spread across the table and Grandad's art supplies on the countertop, a smear of crimson paint on the back of his knuckles, the tube still in his other fist. And he pulled a face, like he wanted to cough, just for a second, before his body went limp. He didn't fall back or forward—he just slumped to the floor in a heap with half of an unfinished sigh.

And Tommy McDaid was gone.

I knew it even when he fell, when I shook him but he wouldn't open his eyes. I got him onto his back and checked for a pulse, pressed my cheek against his mouth to feel for his breath, and then I put my hands together on his chest and pumped until my arms ached.

The paramedics pulled me off him, twenty minutes or two hours later.

Mum told me I wasn't crying. My face was set with determination. But the grief hit me when the ambulance crew carried him away on a stretcher with a sheet pulled over his face. I stood on the grass that I'd cut the day before while he'd watched from the porch and said, "You missed a bit," and my legs buckled from under me. I knelt in the fresh cuttings that hadn't been raked and no amount of coaxing from my mum or stepdad would get me to move, not until my friend, Ryan, came over and gripped my face in his hands, forcing me to look at him. Forcing me to stand up.

He led me inside, walked me up the stairs to my bedroom, and helped me onto the bed where he sat on the floor beside me until it was dark out and darker inside.

We didn't speak, and at some point, my tears stopped, dried and crusty around my swollen eyes. I stared at the wallpaper, knowing Ryan was there but not really caring.

Not until he said, "I need to go home. Will you be all right?"

I didn't answer him. He patted my leg, hauled himself off the floor where he'd been sitting for hours, and I heard him go downstairs, heard him say something to my mother. "I'll tell the teachers. Don't worry about school."

Mum tried to give him money, he told me later. I'm not sure why. I don't even think she knew why. But friends are there for each other. That's what they do.

He was there for me at the funeral, too, staring at me while I had to get up and recite a poem. Something about the end. Something about beginnings. Before we went into the church, he said, "Just look at me. Imagine nobody else is there."

I'd nodded. Tried to say something snide to make him laugh. But the words wouldn't come out. And I couldn't look at him while I stood at the lectern and read the lines on the page. I couldn't look at anyone.

After the funeral, everybody came back to the house for tea and sandwiches—except there were more wine glasses and beer bottles than teacups. Ryan stood by my side, fielding condolences, saying, "I know. Such a shame," when people kept saying, "I can't believe it," or "He's in a better place now."

But the ground wasn't a better place. How could it be?

Later, when everyone had gone home and the house smelled like perfume and cigarettes, I sat at the kitchen table, staring at the spot where Grandad Tommy had been just a few days ago. Ryan walked across the room, right where Tommy should have been, and he scraped out the chair beside me, sitting down heavily. His tie had been loosened and his suit jacket was off. I'd seen him in a maroon school blazer for years, but in a black funeral suit he looked different. Older.

He said, "You good?"

I twisted my hands in my lap. I knew what he'd said, but

it didn't register as a question. He had to ask it again before I nodded.

There was an open bottle of whiskey on the countertop and Ryan reached for it, sniffed the neck, and then held it towards me.

"Piss off," I said.

"Nobody's watching. And you could be doing with it."

"I'm all right."

He took a quick swig from the bottle, wiped the back of his hand across his lips, and then smeared it on my jacket sleeve. "You smell like booze now; you might as well take a drink."

So I did. It burned on the way down and threatened to come back up, but I sealed my lips until the feeling passed.

"Better?" he asked.

I shook my head. What was better supposed to feel like?

Ryan drummed his fingers on the polished wood of the table, then he tilted his head, angling it into my view. "Owen," he said. "O when the saints go marching." Owen the Saint, that's what he called me. But I felt far from it.

"I'm all right," I told him.

"You don't have to be," he said.

I looked at him then. We'd been friends for more than eight years, but every time I looked at him, I saw a different Ryan. I used to say he was made of playdough—he had a face for every occasion. Not in a two-faced way, but in a way that slotted neatly into whatever situation he found himself in. Sad Ryan, happy Ryan, enthusiastic Ryan. He'd shift his mouth, mould his eyes, and there'd be a new Ryan, ready to step up.

"It's okay not to be," he said. Motivational Ryan. Like a poster on a classroom wall.

I pushed the bottle of whiskey away from me just as Mum came into the kitchen, still wearing her black dress but with her heels removed. She looked tired. More than usual.

She smiled, briefly, flicked the kettle on and stood by the window, facing away from us.

And Ryan put his hand on top of mine, warm fingers full of sympathy. "I better get going."

"See you," I said.

He touched Mum's shoulder for a second when he passed her, and her smile returned, just for a moment, until we were alone. Then she stared through the window at the darkness of the garden, listening to the marquee flapping in the cool breeze. The funeral home had brought it, a rental. I didn't know when they'd remove it. Tomorrow, probably, along with every shred of evidence that Grandad Tommy was ever here.

"Where's Mick?" I asked, but I could see the glow of my stepdad's cigarette under the marquee outside.

"He only smokes when he drinks," Mum said. "Don't ever start," she told me.

"I've grown attached to my lungs. I don't think I'd get along well with somebody else's."

She nodded. "Don't let Mick hear you say that or he'll be asking for one of yours soon."

Grandad Tommy used to smoke, I was told, but I'd never seen him with a cigarette. It wasn't lung cancer that killed him, it was a subarachnoid haemorrhage. Nothing to do with spiders, apparently.

"Where's Tommy Two?" I asked. The kettle boiled and the

switch flicked off. Nobody called Mum's older brother Junior the way they do on TV when you're named after your father. They called him Tommy Two because Grandad was always number one.

Mum didn't pick the kettle up, didn't grab a mug. She leaned against the counter and stared through the window at the dark, at the pull of Mick's cigarette. "He's sleeping it off on the sofa. He'll have an awful headache in the morning."

I looked at the whiskey bottle on the table and wondered how strong the smell was. If I kissed Mum's cheek, would she know I'd had a sip?

"Go on up to bed," she said.

I looked at the spot on the floor where Tommy had fallen and when I stood up, I walked the other way around the table, avoiding the weight of the emptiness.

Mum rubbed my back on the way out of the kitchen. She said, "Hang your suit jacket up. I'll wash your shirt in the morning."

"I'm not going to school," I said, unprovoked. Tomorrow was Friday.

Mum shook her head. "You've missed all week. One more day won't hurt."

At the top of the stairs, I stopped. Tommy's bedroom door was opposite mine, the door ajar, a black ribbon pinned to it. Anyone who ventured upstairs during the wake, while his body had been on display in the living room for the previous three days, would have known not to open the door. You don't enter the sanctuary of the dead. But the door was open now, just a crack.

I hesitated. I'm not sure if I wanted to go in or just close the door properly, but when I put my hand on the brass doorhandle, instinct made me push it wide. It smelled like Grandad inside. Paint and woodsmoke. Distinctive.

The room was dark, the curtains drawn, and the mirror on the wall had been covered with a dark sheet. Tommy's collection of easels was propped against the side of the wardrobe where they always were, blank canvases stacked beside them. His paints would be in a purpose-built chest of drawers at the other side of the room, behind a combination lock that only two people knew the code to—Grandad and me. The lock was there to stop my younger cousins from getting at them and either smearing them on the walls or eating them the way kids always do with stuff they're not supposed to.

I pushed the door wider and stepped over the threshold. There was a single black shoe at the bottom of the bed. Not one of Grandad's. When I stepped around the door, I stopped. Tommy Two was sprawled across the bed, lying on his stomach, one shoe on, suit jacket buckling at the shoulders where he'd pushed one hand under his cheek. There was a glass of dark amber whiskey on the nightstand beside the large-print novel Grandad would never finish reading.

I crept across the floor. He was drunk, drooling, and his breathing was heavy and wet. I took the glass to the bathroom, poured it down the sink and filled it with water before returning it to the nightstand beside him. He didn't wake, but I heard him whimper as I pulled the door closed behind me.

I couldn't sleep that night. I lay in bed, staring at the ceiling, listening to Tommy Two's noisy snores and Mum's whispered voice from her bedroom with Mick. And then I sat up, propping the pillows behind me, and looked at the collection of sketches on the floor in the corner of my room, the ones that had been on the table the day Grandad Tommy had fallen down and didn't get back up.

Art was his life. He wasn't famous, but he sold enough paintings over the years to be able to afford new supplies when he needed them. In the nineties, way before I was born, one of the smaller galleries in Dublin had displayed a dozen of his landscapes.

Watercolours weren't my thing. Paint wasn't my thing, to be honest, no matter how often he tried to convince me to give it a go. I was better with a pencil or charcoal. When I was six, he took me to the cemetery—the same one he was spending the night in now—and he beat down the bracken by the older gravestones, the ones from the 1800s. We held sheets of paper against the stones and rubbed charcoal over them and then he bought me ice cream. Because morbidity loves dessert.

I still had those rubbings, somewhere in the attic, rolled up and tied with string.

There were a million sketchbooks at the bottom of my wardrobe, filled with anime characters and Lamborghinis and trees with no leaves, twisting branches sprawling across the pages. By the time I hit high school, I had gone through a phase of drawing fruit with no outlines, just shadows made by holding my pencil at an acute angle to the paper, sweeping into circles of apples or the stretch of a banana.

And there was a spiralbound book filled almost entirely with half-finished sketches of Ryan—his face, his eyes, his smile, back when we were fourteen. A Frankenstein collection of body parts on different pages. I kept meaning to throw it away, but I never did.

Maybe I never would.

A car turned at the end of the street, headlights playing across my ceiling, and when the room went dark again, I shuffled back down the bed, burying my head in the pillows where I could muffle the drone of Tommy Two.

Mum and Mick had gone quiet, and I couldn't tell if they were asleep or if they were staring at their ceiling the way I was staring at mine. Most kids get two grandads and only one dad. I only ever had one grandad, and Mick was a second father. Not that he ever asked me to call him that.

But now I had no grandad.

And an ache where he used to be.

The sketches in the corner of the room were silent, and they remained that way until morning when the sunlight brightened the corner, catching the edge of the paper in a way that made them glow.

At nine-fifteen, I got a message from Ryan. A link to an American high school band on a football field, trumpeting out a terrible rendition of "Oh When the Saints Go Marching In".

Then a follow-up text. *If you provide the fish and chips, I'll bring your homework tonight. Mr Madden misses you and sends you sloppy kisses.*

I left him on read, like I'd been doing all week. Not because I didn't want to reply, but because I didn't know what to say. And Ryan understood that.

A few minutes later, he sent a new text. *I see you peeking. Go back to sleep. That's an order.*

And then another. *Seriously. If I have to come over there and bop you on the head to knock you out, I will.*

He would, too. So I swiped the final notification away and I closed my eyes.

But sleep never came.

CHAPTER 2

Nobody got out of bed on Friday until eleven. I slept in short bursts, jolting awake for no reason, knowing I'd nodded off but not really feeling it, and eventually I heard somebody shuffling around in the bathroom and going downstairs.

I sat on the edge of my bed, feeling the chill of a spring morning against my legs. It was that time of year when the central heating had been shut off, but the mornings were still lacking. I pulled on yesterday's socks, just because they were right there, and when I was done in the bathroom, I crept downstairs in my dressing gown, expecting to see Mum making toast or clearing up what was left of yesterday's post-funeral party. The rest of the world might call it a celebration of life. In Ireland, it's most definitely a party. Alcohol and music and somebody's awful singing. A solitary voice letting an old folk song into the room that made everyone else fall silent to listen and applaud and ask for another.

Another song.

Another drink.

In the kitchen, it wasn't Mum or Mick. It was Tommy Two, still in yesterday's suit. He stood with his back to the fridge, a cold glass of water pressed against his forehead, and his tie was hooked up around his shoulder like it didn't want to be there. His hair—dark with slender fingers of grey—stood up in clumps like lazy sentries.

"Morning," he croaked.

I nodded. "Headache?"

The cold glass was sweating against his skin, and he rolled it across his forehead before drinking from it. "What time is it?" he asked. I could hear the sickness in his voice.

"Eleven."

"Jesus," he said. He pulled out a chair at the table and slumped into it, scratching the stubble at his cheek. He was divorced, living alone in a small flat on the south side of Dublin, thirty minutes away, but he would swing by the house to see Grandad about once a week. They used to go fishing together. Or at least Tommy Two would fish while Grandad would set up an easel and wash green paint across his canvas as if he was mocking the murky brown of the bay out at Bull Island.

I filled the kettle and switched it on. My stomach wasn't ready for food and Tommy looked like he might hurl if I mentioned toast or eggs. I stood by the counter, looking at the floor, remembering the slump of Grandad Tommy's body, and my uncle pressed his elbows into the table and covered his face with his hands.

I made him a milky tea, just the way he liked it, but instead of two sugars, I dropped in a third. That was good for hangovers, wasn't it?

He took it without a word and when I sat opposite him, he stared at me as if he wasn't really seeing me.

I didn't know what to say.

Tommy Two swallowed his tea and I heard the noise of it going down in the stillness of late morning. There was a creak of floorboards above us. Mum or Mick was getting up.

Behind me, the door to the living room was closed. That's where the coffin had been for three days, and I wasn't sure I ever wanted to go in there again. How could I watch TV, knowing that Grandad Tommy's remains had been laid out where the sofa usually sat? It had been pushed against the far wall for the duration of the wake, and somebody had moved it back yesterday once the coffin had been carried out to the hearse. Funeral fairies, cleaning up after the dead.

When Mum came into the kitchen, she touched the back of my head, a greeting, and then leaned across the table and kissed her brother's cheek. She switched the kettle on even after I told her it was just boiled, and then she said, "You stink of booze."

I thought she meant me, that single sip of whiskey Ryan had made me drink, but Tommy Two said, "So be it," which was his way of telling her to mind her own business.

I looked at him, then her. Mornings weren't always this awkward.

Mum said, "You all right?"

I nodded. Shook my head. I wasn't sure. "I don't know

what to do today," I told her. I didn't really know what to do with my hands, never mind the rest of the day. I picked up a coaster and flipped it in my fingers. Sat it down. Slid it across the table. Pushed my hands into the pockets of my dressing gown. Both of my legs were bouncing with restlessness.

"Go for a walk," Mum said.

"Paint the fence," Tommy Two said.

Mum got a mug and dropped a teabag into it. "Mick painted the fence two months ago. What's wrong with it?"

But Tommy Two only shook his head and then finished his tea. He stood up, wobbled, and said, "I should go."

"You can't drive home like that," Mum told him.

And I left them to their argument while I showered and crawled back into bed.

There was an absence of sound from Grandad. It wasn't just him missing but all the noises that went with him. The soft stamp of his cane on the tiled floor of the kitchen or his coughing in the bathroom. The classical radio station that would probably never be switched on again. The scrape of heavy plant pots in the greenhouse as he rotated his tomato plants and strawberries. And the slap of his three-inch paint brushes on the side of his easel when he cleaned them.

For the whole weekend, the only thing there was absence.

When Monday barged into the back end of Sunday, I was grateful for the change at last. I didn't want to go to school, but it was better than sitting at home doing nothing, listening to the silence that filled the gap between Mum and Mick, eating dinner without words because a mouth full of food meant not having to speak, and not speaking was easier than stuffing the void with emptiness.

Nothing was any different than before—the bus ride, the school gates, the packed hallways and dented lockers. The smell of disinfectant that failed to cover the stench of mildew and the sweat of teenage boys that had seeped into the woodwork over the course of a hundred and fifty years. When you breathed in, you were inhaling the memory of a million boys since the school opened in 1874. It used to be a Christian Brothers school, where monks would beat the crap out of you if you got your sums wrong. It became a state school forty years ago. But the smells never changed.

The only thing that was different was the looks that people gave me, at least the people that knew me. Grandparents died, I knew. People die all the time and nobody bats an eyelid. Andrew McGovern's grandad had passed away at the start of the year and he took two weeks off, and when he came back, he acted as though nothing was different. Like life just carries on regardless.

"Hey," Gavin O'Neill said in the corridor. I sat beside him in maths class.

I nodded.

Gavin's smile was tilted and nervous, like it always was. "Heard about your Grandad. Sorry, man."

"Yeah."

"You okay?"

I nodded because the question didn't deserve a true answer. I carried on down the hall, hoping the bell would ring soon, but it didn't, and Gavin kept walking with me.

"Was he old?"

I stared at him.

"I mean, did he have a long life?"

I adjusted the weight of my backpack and shifted my sketchbook from under one arm to the other. It was too big to fit in my schoolbag. The bell broke into the crowded hallway and Gavin was watching me until the ringing stopped.

"Not long enough," I said. And Gavin lowered his gaze, his smile gone. He slipped into his classroom and I watched him go. When the hallway was empty, I turned, wondered if I should go to the office to explain my few days off last week, but thought better of it. Mum had probably spoken to them days ago, before the funeral.

I stood there, in the empty hallway, listening to the murmur of kids in classrooms, the scrape of chairs and the quiet noise of chalk on boards. And then I had to think about what day it was, what class I should be in. I checked my phone to make sure. Monday. English.

I could cope with that.

I took the stairs to the next floor and kept my head down as I slipped into class. The teacher said, "Thanks for joining us, Mr Kelly."

I shrugged and took my seat beside Ryan, who nudged his elbow against my arm and smiled one of those dimpled grins that I used to love but didn't enjoy this morning.

"You good?" he whispered. Somebody needs to write a book on what to say to people after their grandad dies that isn't just *you good?*

I smiled at him. I didn't really want to say it out loud. And Ryan put his hand on top of mine, as tactile as ever, filling the space between us with normality. He used to say, "No homo," when he did it, back when we were twelve. But now he threw himself around my body like he belonged there, even though he was straight. He was comfortable like that, knew who he was before most people did. And I admired him for that.

"It's Bolognese for lunch," Ryan whispered, as the teacher wrote something on the board about Hamlet.

"How do you know?"

"I'm not at liberty to say."

"Your mum?" I asked. It wasn't a yo-mamma joke—Ryan's mum worked in the canteen—but Ryan always took it that way.

"*Your* mum," he said, stamping on my foot to trip me. "But seriously. Are you okay?"

"I'm fine."

"I mean about your grandad, not the Bolognese."

I smiled, couldn't help it. Then I let it slip away when the teacher said, "O that this too, too solid flesh would melt." He could quote Shakespeare at you until your ears bled.

Ryan muttered, "That's what she said."

But I was done smiling for the day. I'd let one escape me. There wouldn't be another.

At lunchtime, we sat together at a table near the window, and I watched Ryan roll spaghetti onto his fork and chase after a meatball that refused to be speared. The Bolognese was claggy and cold, but Ryan would eat anything if he had enough salt to cover it with.

"Are you getting the bus after school?"

I had my sketchbook on the table, a brand new one that I'd bought two weeks ago, its pages still empty except for a smudge of charcoal on the cover near the spiral binding, and I pushed the food around my tray without eating it. "I'm going to head to the art room after class."

"What are you working on?" Ryan asked. He wiped sauce from his chin with the back of his hand, picked up my sketchbook, and flipped through the empty pages. He glanced at me over the top of it, then back at the book. "Is this your minimalism phase?" He turned the page, twisted the book so it was landscape. "What do you call this one?" Then he flipped the page again, held it out like it was a centrefold pin-up, and he whistled, low and seductive. "Gorgeous," he said. "You should frame this one." He turned it so I could see and pointed at the corner. "You forgot to sign it."

"My bad," I told him. The blank page mocked me. "I never know how to start a new book."

Ryan closed it and put it back on the table. "Start where you always start: with me." He tilted his head, fingers under his chin like he was posing, and the light from the window caught him in a way that used to make my chest ache. In a way that would look amazing on paper.

"I'm good," I said, turning my attention back to the tray of stodgy food.

"Fine," Ryan complained. "I'll pose naked for you. Just once. Still life. But you've got to make me look good. Everywhere."

"Piss off," I said. There wasn't a smile.

"Is that a smile?"

"No."

Ryan leaned across the table. "Are you sure? That's totally a smile."

"Are you done?" I asked. And Ryan sat back, finally speared that wayward meatball, and chewed it with a frown. His teasing came naturally and usually I liked it. It never came in anger, always love.

"I'm an ally," Ryan had told me once, when we were thirteen.

"A what?"

"An ally. I'm here for the people."

"What people?"

"All the people. The LGBTQ+ community."

"Okay," I said. We hadn't been talking about that when Ryan brought it up out of the blue.

"I'm just saying," Ryan said. "It's important that people know."

"What people?" I asked again.

And Ryan had smiled. "All the people. Anyway. That's all I'm saying. I'm an ally. Okay?"

"Okay," I said. And I sort of didn't say I was gay but sort of didn't say I wasn't, either. And Ryan went to Dublin Pride with me that summer.

After lunch, I sat through my classes in a quiet numbness that hadn't left me since last week. If I thought hard enough, I could drown out the swell of voices. I didn't have a lot of classes with Ryan any longer—he was in the advanced sets for most subjects because cool people can study too—and when the final bell sounded, I packed up my things and headed to the art department.

Ryan was at the end of the corridor under the strip-light that was yellowing with age and when I approached, he waved.

"I'm not sketching you," I said.

"Spoilsport," Ryan said. "I'm just checking on you. Making sure you're still with us."

"Where else would I be?"

Ryan threw his arm around my neck, half a headlock, half a hug, and said, "Want me to wait for you? We can walk into town together and get pizza. My treat."

"Why are you always thinking about your stomach?"

"Somebody has to."

I shook my head. "I'm all right. See you tomorrow?"

When I was alone, I went into the art room, spoke to Mr Madden briefly, and then sat at the back of the room with my sketchbook for as long as Mr Madden would allow me. The art teacher was grading Year 7 projects, the scratch of his pen interrupting the silence, and I opened my sketchbook to the first page. I really did hate a brand new book that had no essence of anything inside it.

I pulled out a 2B pencil and sharpened it with a craft knife. Mr Madden said using a mechanical sharpener was like grating cheese with a tennis racquet—it gets the job done but there's no passion in it. And art wasn't art if there was no passion.

When I finally put the pencil to the paper, I closed my eyes. I didn't know what I was going to draw, but I slid the lead across the page with purpose. The first stroke was done. Whatever came next would happen or it wouldn't. That was art.

As the pencil bled onto the thick paper, I kept the momentum going. A bird. A tree. Abstract in the long strokes. Just shapes and textures and motion. The faint twisting of jagged branches and the hoot of an owl lost somewhere in the dark of the pencil marks.

My strokes were harder now than they used to be, less

delicate, more deliberate than they needed. But the weight was in the detail, because the pencil was crying where I couldn't. I knew that in a way that I shouldn't.

And when I paused, wiping a smudge from the side of my hand, I saw Grandad Tommy in the rough texture of the shadows. And again on the previous page. Faceless and featureless but there.

I closed the book.

Mr Madden said, "You finished? I'm about to lock up."

I hadn't realised I'd been sitting there for ninety minutes. I packed up my things and when I got to the door, Mr Madden cleared his throat.

"I'm sorry for your loss." Teachers always knew these things, like there was a weekly email blast or something.

"Thanks," I said. Had said it a thousand times today.

"You can put it in your art," Mr Madden said.

"Sorry?"

His beard was an art piece, like something from a Dali painting, angled and untameable. He eased his hand over it now before saying, "I don't mean to insinuate myself into your grief, but what better way to let it out than in your art? Art is driven by emotion—I've been telling my students this for years."

"I don't know how," I said, but I knew I was already doing it, finding Tommy's shadow in the darkness between strokes. "What if it doesn't help?"

"Why wouldn't it?"

I didn't have an answer to that. So I nodded, slipped out of the classroom ahead of Mr Madden, and stood outside the school gates at the bus stop, long after everyone else had gone home and the spring sunlight had cooled and turned from gold to grey.

At home, I ate dinner in my room. Mum tried to convince me to sit downstairs with her and Mick, but I told her I had a lot of homework to get through. I had a week to catch up on, so it wasn't a lie.

She checked on me twice that evening to make sure I'd eaten, while I sat at the desk in the fading light, reading *Hamlet* and not recognising a single word. Finding recurring decimals out of fractions. Ignoring my sketchbook.

Because ignoring it was better than seeing Grandad again.

Anything was better than that.

CHAPTER 3

Last night, my dreams were filled with texture. Light and shade, but with an absence of colour. I'm not sure what that meant. I heard a dog barking but I couldn't find it and when I turned my head, everything was dark. In the opposite direction, there was only light. And in my terror, I walked towards the darkness, groping blindly in front of me and calling the dog's name. I heard him barking and I clapped my hands.

But I was alone.

I woke before dawn, shivering, with my quilt on the floor, and there was an actual dog barking somewhere outside. I got out of bed and pulled the curtains wide to look, but the street was too dim to see much, yellow puddles of light under the streetlamps that lit up nothing but the pavement and the bins that had been put out the night before.

The dog barked again, lonely and pitiful, and then it was silent.

I couldn't get back to sleep, waiting as the sun rose, inching across my carpet like ants pulling the sunlight behind them, and I buried my face in the blankets until my alarm broke the silence. I snoozed it, and snoozed it again, and finally got out of bed, more tired than when I got into it last night. I wanted to have the flu, a cough, anything that would get me out of going to school, and when I looked in the bathroom mirror, I was certain my eyes were bloodshot and my cheeks were burning.

But downstairs, Mum pressed the back of her hand to my forehead and said, "You're all right."

I tried to cough.

"Owen," she said. "I know you're sad. You're allowed to be. But you'll have to be sad at school. You can't miss any more pop quizzes."

"You sound like a teacher," I told her.

"I sound like your mother," she said. She pushed my fringe off my forehead and tapped it twice with her finger. Mum's rules.

So I stood at the bus stop and I stood at the school gate and I stood at my locker that had the faded remains of some long-past graffiti that discoloured the grey paintwork. I pressed my head against the metal and waited for the second bell to ring, the one that meant get the hell into your class-room or you'll be sorry.

And I felt Ryan step into the space behind me, his breath on my neck, and he whispered, "Rise and shine, Clementine."

I stood up straight. Looked at him.

And he said, "What's wrong?"

Was I that transparent? I shrugged. "Nothing," I said. And then the bell sounded, glaring above our heads. Lockers were slammed and classroom doors were shut.

And Ryan caught my arm to stop me from walking away. When the hallway was empty, he said, "Shall we welch it?"

That was our code to take an unsanctioned mental health day. A Raquel Welch day. Ryan came up with it after we'd watched *Shawshank Redemption* where Andy escaped from prison behind a Raquel Welch poster.

I nodded, and Ryan pulled my sketchpad out of my locker, gripped it under his arm, and nudged me towards the end of the hall where it opened into the offices and school reception. We hovered at the corner until Maisie the receptionist turned from the desk to photocopy something, and then we made a break for it, dashing through the doors, down the slope of the wheelchair access, and around the side of the building into the carpark.

"Boys!" somebody shouted from behind us.

We stopped. Turned. We hadn't even made it as far as the gate.

"Did you not hear the bell?" Mr McLaughlin said. "What are your names?"

Ryan waved my sketchbook above his head. "Art project, sir. We're drawing cars."

Mr McLaughlin looked at his watch. "Does Mr Madden know you're out here?"

"Yes, sir."

He looked like he was about to haul us inside by the ear, but then he said, "You're the Kelly boy, aren't you?"

I nodded. "Yes, sir. Owen Kelly."

"You won the art award last year?"

"First place."

Mr McLaughlin checked his watch again. I could see in his face that he knew about my grandad. "Make sure you don't leave the school grounds," he said. "I'll be watching."

We smiled. Ryan opened the sketchbook and looked around the carpark. And when Mr McLaughlin had gone inside, we ducked between cars and slipped through the gate onto the street.

"I knew your art would come in handy one day," Ryan said.

I shook my head. "Having a dead grandad did that, not my art. Didn't you see his face?"

Ryan shrugged and handed the sketchbook to me before we jumped on a bus and headed into town, making sure our jackets were zipped up so any undercover truancy officers wouldn't see our school crests and know which school we'd escaped from. "Welch Day," Ryan said, offering me a fist to bump.

We had breakfast at a tiny café in a narrow street on the north side of the river, and while Ryan was shovelling a mountain of baked beans onto a slice of dark toast, I said, "It's Tuesday, isn't it?"

He nodded and licked his fingers.

"Your mum works Tuesdays, doesn't she?"

"Balls," he said. He tapped his phone screen as if it would lie to him and tell him it was any other day but Tuesday. "I'll have to go back for lunch. If I don't wave at her in the lunch queue she'll know we made a break for it."

"So much for Welch Day," I said.

"A half day will have to do."

After breakfast, Ryan bought snacks—the only time he wasn't eating was when he was sleeping, and even then he was probably dreaming about food—and we headed into the back streets towards the west side of the city, where the shops gave way to houses and the roads narrowed. We slipped down an alleyway and crossed a wasteland area that smelled like a sheep had died there recently among the upturned shopping trolleys and busted footballs, and then we skidded down a grassy slope where a wide stream trickled along a rocky bed.

It used to be a river, Ryan told me once, but I didn't believe him. "Industrialisation," he said. "We take from the land and give nothing back."

"Since when have you been an ecowarrior?" I laughed.

We sat on the rocks at the back of the stream and Ryan shared his bag of snacks, and when the sun was high enough to breach the nearby trees, it shimmered in the gurgling water, coins of light spilling among the stones. I opened my sketchbook and got the tin of charcoal sticks from the bottom of my bag, then I mimicked the flow of the stream on my page, swooping around rocks and over pebbles, tufts of grass and the spread of moss.

Ryan chugged on a can of Fanta and I flipped the page, drawing in the side of his face, his hand, the drink's can.

"You're doing it again," he said.

"Doing what?"

"Staring."

I looked away from him. "You said 'sketching' wrong."

"Let me see," he said. When I held it up, he smiled. "Is my

ear really that small?"

"I drew it bigger so you don't get a complex about it."

Ryan covered his ears with his hands. He said, "You know what they say about a guy with small ears."

"What?"

"Anything they want—he can't hear them." He threw a stone, unwrapped another sweet, and then said, "How's your mum?" he moulded his face to become Caring Ryan. When he looked at me, I saw the compassion in his eyes, like he actually cared. Not the false pity I saw in everybody else.

I shrugged and closed my sketchbook. "Sometimes she's normal. Sometimes she's not. She burnt the spuds last night."

"How do you burn spuds?"

"No idea, but she did it. I still ate them, though. Didn't have the heart to say anything."

Ryan crunched his sweet and waited until he was finished with it before speaking again. He picked up a pebble, rubbed it between his thumb and finger, and then dropped it into the stream where the water was running too slowly to splash. He said, "It'll take time. She'll be all right soon enough."

"Mr Madden says I should put my grief into my art," I told him.

"How do you do that?"

I shrugged again. "Cry on the paper? I don't know."

"Will you draw Tommy?" Ryan asked.

I remembered the shadows of him in the sketches I drew yesterday, the curve of his back and the wave of his hand. "Maybe," I said, because those shadows hadn't been intentional and if I tried I'd probably fail to capture him right.

Ryan stood up. "We should head back to school now

before the dinner bell. And you," he said, "should paint."

"Paint what?" I asked, packing up my charcoal sticks and licking my fingers to wipe the dust off my hands.

"Whatever you want," Ryan said.

"I'm no good with paints. You know that."

He turned to me. "You don't have to be good. You just have to do it." He picked up his discarded sweet wrappers and stuffed them into his pockets. "For Tommy," he said. "For G-Dawg." Ryan was the only person in the world who could get away with calling Grandad G-Dawg. Tommy would beam with pride when Ryan said it. He was everybody's grandad, not just mine.

When we got back to the bus stop, I had the idea that maybe Ryan was right. I wasn't any good at sketching with pencils when I started. Why should it be any different with paint? I didn't have to be good at it. I just had to do it, like he said.

The bus pulled up and Ryan got on ahead of me, but I stayed on the pavement under the shadow of the bus shelter. Ryan turned, looking out at me, and I said, "You go."

"What about lunch?" he asked.

"I'm going to paint," I told him.

"Now?"

I shrugged. "Why not?"

And he nodded. "Make sure you draw a car," he said, "in case Mr McLaughlin checks up on us." And then he waved and I crossed the street to catch a bus in the opposite direction.

At home, I slipped in the back door and announced loudly that I was home, just in case anyone was there, but the house was empty. I dropped my bag and sketchbook in my room and then stood on the landing, hovering outside Grandad Tommy's room, breathing into the shallow of sadness and apprehension.

I pushed his door open. The curtains were still closed, and I don't think anybody had been in there since Tommy Two on Friday morning. I didn't turn the light on. I went to the far wall, to Tommy's tall chest of drawers, and I twisted the wheels on the combination lock to open it.

Oils. Acrylics. Watercolours.

Brushes that ranged from narrow points to four-inch blocks. Palette knives and masking fluid. Everything was meticulously organised, even the paint tubes, from light to dark, colours chasing into each other towards Mars Black, like me chasing dogs in my dreams.

I returned to the watercolour drawer and picked out a handful of tubes in colours that I figured would be enough, and then I took one of his unused canvases and a small easel, and I looked around his room as if he was standing behind me, encouraging me, before I closed his door and carried everything down to the park.

We'd had an unusually warm week—"Tommy's doing," Mick had said, pointing at the sky like Grandad was up there pulling cranks and levers to bring the sun out—and some of the spring flowers were beginning to open. Yellows and oranges and blues. Leaves were budding on the trees that hung over the path from the wide gate to the duck pond and I heard the coo of pigeons on the hunt for food from passing strangers.

I found an empty bench near the pond, one that Tommy and I would sit on years ago while he painted and I sketched the ducks, and I erected the easel in front of me, which was easier to set up than it looked. I locked the canvas into place with the top screw, and I didn't care that people were watching me. They would stand by Grandad Tommy's easel and stare while he talked to them about the weather or the ducks or his painting techniques and say, "No, it's not for sale," when some businesswoman in a pantsuit would offer to buy one of his landscapes.

I sat my bag of supplies on the bench beside me and pulled out an empty jam jar that Tommy would use for water. I didn't dare leave everything sitting there unattended to grab a bottle of water from the kiosk near the entrance of the park, so instead, I dipped the jar into the murky pond. The water was grainy but it wasn't dirty so I didn't mind too much. Besides, I wasn't here to create a masterpiece, just a piece.

I squeezed a variety of paint colours onto a plastic palette, selected a brush, and then I stared at the blank canvas.

At the pond.

At the trees.

And all of my inspiration left me. What the hell was I doing? I was never any good with paints. I knew that. Mr Madden knew that. Grandad Tommy knew that. But still, Ryan's words were echoing in my head. You don't have to be good.

I mixed some blue paint together with red and yellow, making a dirty brown colour, and I added some white to lighten it before sweeping my brush across the canvas. It was a duck pond. Sort of.

But at least it was something.

I filled it in, added some green around the edge, and then

washed the brush in my jar of water before painting in a blue-white sky above the pond, fading towards the white canvas. But when I looked at my creation with a critical eye, there was something missing. A focal point. I looked around. It didn't matter what was in front of me, what mattered was what I could put on the canvas that felt natural, as though it belonged. A tree, a person. Anything. But nothing felt right. Or maybe the painting was all wrong. The water was too brown, the sky too blue.

"It doesn't matter," Tommy would have said. "You did it, that's what counts."

I did it. But it looked terrible. Like Constable if Constable had been a turf-cutter instead of an artist.

I cleaned the brush in the dirty water jar, wiped the bristles on my jeans, and decided I wasn't going to sign the canvas. It didn't deserve it.

When I stood, I almost knocked the jar over as I pushed the easel aside and the brush fell between the slats of the bench. I stooped to pick it up, bumping the easel, and it collapsed behind me. Grit from the path exploded across the painting and, for a second, I just stared at it, too shocked to react. And then I laughed, because the grit put some texture on the canvas that had been lacking.

"Thanks, Tommy," I muttered, and as I picked up the jar of dirty water from the bench, I imagined him saying, "You're welcome."

I turned, leaving the canvas on the ground, jar in hand to rinse it in the pond, and walked straight into somebody.

The water sloshed out of the jar.

And I jumped back to avoid it, brown liquid coating my

hands.

I looked up. "Sorry," I said, an automatic impulse.

And the boy in front of me stood there with his arms wide, his mouth open in shock.

Brown water dripping from his cream sweater.

"Shit," I said. "I'm so sorry." I tried to wipe his sweater with my fingers but he stepped back. When I looked up, his eyes—so brown they could have been black—stared at me. He was Asian, dark hair parted off-centre, a perfectly straight nose—straighter than Ryan's—and his lips were pink and parted, like half of a scream that never came.

The brown paint-water soaked into the wool of his sweater and dripped onto his shoes.

I held the jar up. "It'll wash out. Or I can pay—for the drycleaning or whatever."

He looked at me. I couldn't read his expression. Then he stared at the half-empty jar in my hands, at the fallen canvas on the ground that looked like a child had crapped all over it.

And then he made a gesture with his hands.

Like he was cursing me out without words.

CHAPTER 4

I didn't know what he meant when he made the hand motion, but it didn't look like, "Screw you."

I turned from him and sat the jar on the bench. I wiped my hands on my jacket and then reached towards him again, as if I could wring the dirty water out of his sweater and make it magically disappear. But again he stepped out of my reach, the water still dripping on his shoes and the cracks in the pavement around him.

"Sorry," I said one more time, lame and limp. I got my wallet out, but all I had was five euros. "Here. It's probably not enough but I can get more. I don't know how much dry-cleaning costs."

The boy blinked. He closed his mouth at last and stared at the five-euro note. Then he held a hand up to stop me and shook his head.

"It was an accident," I said.

He pulled a sleeve down over his hand and wiped the spreading stain, making it worse. Then he wiped his dirtied sleeve with the other one. He looked at me again. Why wasn't he screaming at me like anybody else would?

His eyes—I wanted to say they were almond-shaped, but that wasn't exactly right; more like a paintbrush, tapered at the edges—stared at me in an unasked question.

"Sorry," I said. Again. Like it meant anything.

The boy with the dark hair and questioning eyes shook his head. Not in an angry way. More dismayed than anything. And then his smile was clipped, short, meaningless. He gave his sweater one last swipe with a sleeve, stepped over my fallen canvas, and walked away. He hadn't said a word and I wondered if he spoke English. Dublin was a hotbed for tourists in the summer, but not so much in spring.

I sat on the bench and kicked the leg of Grandad's easel. Then I let my gaze follow the path in the direction he'd walked. There was a trail of dirty water fading across the path and I thought about the shape of the boy's face, the angle of his jaw. The colour of his skin, like Naples yellow that had been watered down with some titanium white.

That was a colour I wanted to paint.

If only I was any good at painting.

When I got home, Mum and Mick were still at work. I kicked my shoes off by the front door, like I would if I'd just come home from school, and I put Grandad Tommy's easel back in his room, the paints in the drawer, and I looked to see if he had any Naples yellow. Just in case.

At school the next day, I saw Mr McLaughlin in the corridor near the lockers, but although he nodded at me as he passed, he didn't stop to ask about sketching cars in the car-park. He probably knew the truth. I'm sure some teachers are actually all right and weren't created in a teacher-training lab. Mr McLaughlin wasn't one of my teachers, so I didn't know for sure, but I was grateful that he didn't ask to see my sketchbook, because I'd forgotten to draw a car like Ryan had told me to.

I suffered through ninety minutes of our English teacher quoting Shakespeare at us in a way that sounded like he was declaring his impassioned love to the first row, and in the corridor afterwards, Ryan gripped my wrist and pulled me aside just as a football flew through the air. It would have hit me in the back of the head if he hadn't been so quick. It bounced and rolled among the students, and nobody owned up when a teacher asked who it belonged to. "It's mine now," the teacher said, taking it down the corridor to the teachers' lounge.

"Did you paint?" Ryan asked.

I shrugged. "I mean, I used some paints. Put them on canvas. Does that count?"

"Show me," he said.

"I didn't bring it. It was awful."

"Awful is good," Ryan said, steering me towards the canteen. He always wanted to get in the queue early. "Awful is better than non-existent, right?"

"Says who?"

"Jacob van Ruisdael."

How the hell did he know the name of a seventeenth-century Dutch painter? "Is there anything in your head that gets lost?" I asked.

"Nope. Except for the twenty euros I owe you."

"What twenty euros?"

"Exactly."

We stood in the lunch line behind a group of boys in the year above us who were picking on a kid from the year below, flicking his ears, tugging on the tail of his blazer. Ryan tapped one of the older boys on the shoulder and when he turned with a scowl, Ryan said, "Cut it out, will you?"

The younger boy looked at us like he was desperate to get away.

"What's it to you?" the older boy said.

Ryan put his elbow on my shoulder, casual and nonchalant. "You're holding up the line."

"What are you going to do," the guy said, "cry to your mammy?"

Ryan tilted his head to crack his neck like a bigshot, but I put my hand out between him and the older guy. I said, "Leave it out, buddy."

"Buddy?"

I squared up to him. "I just buried my grandad and I'm not in the mood to get blood on my uniform. Yours or his," I said, pointing my thumb at Ryan beside me.

The guy narrowed his eyes, like he didn't believe me or didn't care. Then he patted my shoulder. "Respect," he said, and he turned back to his friends. The kid in front of them had been served and was standing at the till, and he kept his head down as he walked through the tables to find a seat.

Ryan said, "Where did that come from?"

I shrugged. My heart was thumping under my shirt. I'm

not sure I could have taken a swing at him if he'd given me the opportunity.

Ryan put a bread roll on his tray and pointed at the lasagne, waiting for the lunch lady to scoop some up for him. His mum was behind the prep station in the background, too far to have seen anything. He said, "Using your grandad like that was ballsy."

"Tommy would understand."

"G-dawg," Ryan said, and I punched his arm for no reason.

After lunch, I saw the older boy again in the hallway. I was on my way to my locker from the boys' toilets and he stopped in front of me. He was alone too. I'm not sure if that made any difference.

He looked at me. Then he said, "Your lace is undone."

I didn't want to look down, like it was a trick, like he'd clock me if I did. But he nodded and then walked away. I clenched and unclenched my fist, then looked at my feet. My right shoelace was spread out like two snakes trying to escape. I stooped to tie it, wondering if bullies were just one shoelace away from being nice.

One dead grandad away.

In history class, I sat beside a boy called Connor. We never spoke unless he needed to borrow a pen when his stopped working—he was one of those boys who always had an empty pen, like he'd used up all the ink the night before. Miss Cleary flashed a British political cartoon from the 1940s on the overhead projector. It was a line drawing, badly done, of a queue of people entering what looked like a soup kitchen, and another line of people coming out a second door, looking skinnier than when they went in. A war plane overhead.

"What's interesting here," she said, gesturing to the in and out doors, "is how much is being communicated without words. Without dialogue. What do you think the artist is saying?" she pointed at somebody in the front row.

He said, "War makes you hungry?"

We laughed and Miss Cleary smiled. "I'll accept it," she said. "But what's the political statement here? Is it pro-war? Anti-war?"

It was against the war, we agreed, and I took some notes in my workbook, doodled the outline of a bowl of spaghetti in the margin, then a few stars around the edge. Mostly, my exercise books were filled with more pictures than words, which I guess is what Miss Cleary was trying to get at.

"There's no caption," she said. "No dialogue, no speech bubbles. But it still says everything it needs to, just from symbolism. Positioning. Body language."

"Look, Battersly," somebody said. "Your mum's in that queue. The skinny one."

The classroom erupted, but Miss Cleary picked up the whiteboard eraser and slapped it against the board to settle everybody down.

"Shush," she said. And she waited until we were silent again. "Listen," she said. "Listen to the picture. Sometimes, silence says more than words ever could."

And somebody at the back said, "Would I get an A if I handed in a paper with no words?"

"Absolutely," Miss Cleary said. "In art class."

The boys erupted again, and somebody chanted my name a few times, because everyone in my year knew I was half good at art. I stood and took a bow. Not because I deserved it, but because I was trying to be funny, to fit in, even when I didn't want to.

Because, in high school, if you don't fit in, you stand out.

And nobody wants to stand out.

At the end of the day, I realised I'd thought about Grandad Tommy one or two times fewer than yesterday, longer gaps in between my sadness. And that cut into my veins like a knife.

Ryan met me at my locker, draped his arm around my neck, and said, "Are you getting a lift or catching the bus?"

"Bus," I said, the joys of having two working parents. "Is your dad picking you up?"

Ryan's dad worked at the docks, alternating between the day shift and the night shift, and I could never remember which day was which. He said, "Nope, I'm all yours. What do you want to do?"

"You can help me with my homework."

"Homework is for wimps," he said. He often did his on the bus in the mornings, because he was clever enough not to have to study like a normal human being.

We rode the bus together and when we got off at the end of our road, he slapped the back of my head, said, "No back-sies," and ran home. I pretended to chase after him for a few steps, and when he waved from his doorstep, I nodded and went home.

Mum and Mick were still at work, and I stood outside Grandad Tommy's bedroom door. I didn't go in this time, didn't want to disturb the quiet. But I didn't know what else to do with myself. Ordinarily, he'd be standing in the kitchen at this time of day, peeling potatoes or dicing carrots, prepping dinner for when Mum got home. On Friday's, he'd gut the fish that Tommy Two brought over and there'd be a bottle of beer beside him, opened but untouched. He'd sip it over dinner and when the dishes were being cleared away, he'd pour what was left of it down the sink. I think he only drank it to be polite.

I got my sketchbook and stuffed a couple of pencils into my back pocket, and because there was at least an hour before Mum would get home from work, I walked down to the park again. I didn't take any of Grandad's paints or the cumbersome easel. I was far more comfortable with a pencil and my sketchpad on my lap where I could avoid any water-based accidents this time.

I went through the park gates, down along the path on the left that led to the duck pond. I wanted to sketch the same scene I'd attempted to paint yesterday. Maybe if I could figure out what it should look like in pencil, I might be able to better imagine it in colour.

But when I got to the bench, the Asian boy was sitting there, alone, a coffee cup in his hands.

He looked up when I approached, stood, looked at the coffee in his hand and then carefully sat it on the bench, away from me.

I smiled and held up one hand, the other one gripping my sketchbook. "Lesson learned," I said.

He was wearing a dark navy jacket today. Waterproof. Was that on purpose?

He moved his hands, put them together, slid one away and twitched his fingers. And it took me a second to realise what it was. Sign language.

That's why he hadn't spoken to me yesterday.

I looked at his face. There was a smile there. A tiny one that coloured the corners of his lips. I said, "I'm sorry. I don't understand. And I'm sorry about yesterday. It was an accident."

The boy pulled out his phone, typed something, and then showed me.

Hi, it said.

I smiled. "Hey."

Then he typed again. When he held his phone up, there was a grinning emoji after his words.

Draw me?

I narrowed my eyes, studied his face for a second, and then shrugged.

"Sure," I said. "Why not?"

CHAPTER 5

He sat on the bench, picking his coffee up and gripping it in his lap like a prop, and I wasn't sure what to do. I'd only ever sketched people from photos before, or from memory, except for Ryan, but that was often when he wasn't staring at me and didn't know I was drawing him.

The boy flattened his lips for a second, then gave me a short twitch of a smile, self-conscious in its haste. So I sat at the other end of the bench, facing him as best I could, and I opened my sketchbook to a blank page. I tapped my pencil against it, hesitant to look up, and then I blinked and stared at him, not in a creepy way, but I needed to see the detail, needed to understand his face.

He stared back at me, unblinking, unnerving. He took a quick sip from his coffee and then lowered it. And I made my first pencil strokes, rough, light, just a shape to begin with.

I looked at him, at the curve of his cheekbone, then at the page, mimicking that sweep with my pencil. And I said, "I'm Owen." It kind of felt weird, sketching somebody and not knowing their name.

The boy moved his hand, touched my arm, and I looked up. There was a question on his face and I realised that, if he could read lips, those lips needed to be facing him, right? So I said again, slowly, "I'm Owen."

He nodded and tilted his head in a bow.

But he didn't offer his own name, so I pointed my pencil at him. "And you?"

He didn't sign it, which I was grateful for. He picked up his phone and typed his name, then held the screen up for me to see.

Lee Jun-ho.

"Lee," I said. "Nice to meet you."

But he deleted it and typed again: *Jun-ho Lee.*

"Oh," I said. Last name first.

More typing. *Just call me Jun. Like "June".*

I nodded and turned my attention back to the sketch on the page, saying, "Jun," and sounding it out. "Jun."

I looked at him, then shaded in the dark side of his face, away from the sunlight that brightened his dark brown hair with hints of sun-kissed auburn. He didn't move, barely blinked, and there was no smile on his lips as I sketched them onto the page in short, light strokes.

"This is weird," I said, looking down. He nudged me to say it again while looking at him. "I said it's weird. Sketching somebody. Like, normally I just draw the trees or the pond or whatever I see. Not people."

He shrugged, took another sip from his coffee, and the sheen of it made his lips glow. I flipped my pencil over and erased some of the shading on his lower lip to match the liquid shine.

There was a single freckle on the side of his chin, just above the jawline, and another near his left eye. And one side of his mouth was curled up slightly higher than the other—not a lot, just enough that I noticed while I studied him. These are the details we never see in strangers, because we don't pay enough attention. I don't think I'd looked at my own mother's face this much in one go, never mind mine, even though I'd once tried a self-portrait, staring at myself in the mirror. But I didn't like that my left eye was a little bigger than the right and my eyebrows tapered out like they were half finished, like the universe had run out of eyebrow hair.

I turned the sketchbook sideways to shade in his hair at a better angle, and Jun typed quickly on his phone. *Is it good?*

I smiled. "It's not finished yet."

But is it good?

"It's amazing," I said. "Because I'm amazing." I didn't mean it, it was a joke, but Jun just blinked and returned his head to the pose he'd been holding. He sat there with his back straight, ankles crossed under the seat of the bench, and coffee cup in his lap. And I moved my hand slowly now, making careful, deliberate strokes. He didn't fidget, didn't smile, just held himself erect like a statue, and every time I looked at him, he was staring back at me with those big brown eyes that were asking questions I didn't have any answers to.

"Jun," I said again, absently, glancing at the page as it

shone in the sunlight. I filled in the line of his neck, the collar of his jacket, and then shaded in a faint background behind him. And when I was done, I pushed the pencil into the wire spiral at the edge of the book, and sat it flat on my lap, covering it with both hands. I said, "I don't normally do people."

Jun typed. *Show me.*

It was light on detail, but it was enough of a resemblance that it looked like him. I held it up, self-conscious, and prepared myself for laughter.

Jun looked at it without smiling, studied it for a minute, and then he glanced at me and nodded once.

I relaxed enough to ease the tension in my shoulders, and then I took the pencil again and wrote his name at the top of the page. *Jun-ho Lee.* Then I erased his family name and put it before his given name. *Lee Jun-ho.*

He smiled, pointed at the page and then himself.

"Can you keep it?"

He nodded. And I shrugged. Ryan never asked to keep any of the sketches I did of him, but that was probably because he knew I'd say no. But when Jun asked, I smiled and tore the page out of the book.

He held it up, admiring it, and then he passed it back, scratching his finger at the edge of the page, reminding me to sign it.

When I did, a squiggle of a signature that was nowhere near as impressive as Grandad Tommy's curve-curve-stroke, Jun put his fingers to his chin and moved his hand away in front of him.

I guested he was saying thanks, so I said, "You're welcome?" and when he smiled I nodded.

Jun took the sketch and folded it into quarters. He stood, said thank you again, and then he bowed his head, deeper than a nod. And he turned to walk away.

I called after him. "Hey."

But he didn't turn around, and I watched him leave until he disappeared beyond the trees at the bend in the path.

I looked at my sketchbook, at the blank page that was left behind after tearing out the likeness of Jun-ho Lee. There were some frayed strips of paper trapped in the spiral binding, and I left them there as a reminder.

I wondered if I could draw him again, from memory.

And the answer was probably yes.

I closed the book. I couldn't even remember why I'd come to the park, and it was getting busy now, schools finished for the day, people milling about. So I left with my pencils in my back pocket and my sketchbook under one arm. I walked up the hill and down the other side, away from home, not really knowing why but unwilling to feel trapped inside the shell of our house until my mum came home from work.

I just let my feet carry me, realising where I was going but refusing to admit it. The church. The cemetery. My grandfather.

The gate was open but the church doors were closed, and I carried on around the side, crossed the small carpark, and into the graveyard. In my grief, I couldn't remember which row he was buried in, but I knew it was just beyond the huge statue of an angel—Michael, maybe; I wasn't sure. I walked along the path, up one row, down the next, and when I found him I realised I probably could have spotted it from the top of the graveyard because the fake grass they'd placed around the grave on the day he was buried was gone, and the damp soil that covered him was fresh, not quite a mound but not flat either.

It had been almost a week since I stood here in a black suit, watching as they lowered him in. The gravestone said *Sandra McDaid, beloved wife, mother and grandmother. 1942-2008. Forever in our hearts.*

But Tommy's name hadn't been etched into the marble yet, like they'd forgotten about him.

I blessed myself, because that's what you do at somebody's graveside, and I lowered my head, the sketchbook still in my hands. The soil was uneven, unsettled, like it hadn't figured out how to lie flat, and I wondered if Grandad Tommy was up there—if there was an "up there"—complaining about the dampness of the earth and the chill of the wind that skittered through the headstones, night after day, keeping the dead awake.

I crouched and flicked away some small twigs that had half-buried themselves in the soil. I wasn't crying, but I knew that I could if I let myself. The flowers in front of the stone were withering, left out in the sunlight with no water, and I made a note to bring some fresh ones next time.

I dusted the soil off my fingers and then rocked back on my heels, sitting on the cold stone pavement at the foot of my grandparents' grave. I put the sketchbook on the ground beside me and pulled the pencils out of my back pocket before they broke. I wasn't going to do any gravestone rubbings. Not today. Not ever, because it felt like a violation now, and it made me realise the rubbings we did years ago, Tommy and me, had been an invasion of a dead person's privacy. It didn't matter that there was nobody around to visit them, to cut back the bracken and lay fresh flowers. We were stepping over their remains with disrespect. And I'd dread to think of anyone doing that to Tommy's grave two hundred years from now.

Where would I be, two centuries in the future? Not here. The plot at either side of my grandparents was occupied, and I'm pretty sure you can't move house once you're gone. They don't dig you up and put you someplace else. Maybe we'd be further down the graveyard where the newer plots were, my mum, Mick and me. Or maybe I'd be buried somewhere else, with a husband and my own headstone. My own berth for two, just like Tommy and Sandra.

Who knew?

I shrugged. Then I smiled because I was answering my own questions, and Grandad Tommy would have said that was a sure sign of madness. "Talking to yourself is bad enough," he'd say, "so long as you don't answer back."

I sat there, listening to the flutter of the pages in my sketchbook where the wind caught the edge of it, and I stared at the empty space on the headstone below my grandmother's name. There should be something there. Something simple. *Tommy McDaid. Everyone's Grandad.*

I stood up when the cold started to seep into the seat of my jeans. I picked up my sketchbook and chased after one of the pencils that had rolled away, the one I'd used to sketch Jun.

And I took one more look at the headstone. I didn't say goodbye. I just bowed my head, deeply.

And then I put my fingers to my chin and moved my

hand away. Jun had taught me that.

Thank you.

CHAPTER 6

The weekend arrived without anyone else dying, which I took as a win. On Thursday night, a week after we'd buried Tommy, I dreamt that Mum and Mick were in a car crash and Tommy Two drowned while fishing and Ryan's kitchen exploded from a gas leak, killing him and his dad and wiping out half of the lower end of the street. And a policewoman stood in the ash that coated the road and told me I was all alone. And then she laughed.

Dreams are awful.

On Friday morning, I got out of bed and stood outside Mum's bedroom door, listening, just to make sure they were still alive. I almost knocked, but it was still early, nobody's alarm had gone off yet, and at least I could hear their breathing. So that was something.

I moved through Friday under the static hum of humanity carrying on with its day—kids on the bus, adults on the streets, teachers in the halls. Nobody gave a crap about anybody else, I noticed. At least not anyone outside their immediate sphere of connection.

I sat beside Connor in one class and Ryan in another, and at lunch, we ate fish and chips at a table for six in the school canteen, just me and Ryan and four empty seats. Ryan said something about the weekend, about doing something fun, but we didn't settle on any of the specifics and, by home time, my brain had already shut down for the day.

Saturday came like a quiet sigh at the end of the week and nobody asked anything of me. I stayed in bed longer than I should have, the duvet cocooned around my legs. My sketchbook was open beside me but I hadn't drawn anything yet, not since I tore out the likeness of Jun earlier in the week and gave it to him. I still wanted to draw him again, the shape of his eyes, the fullness of his lips, but I couldn't muster the effort to pick up a pencil.

Mum or Mick was moving around downstairs, the kettle bubbling, a cupboard closing, but there was nothing urgent. No footsteps on the stairs, no calls for me to go down. Just the quiet of a Saturday morning with nothing to do, nothing to smile for.

We'd felt Grandad's absence last night at the dinner table when Mum absentmindedly put out four plates instead of three, and when she'd stopped crying, Mick said it was all right, these things happen.

"Death?" Mum asked.

Mick held her while I sat at the kitchen table beside

Grandad's empty seat. "Yes," he said. "Death happens. It isn't easy, so we need to allow for mistakes. You don't think he's up there, wondering what's for dinner?"

She slapped his chest because it wasn't even funny, and then Tommy Two came in the front door and looked at us in the kitchen.

Mum said, "I didn't know you were coming. Mick, get that plate out again."

Tommy Two sat down and he looked at the table and he looked at my mum. Then he said, "I didn't know I was coming either. I was going home after work."

"Then why are you here?"

He reached for the bottle of water on the table. "Auto-pilot," he said.

"Auto-pilot," Mick agreed. "The same thing that made you set an extra place. See? These things happen."

We ate dinner together, the remnants of a family in the wake of loss, and before he left, Tommy Two said, "The stonemason will be adding Dad's name to the headstone on Tuesday. You agreed the wording, didn't you?"

Mum nodded, her eyes still puffy, and she put a pod into the coffee machine.

"What will it say?" I asked quietly, not really sure if I wanted to know.

Mum covered her mouth like she hoped she could trap the words inside, but then she said, "Even death is not to be feared by one who has lived wisely."

And we thought about that for a while, in silence, sipping coffees and pushing cake around our plates without really eating it.

When Ryan sent me a text on Saturday afternoon, I was grateful for something to do that wasn't nothing, because after a while even nothing gets boring.

We got the bus into town, sitting beside each other in silence as it rattled through the streets in a cloud of diesel fumes. When we stood on Argan Street, Ryan coughed and said, "We can walk around the shopping centre. Like nineties kids."

"I didn't know we were going for a nineties vibe," I said. "I would have worn double denim."

"Wasn't that the eighties?"

I shrugged. I'd seen pictures of Mick in blue jeans and a matching denim jacket, his hair slicked up like he was trying to add five inches to his height—before it started to thin out. It was comically attractive. Maybe that's why Mum fell in love with him after my dad left. He always made her laugh, especially when she didn't want to.

I think that's what I wanted in life—laughter. The kind that makes you snort Coke out of your nose because you can't control it. Ryan made me laugh a lot, but he'd never be the one to put his hands on me the way I wanted somebody to. Ryan wasn't my One & Only.

He'd been my first crush when puberty snaked into my body with its cruel—and somewhat hairy—invasion. My training wheels. But now he was just Ryan. Best friend and confidant.

I trailed behind him as he led me from one store to another, looking for a hoodie without a slogan on it. "Why does everything have text?" he asked, holding one up. *Born to Nap.* "We're sixteen, not six. I'm not *Mummy's Little Soldier.*"

"But you love to nap," I said.

He pointed at the slogan. "Doesn't mean I have to tell the world."

I rifled through the rack. "There has to be one that says *No Slogan Necessary*."

I pulled a T-shirt off the rail and held it against me as I checked it out in a mirror. Mall mirrors never tell the truth. It must be the lighting or something, but if it looks great in the store, it looks awful at home. That's the rule.

We ended up in the food court after a fruitless search for a hoodie, and Ryan bought a bucket of fried chicken that could have fed the twelve apostles and still had some left over for seconds. I'd bought a new box of pencils, a mix of 2H and 3H. I didn't use hard leads often because they made everything too sharp, but whenever I needed to I could never find one. I still hadn't drawn anything new in my sketchbook. I don't think I was in the mood.

I had started to wonder about my end of year art projects, what I would do if the mood didn't return to me on time. I could sculpt something out of clay or papier-mâché. I could silkscreen *No Slogan Necessary* on T-shirts and get an A. But what I wanted to do was draw. Drawing was my comfort zone and without it I'd have no Grandad and no purpose.

Ryan said, "Close your mouth before the rest of it escapes."

I looked at him. I'd zoned out, letting the busy background noise carry me away. Ryan reached across the small table with greasy fingers and touched the underside of my chin.

"You were doing that thing where your soul falls out of your mouth and your eyes go dark."

"Was I?"

"What was it this time? Boys?"

"Piss off," I said, reaching for one of his chicken pieces.

He slapped my hand away, then he changed his mind and pushed the bucket towards me. "Tommy?" he asked.

I shrugged. I was thinking about my grandad, but also more than that. Sometimes my brain can't settle on one thing at a time and it flits around like a bumblebee in a flower shop.

"Eat," Ryan said.

When we were done, we walked back through the mall, trying on sunglasses we didn't need and didn't buy, and then we headed for the escalators with chicken in our stomachs and still no hoodie for Ryan. I got on the moving stairs behind Ryan, who was still talking about a pair of shoes he almost liked, and as I gripped the rail, I looked down. Sunlight broke through the glass ceiling and turned the floor to gold.

And Jun was on the opposite escalator, coming up.

I recognised him even with his back to me. He was signing to somebody, a woman, who stood on the step behind him. He was wearing the same waterproof jacket as the other day and his hands moved in a dignified and controlled manner. The older woman signed something back to him and then he turned to face forward just as I tried to make it look as though I wasn't staring.

Ryan said something about the shoes he couldn't afford and Jun watched me watching him.

When we passed, me going down, him going up, I kept my hand on the rail and the other in my pocket and I smiled because I didn't know how to say hello in sign language.

Jun turned his head, following me as I passed, and then he raised one hand, palm up, like an unfinished wave. He didn't smile, didn't blink. His hand went up and then it went down.

And by the time we got to the bottom, I looked up and couldn't see him anymore.

Ryan said, "What time's the bus?" He poked my ribs. "Did you forget something?"

I looked at him, then back at the escalator. Jun was gone. Again. I blinked and smacked Ryan on the arm. "Yeah. I forgot you were a moron."

I had to wait for him outside the men's room and while there was an announcement about a sale on the second floor, I took out my phone and looked up the sign for hello.

You won't be disappointed to know that it's a thumbs up, which is the perfect way to say hi.

At home, I skipped dinner because I'd eaten too much chicken and Mum put the leftovers into containers in the fridge. "You can pick at it later," she said.

I sat on the couch while Mick watched the news and Mum read a book, and while everybody was doing something that meant conversation wasn't necessary, I went to my room. At the foot of the stairs, Mum said, "Don't forget to eat something."

I told her I wasn't hungry and I heard her complain to Mick as I went upstairs.

I looked up Irish Sign Language and found some blog posts and YouTube videos, a few clunky-looking apps that gamified learning in a way that always annoyed me. I wanted to learn a language, not gather XP to exchange for stars that could be used for coins.

I watched a video of a man signing while he spoke. "Sign language isn't universal," he said. "There are some similarities, like 'yes' or the sign for applause"—he shook his hands at either side of his head—"but for the most part, each country's sign language is as unique as its spoken language."

I looked up the alphabet and learned to sign J-U-N. I ran it back, over and over, until I'd perfected it. And then I learned O-W-E-N. And by the time I'd mastered my own name, I'd forgotten the signs for J and U.

As I scrolled through the search results, there was an ad for an online class, but even though it said it was for Irish sign language, the class times were at eleven p.m., as if it was held in America.

I did another search and found a community centre in town that had weekly lessons for seven euros. I looked up the address and checked out their website. The ISL class was sandwiched between macrame and Mums, Bums and Tums. Maybe I'd go. Maybe I wouldn't.

But it's not as though I had anything better to do with my Tuesday nights, and it might take my mind of Grandad Tommy and my art.

Before I got into bed, Mick knocked on my door and didn't open it until I said he could come in. He stood in the doorway and said, "How are you doing, son?"

I looked up from my phone screen and blinked. He never asked me how I was. He just assumed I was all right.

"Fine," I said.

"Good," he said.

He looked at me. Then he came into the room, studied the books on my shelf, kicked the heel of my shoe to line it up with the others beside my desk.

"Mick?"

He made a noise, something like a question. Then he said, "How's school?"

"Fine," I said again.

"Good," he said again.

"Did Mum send you in?"

He sat on the edge of the bed. "She's worried you're not eating."

I rolled my eyes. "I ate with Ryan."

Mick nodded. He didn't face me. "She's just looking out for you, son. She doesn't want another do like last time."

"Jesus."

Mick shot me a look that told me off for swearing.

Last time. We didn't speak about that any more. And Mick wasn't even around then, anyway. I was overweight. Or I thought I was. But that's how it starts, isn't it? And anyway, it was my dad's fault for disappearing when I was nine and Mum's fault for not explaining it to me properly. For over a year, I blamed myself. And I got into this thing where food became my enemy. I wasn't refusing food in order to starve myself, I was protesting. At least at first. Then it became something more. Something bigger.

Bigger than me.

"That was years ago," I said. "I was a kid."

"I know," Mick said. "She's just worried. Now that your grandad's..." He didn't finish.

"Gone?" I asked. "I know he's gone. And I know it wasn't my fault." I felt the heat rising in my chest to tighten my throat and I remembered kneeling in front of Tommy's body on the kitchen floor, pushing my hands against his sternum like I could bring him back to life.

Two minutes ago, I was waving hello and learning my name in another language. And now the room was dark and Mick's presence was weighing on me like an anvil inside my chest. That's how fast things can change.

"So, you're all right?" he asked.

I stared at him. The darkness wound down my arm and into my fist where I gripped my phone so tight it hurt.

"I'm sorry," he said. He patted my leg.

And when he left my room and closed the door, I said, "Me too."

CHAPTER 7

The bell had just rung for lunch and the corridor was a mess of opened lockers, slamming doors and the echo of somebody shouting, "Wait up!" down the stairwell. I slumped out of the classroom ahead of Ryan, knowing he'd catch up to me, but hoping maybe he'd stop to talk to somebody and I could disappear into the art block or the library.

After the awkward conversation with Mick at the weekend, I locked myself in my room, coming out only for dinner on Sunday where I made a point of clearing my plate and asking for more. Because sometimes I can be petty like that. Then I took a slice of cheesecake up to my room but when I realised I didn't have any room left for it, I let it sit on my desk until nighttime when Mum collected it without a word. It wasn't in the fridge on Monday morning, so she must have thrown it out. She didn't apologise for sending Mick in like a general, and I didn't apologise for being a dick about it.

So I guess we were even.

I kind of let the weight of Tommy's absence fall on top of me today. I showered under the darkness of it and brushed my teeth with the thought of him stuck in the corners of everything, and I rode the bus to school with a cloud of noxious angst around me, enough that even Ryan didn't speak to me on the way. He just slapped my back in the hallway after homeroom and headed to his first class, advanced physics or advanced chemistry or advanced something. I knew his schedule as well as my own but today my brain was on vacation.

We met up again for maths before lunch and when the bell went, I pulled my jacket from the back of the chair and scooped my bag up without a word. "Hang on," Ryan said, throwing pens into his pencil case, but I went into the hall with the press of bodies behind me, all eager to get to the lunch queue before everyone else.

He tugged on my sleeve in the stairwell. "What's gotten into you?"

"Nothing."

"Yeah," he said. He wasn't buying it.

"Come on," I said, going down the stairs ahead of him. "I'm starving."

When he caught up with me again, he nudged my arm with a smile and said, "Now you're talking. My stomach feels like my throat's been cut."

Somebody jumped down the stairs beside us, three at a time, and shouted at a boy further down. "Smells like pizza!"

Ryan shook his head. "It's not pizza. He's going to be disappointed."

"What is it?" I asked, not really caring, and I stepped through the door of the canteen when he held it open for me.

"Steak bake," he said with a frown, which I guess means he wasn't a fan.

We found a table with a few empty seats at one end and while we were eating, a kid from one of Ryan's advanced classes joined us, a half-empty packet of crisps in his hands. "All right, boys?"

Ryan gave him a one-shoulder shrug and poked at the food on his tray.

Brendan O'Rourke was one of those students who sailed through with straight Bs but didn't care about school. Apparently, his girlfriend was pregnant and the boys in his class called him Bren*dad* instead of Brendan.

"Where were you the other week?" he asked me, and for a second I didn't know what he meant. "Ryan sat with me like a lost puppy all week."

I glanced at Ryan. I could imagine the look on his face, the puppy-dog one.

"Leave it out," he said to Brendan.

"Did you go on holiday during term time?"

"Brendan," Ryan said sharply.

"What?"

I cut the edge of my fork into the steak bake to let the steam out before I said, "My grandad passed away."

"Shit, man," he said. "That sucks. But you're all right now?"

"What do you mean?"

"Brendan," Ryan said again.

"What?"

"He's just lost his fucking grandad."

I stabbed the fork into the meat because I couldn't stab it into his face. And when I stood up, the chair scraped out behind me and fell over.

"I didn't mean anything," Brendan said.

As I walked away, I heard Ryan say something about Brendan's own grandkids one day. But I didn't care. In the hallway outside, Ryan ran up behind me and gripped my arm. "He's just a dickhead," he said.

I nodded. "It was cruel."

"I don't think he meant it," Ryan said. "At least not the way it came out."

"Then he shouldn't have let it come out that way."

We walked down the hall. We still had twenty-five minutes of lunch left and we couldn't exactly go back into the canteen and reclaim our half-eaten food.

Ryan said, "How is it that I'm spending all day chasing after you?"

"You're getting slow in your old age," I said, and I side-swiped his ankle before running from him.

"No running," a teacher shouted.

But you don't stop when a teacher says that. You just slow down. Speed walk.

When Ryan was beside me again, he said, "You owe me lunch."

I smiled. "Come on. I'll buy you a Snickers."

The rest of the day was no better, and when I got home, the house was swallowed in emptiness. No, Brendan O'Rourke, I'm not all right now, thanks.

I stood in the kitchen, on the tiles where Tommy had collapsed, and I looked in the fridge and opened the freezer and then slammed them both. I grabbed my sketchbook from upstairs and walked down to the park. It was overcast, but it wasn't raining, and I swear I wasn't looking for Jun.

But I wasn't not looking for him, either.

I got to the bench and there was a girl sitting there, a year or two younger than me. She was alone, texting on her phone, her hair falling around her face, and I couldn't tell if she was waiting for somebody or if she had already been stood up. She kept glancing along the path.

When she looked at me, she turned away, tapped on her phone, then turned to me again. "What?" she said, like I was invading her space.

"Nothing." I flapped the sketchbook under my arm. "Can I sit there?" I asked, indicating the empty side of the bench.

She turned from me again, saying, "Free country," and I sat, awkwardly, the sketchbook on my lap and a 2B pencil in my hand. I didn't open it. I stared ahead or to the left, but never in her direction. I didn't want to be creepy. And my leg jittered with nerves until two other girls approached and my bench partner said, "Finally."

She left without even acknowledging me, and I waved at her back as they took off down the path. "Good talk," I said. To myself—not loud enough for her to hear.

I finally opened my sketchbook, looking at the frayed curls of paper that were trapped under the spiral binding from when I'd torn out Jun's portrait. The empty page glared at me with its freshness and I drew a straight line across the middle of it for no reason. You can draw a straight line on a page without a ruler by guiding your pinkie finger along the edge as you keep the pencil steady. Mr Madden taught me that, and when I showed it to Grandad Tommy, he smiled and said, "Well, what do you know?" And then he drew a straight line across my page without any guide.

I spent an hour that day trying to replicate it, but there was always a wobble in my hand, a kink in the line.

I turned the pencil stroke into the horizon and sketched some trees at either side of the page, a pond in the middle. It wasn't the scene in front of me, not strictly, but it was similar enough that Tommy would approve.

Somebody sat at the other end of the bench and I didn't bother looking up. I tilted my sketchbook and shaded in the darker spikes of a picket fence that my brain imagined, then I added the rough outline of a dog because that's as close as Mum's allergies would allow me to get to a real one. I let the dog chase after a ball before returning my attention to the ripples of the water in the pond.

And a hand came into my view, a phone easing closer.

"Shit," I said. I looked up. It was Jun, his face soft with recognition, smiling now, with his eyes wide and his hair parted perfectly above his right eyebrow.

He nudged the phone closer to me and I looked down. *You're good*, he'd typed.

So I signed, *Thank you*, and his smile widened.

And then I tucked my pencil into the spiral binding and put my hands in front of my face. It took me a second to remember it, but I signed *J-U-N*.

And his eyes disappeared when he laughed.

I grinned.

Jun reached out and corrected my right hand, making the J sign again, and I said, "Oh. Like this?"

He nodded and I signed his name one more time.

And Jun said, *O-W-E-N.*

"You remembered."

He shrugged like it was no big deal.

When he turned his head to look at something on the bench beside him, I confirmed my suspicions from the last time that I'd drawn his face—he wasn't wearing any hearing aids. It hadn't registered in my brain before because I'd been concentrating on drawing the parts not the whole. But then I figured I knew very little about deaf people—do you even call them that, respectfully?—but I guessed hearing aids were for the hearing-impaired, not the deaf. Right?

I'd ask him. One day.

He picked up the object beside him—his own sketchbook, half the size of mine, and he opened it to the first page. Blank, new, painfully empty. I pointed at it and said, "Are you any good?"

Jun shook his head and signed something, then typed, *Do stick figures count?*

I nodded, stifling the grin on my face. Had he bought the book just to sit here with me? I looked back at my unfinished sketch, and Jun settled against the back of the bench, looking for something to draw. When he started to add some faint lines to the page, I watched him, and when he noticed, he turned from me like he was trying to protect his answers in an exam hall. I laughed and he showed me what he'd drawn so far.

It wasn't much, just a few strokes, but I could already see

the outline of the pond and something floating in it. "Is that a duck?"

He pressed his hand on top of it to hide it and I could see the embarrassment on his face.

I tapped the eraser side of my pencil against the back of his hand. "It's good," I said, and I didn't mean it in any patronising way. "At least I could tell what it was, right?"

We sketched a bit longer in silence, and I kept glancing at his page. His linework was straighter than mine and what surprised me was his ability to be literal on the page. We were both drawing the same pond, but whereas I saw something and drew what I imagined it to look like, Jun drew what it was, exactly what he saw, with no room for interpretation.

I gave him a thumbs up and then he pointed at mine. I turned it to let him see and he studied it for a long moment, then nodded. His approval—like everything else about him—was quiet.

I smiled. I couldn't help it.

When Jun closed his sketchbook and made a sign, I understood it. It was one simple action, a careful movement of his hand, but it said, *Do you want to grab a coffee with me?*

And my smile said, *Absolutely.*

We walked, slowly, to the kiosk near the entrance of the park. He was a couple of inches shorter than me, I noticed, and when we got to the counter, the girl behind it smiled and signed something. Jun signed back, then pointed at me.

Was I the only person in the world who didn't know sign language?

The girl said, "One caramel macchiato and…?"

I didn't know what a macchiato was—I'm basic when

it comes to coffee—but I shrugged and said, "I'll have the same."

Jun paid, despite my protests, and we sat at a small table on the grass in front of the kiosk.

"She knows how to sign?" I asked.

Jun typed, *She knows my order.*

"You come here a lot?"

He spread his fingers flat and wobbled his hand. *So-so.* He sipped his drink and then licked foam from his lips.

There was a zigzag of thick caramel over the whipped cream and when I tasted it, it was sweet and sickly and creamy in a way that meant I'd never have a second one.

Jun must have seen the repulsion in my face because he laughed, then typed, *You don't like it?*

"It's not an Americano, that's for sure," I said.

He stood, and I knew he was going to go back to the kiosk and order an Americano for me, so I gripped his wrist to stop him.

"No, it's fine. I like it."

He narrowed his eyes.

"I do. It's just sweeter than I'm used to. But it's nice."

He sat down again and I took a deliberate sip from my cup.

Then I said, "I haven't seen you around before. Did you just move here?"

Jun typed on his phone and then presented it to me. *Been here for about four months. We moved from South Korea. My mum is Irish.*

"Awesome," I said. "She came here for work?"

Jun blinked, typed, *Yeah*, but I sensed there was something he held back, so I didn't pry any further. It wasn't any of my business.

So, Jun was half-Korean. But all cute. His dark hair, darker eyes, and those quiet, full lips. I would have stared at him without a pencil in my hand if I thought he'd let me. And when I realised I was doing just that, I blushed and looked away from him.

Jun did something with his phone, then sat it on the table and slid it across to me. When I looked, it was a blank contact screen, ready for my number. In the name field, he'd typed OWEN THE ARTIST.

I grinned and tapped my number into it, then hit the save button and passed it back. He called me and hung up so that I could save his details, and when I did, I showed it to him. I'd stored him as a series of hand emojis, followed by the Korean and Irish flags. No name.

He laughed, soundless but no less real. His eyes crinkled at the corners and I stared at him for a second longer than I probably should have.

Jun signed something with his hands and when I said, "What?" laughing along with him, he refused to tell me what he'd signed. I said, "There is a universal sign I can give you but you're not going to like it."

And Jun offered me two middle fingers before I had the chance to offer them to him.

And his blush was as deep as my own.

CHAPTER 8

When it started to rain lightly, I wiped cream from my lips and couldn't help frowning when I said, "I should probably head home. Mum'll be wondering where I am."

Jun tidied the table, carrying our cups back to the kiosk, and he waved at the girl behind the counter before turning back to me. He spread his hand out, asking me to lead the way, but as soon as I started walking, he fell into step beside me.

At the gate, we stopped. "Which way are you going?" I asked.

He pointed.

"Ah. I'm going this way."

Jun nodded, and it kind of felt like a bow, or maybe I was imagining that. Then he waved, once, and when I raised my hand to reply, he smiled, like he was hesitating, but then he turned and walked away.

I watched him go and when he looked back, he waved again.

And I walked up the hill as if there was glue on the pavement that didn't want me to reach the top.

Mum was home and I could smell whatever she was cooking as it wafted out of the kitchen. I sat my sketchbook on the counter and, without being told, I grabbed a fistful of cutlery and set the table. "What's for dinner?" I asked.

"Steak bake," she said.

And I laughed.

"What's so funny?"

"Nothing," I said. "I should invite Ryan."

While we ate, Mick talked about his day at work and I sat my phone on the table beside my plate, wondering if an hour after getting Jun's number was too soon to text him. He hadn't text me yet, so maybe it was. Or maybe he was just being polite and was never going to text me.

After dinner, Mum poured a glass of wine and kissed Mick on the cheek. She said, "I'm going for a bath. I don't care which one of you does it, but please fill the dishwasher."

Mick put his finger against his nose.

And, honestly, I didn't even mind. I stood up, scraping the leftovers from my plate into the food-waste bin, and Mum leaned against the doorframe with her wine glass and said, "Mick, check his temperature. He must be sick."

"Very funny," I said.

"I've been secretly beating good manners into him behind your back," Mick told her.

"Good." She came back into the kitchen—in no hurry for her bath—and ruffled my hair like I was a little kid. I combed my fingers through it to straighten it out, and Mum said, "Can you run by the drycleaners on your way home from school tomorrow? I forgot to pick up the funeral clothes since I dropped them off last week."

I hunted under the sink for a dishwasher tablet and said, "I can't tomorrow, I've got a study group."

"Since when do you go to study group?"

"Since now," I said. I didn't tell her what it really was, but "study group" was close enough; I just hoped she didn't pry.

"Mick?" she asked.

Mick checked his watch as if it could tell his future. "Yeah, I could probably swing by after work if they're still open when I get off."

I don't know why they were in a hurry to pick up the funeral suits. It's not like we planned to bury anybody else soon—I hoped.

I checked my phone. No texts.

They could bury my desire in six feet of soil and I'd still feel it.

The next day, I stumbled through school with a tightness in my chest. Not because of Grandad Tommy, and not even because of Jun, strictly speaking. At five p.m. I had my first ISL class at the community centre. And that thought made my palms itch.

When I got there, the building looked older than I remembered, red brick with mismatched windows and a community noticeboard outside, the Perspex cover graffit-ied, and the notices behind it were sun-bleached and faded.

Community centres were weird. Where else could you put a baby and toddler group right before an AA meeting? Maybe you went to one and then needed the other.

I stood outside for the longest time, watching others go in or leave from the previous class, and my nerves almost got the better of me. But the force to go in was stronger than the desire to leave, and once I was through the door, I didn't feel too bad.

The middle-aged woman behind the reception desk said, "Sign language class?"

I nodded.

"Down the hall on the right. Room 1C."

"Do I pay you?" I asked.

"Just pay the instructor, love," she said, and I thanked her and shuffled down the narrow hall.

The door of the room was propped open with a metal door stopper that was shaped like a cat, and inside, there were about ten chairs arranged in a circle, a whiteboard, and nothing else. Four of the chairs were occupied.

I took a seat, across the circle from them, and smiled politely when they nodded at me, and I took out my phone, scrolling through my socials without taking any of it in. And then a girl slumped into the chair beside me.

"You're new," she said.

I looked up, forcing a smile. I totally loved how people thought they could just talk to me and not weird me out.

She was eighteen, maybe nineteen, long sleeves pulled down over her hands, her fringe a little too short, like she'd cut it herself in a hurry. She had two nose rings in the same nostril and a strand of red in her hair that looked half-deliberate, half-forgotten about. She smiled. "I'm Ella. You look far too normal to be in a community centre with us reprobates."

"Owen," I said.

Ella signed my name to the others across the circle, and a few more people arrived.

"If I talk too much, you can slap me," she said.

"No, thanks."

"Seriously. My boyfriend says I never shut up. That's why I'm here. I can talk with my hands and he can't tell me off."

"Really?" I asked.

Ella laughed. She signed something and said, "No. But it's a cute story, right? Why are you here?"

I hadn't considered that question. I knew why I was there, but I don't think I'd admitted it to myself yet. I shrugged. "I just wanted to learn."

"But why sign language? Why not French or Yoga?"

"Because my French accent sucks and I don't look good in yoga pants."

"Nobody looks good in yoga pants." She laughed again. "So it's for a girl."

"Not even," I told her.

"A boy?"

I looked away from her.

"That's adorable," she said. "Is he cute?"

"Can you not?" I asked.

And Ella shrugged. She nudged her shoulder against me just as the instructor came into the room and said, "I'm only teasing. I'm sorry. You'll love me after a few classes, I promise."

I sort of loved her already, just from how brazen she was, but I didn't tell her that.

We paid the instructor for the class, and then he introduced himself to me because I was the only new guy in the room. "I'm Sean," he said, fingerspelling it. I recognised a few of the letters from my own name and Jun's.

I said my name, spelled it out as best I could from memory, and they gave me a round of silent applause. Which was not uncomfortable in the slightest.

Sean said, "Try not to panic. We'll be speaking as well as signing so there's no need to overthink anything. And you've got Ella beside you. She'll see you right."

Ella nudged me again and the class began with some basic signs—*hello, thank you, my name is*. We practiced them in a circle, with Sean demonstrating each sign twice, then he showed us how to ask, *How are you?* And how to say, *I'm good, and you?*

He said, "I know most of you are a little further ahead, but it's good to practice the basics so you don't forget them." He made us pair up and ask each other how we were doing. "And try to do it without speaking," he said.

Ella shuffled her chair towards me. She signed something that looked almost like Sean's version, and then she raised an eyebrow, waiting for me to reply.

I signed, *I'm good, and you?*

"Show off," Ella said.

When the class was over, I picked up my bag to leave and Sean shook my hand.

Ella said, "You coming back next week?"

I nodded. "I think so."

"Cool. You've got a good face for this."

I blinked at her. "What does that mean?"

"No idea. But you look like someone who listens with his eyes. Good luck with your… friend."

She grinned, slapped my shoulder, and skipped out of the room before I could tell her off.

On the way home, I put my earphones in but didn't play any music. I kept replaying the class in my mind, the signs, the rhythm. How deliberate everybody's hand motions were, especially when they were asking Sean a question, verbally as well as with ISL. It was a lot. But it was fun. On my walk, I fingerspelled my name a few times, trying to get it perfect. A lot of the signs I'd seen online were American sign language, but the Irish alphabet was different. I had some trouble transitioning from the E to the N, but as I walked, I repeated the action over again, to the point where a passing stranger might have thought I had issues.

I looked at my reflection in a shop window and signed, *Thank you. How are you?*

When I got home, the funeral suits were hanging over the banister at the foot of the stairs, shrouded in plastic, and Mum and Mick were eating dinner in the living room with the TV on.

"It's in the microwave," Mum called, and I passed the suits, went into the kitchen, and nuked my dinner for a minute and a half without even looking to see what it was. While I waited for it, I signed, *How are you? I'm good thanks, and you?* And then I carried my plate into the living room to sit with my parents.

"How was study group?" Mick asked.

"Good," I said. G-O-O-D. I didn't sign it with my hand, but I imagined what the letters would look like.

"Was it art?" Mum asked.

"Sign language," I said. I didn't look up from my plate, but their silence was loud. "What?" I asked in response to their quiet, keeping my gaze on the food in front of me.

"Sign language?" Mum said, like she didn't believe me.

"Yep."

"That'll come in handy," Mick said.

"Yep."

"Did you enjoy it?" Mum asked.

I nodded. Ate.

And that was that. They didn't ask any more. I sat with them for a while once I'd finished eating, and when I went to my room, the sun was going down. I switched on the lamp at my desk and sat on the bed, cross-legged, hair a mess because I was always pulling my fingers through it.

I'd been staring at the same page of my homework for twenty minutes when I shut the book and leaned back against the headboard. The signed alphabet was running through my brain but it wasn't enough. I needed to use it for real. For someone.

I reached for my phone and scrolled through social media for another half hour, trying to cure my lack of attention. The only thing that I liked was a photo of Ryan on the football pitch, an action shot of him punting the ball towards the net. I skimmed the comments, words of encouragement, banter from his football friends, and then I threw my phone back on the bed.

How are you? I signed.

I'm good, and you? I replied.

I was bored. Distracted. Annoyed.

I picked up my phone again, opened my contacts and found Jun's number, the hand emojis and flags. And then I recorded a video of myself signing, *Hello. How are you?*

I watched it back, recorded it a second time, sitting closer to the light now, and then I sent it before I chickened out.

I turned the screen off and dropped the phone back on the bed, turning onto my stomach and pressing my face into my pillows where it was difficult to breathe but I didn't care.

I waited. Turned my head, breathed, pressed my face into the pillow again.

When my phone vibrated, I didn't reach for it immediately. It wasn't him, I'd told myself, and I counted to twenty before sitting up and grabbing the phone.

It wasn't him.

It wasn't him.

It was him.

I opened the message—a video—and I hit play. His smiling face filled the frame, like he was holding the phone too close. Then he pulled it back and signed hello. He propped the phone against something so he could use both hands, and he signed something new. Then he stared at the screen for a second before reaching out and ending the video.

I didn't know what he'd signed. It was too fast, too chaotic, and I was just a beginner. He knew that, didn't he?

I stood up then sat down then stood up again. I watched his video twice more, as if I could decipher it through sheer will alone, and then I admitted defeat and sent him a text.

I'm sorry, I don't know what that means.

And Jun replied a minute later. *You sign well. Where did you learn that?*

And then a second message. *By the way, I'm good thanks, and you?*

CHAPTER 9

"Physics," Mr Byrne said, "is the best way to start a Wednesday, isn't it?"

We groaned. Somebody, somewhere, in their need to punish me, decided that Hump Day was a perfect excuse to start with physics and end with double maths. It didn't matter that I had art before lunch or English with Ryan afterward. The day was book-ended by misery.

I opened my textbook that had more diagrams than an architect's manual. Arrows, objects in motion. Mass and velocity. But everything was blurring together while I had Jun's video message playing around in my head, those quick hand gestures, long, slender fingers. And his eyes.

Those eyes.

Searching for me through the screen.

"Energy," Mr Byrne said at the front, "isn't destroyed. It just changes form. If you burn fuel, it becomes heat. If you drop a ball, it becomes kinetic. If you eat a banana, it becomes Owen not falling asleep at his desk."

The class laughed. I raised my head and gave him a sheepish grin. "It's Wednesday, sir."

"Precisely," he said. "It's potential energy. Just think of the rest of the day as gravitational acceleration towards the weekend."

I wedged my pen between my nose and upper lip in response. Take that for potential energy. I stared through the window at the trees, bowing in the breeze the way Jun had bowed to me in the park, and Mr Byrne said something more about energy. He drew on the board. Calculations, examples, graphs. And I copied them down without even thinking about them. The class ended like it began, with my confusing notes and Mr Byrne's joyless humour.

At lunch, Ryan reminded me about his football match after school and I promised I'd stay and watch. "Like a cheerleader," I said.

"In a skimpy skirt?"

"There are male cheerleaders, too."

"But you'd look cute in a skirt," he said, hanging off my shoulder like I was the only thing holding him up. I was never bothered by how tactile he was—in fact I used to enjoy it more than I probably should have—but I was glad Jun didn't go to St Malachy's and see it.

Not that Ryan would care. "Is this your boyfriend?" somebody said to him once, while he pressed his side against me in the corridor as I fumbled in my locker.

"Are you jealous?" Ryan had asked. It was last year. The year before? The boy tutted and Ryan had said, "Open your mind, man. What does it matter who dates who?"

"Isn't it whom?" I'd said, running along with the joke.

"Whom dates whom? That's not right."

The boy sneered.

"Come on, hubby, let's go to lunch," I remember saying, and I slammed my locker closed, skipping down the hallway with Ryan's hand in mine.

Ryan didn't give a shit, which made it easier for me to be me.

"Hey, boyfriend," he'd say often, in the school gym or corridors, camp and full of energy. If anybody else had done it, I'd have punched him for the mockery, but I knew Ryan was doing it in solidarity. His openness gave me bravery. And he was right—who cares whom dates whom, am I right?

I spread my coat on the damp grass at the side of the pitch after school and cheered him on with the rest of the spectators. He was pretty good. Not that I knew much about football—just about watching him win.

They jogged in wide loops around the pitch, arms loose, heads high. Ryan wore number 11. His hair was already dampened to his head with sweat and he hadn't even started playing properly. He called out something to a teammate and slapped him on the chest, then they ran in opposite directions.

The whistle blew and the match started, though I didn't catch who they were playing against. Another class from our school, I think. They just seemed to be chasing the ball around like it owed them money.

Ryan belonged out there. He was confident, fast. Not

graceful but focused—the kind of focus I only ever got while sketching. Or thinking about Jun. I watched him dart through a gap, shout something at the boy with the ball, and then take off down the wing (football terminology—look at me!). We cheered when he took a shot and his grin stretched across the pitch even though he missed.

I looked down at the muddy toe of my shoe and traced a line in the grass with a stick. The wind was cold across the pitch and I tugged the sleeves of my jumper down around my hands. The whistle blew again, somebody swore, and the ball went out of bounds for a free kick.

Ryan turned and caught my eye across the pitch. He smiled like he knew I was watching him. And then he jogged back into position, confident that I'd still be there when they were done.

They finished 4-3 against, but he didn't seem bothered. I sat on the wall near the school gates while he showered and changed, and when he came out, he was wearing a hoodie and his school trousers. "I saw you cheering," he said.

I waved my hands in the air. "Gimme an R."

He curled one arm and thrust the other out in the shape of an R, and I laughed. Then I fell into step beside him for the walk into town. The school bus was long gone, and walking with Ryan was always comforting.

We stood by a street bin while he tore the peel off an orange, and he threw segments at me even though I was hopeless at catching them in my mouth. And when he was finished, we stopped at a corner shop so he could buy a packet of crisps. I had no idea how he was so slim.

When we stood at a crossing, waiting for the lights to

change, Ryan nudged into me with a smile. "You haven't mentioned Tommy in a couple of days."

Damn it. "Thanks," I said. I had just about found myself happy not to be consumed by his memory every waking second.

"Sorry," Ryan said. We crossed the road. "When's the Month Mind?"

I don't know if it's a universal thing, but in Ireland, they hold a mass one month after somebody's death as a way to remember them. I never understood that. It's not like I was going to forget.

"Next week."

He held his crisp packet towards me but I shook my head. I know he didn't mean it, but he put a weight around my neck that I didn't need. It was bad enough at home with Mum and Mick pretending like they weren't tiptoeing past Grandad Tommy's room all the time. And when Tommy Two came over, nobody even mentioned him anymore.

Maybe it was too hard to talk about, but it felt like everybody was pushing him away.

I changed the subject. "I'm learning sign language."

"Okay," he said. "Don't you have enough homework?"

"I still had a few spare minutes before midnight."

"So you filled them with sign language?"

I nodded and signed thank you.

Ryan said, "You know nothing ever really goes away, don't you?" When I looked at him, he said, "Tommy. I'm not saying he's a ghost or a spirit or whatever. But I do believe he's still around."

"They don't talk about him anymore," I said. "At home."

Ryan stopped walking. "Do you want to talk about him?"

I shrugged. "Maybe. No. Not right now."

And he nodded. "You're allowed to still have a life. It's called moving on, which doesn't mean 'leaving behind', it just means accepting it."

"I know," I said.

"What *do* you want to talk about?" he asked.

I took a second before speaking. "I want to talk about sign language. Because there's this boy."

"Hold up. What boy?"

"Just a boy."

"Owen Theodore Kelly. Have you been holding out on me?" That wasn't my middle name, but that was Ryan all over. "Who is he? Is he from school?"

"Shut up," I said. But I smiled. "He's not from school. I don't know what school he goes to. Or if he's even into me."

"So ask him."

"I can't ask him. Anyway, I've only seen him a couple of times in the park. He's probably straight."

"But you've talked to him?" Ryan asked.

"I mean, yeah, but—" I didn't have a but, so I left it unsaid.

"And he's Deaf?" Ryan asked. "Well, I'm hurt. He'll never get to hear my beautiful singing voice."

"I'll remind him that's a good thing," I said and he punched me in the stomach, just a playful punch that still stung, and he dashed around a lamppost so I couldn't hit him back.

Ryan. Full-time bestie, part-time pest.

When I got home, the house was still empty. Still a Grandad-free zone.

I stood in the hallway and called out, knowing I wouldn't

get an answer, and then I drank some milk from the carton and put it back in the fridge. I kind of didn't mind the silence any more. It gave me space between school and homelife where Mick would be darting up and down the stairs, looking for something he lost, and Mum would be darting up and down behind him, assuring him she saw the missing thing somewhere but couldn't for the life of her remember where.

Usually, it was either in his pocket or on his head and he just didn't know it.

People go through life looking for things they don't need to look for.

But they don't go looking for things they need to.

I went upstairs, my shoes in the front hall, muddy from the football pitch and left there for later-me to deal with. Or Mum. Hopefully Mum.

I did my homework at the desk in my room and then I spun on the swivel chair, trying not to pick up my phone and reread yesterday's messages from Jun because that's what a crazy person does. So I got out my sketchbook and outlined a face with high cheekbones and dark hair and a perfectly straight nose. Eyes that were rounded and wide and darker than my feelings.

I shaded in the line of his neck and the curve of his Adam's apple. Softened the shading with the edge of my thumb. And when I sat back and looked at it, it wasn't right. Wasn't perfect. But it was definitely Jun.

I signed it, like he made me do the first time, and when I sat my pencil down, my phone lit up.

If all it took to get a text message from him was to draw his likeness, I'd do it again.

I was grinning even as I picked the phone up, hoping it would be another video message so I could see his eyes again for real.

But it was just a waving emoji.

I waved back.

And then he sent, *You're probably busy, but do you want to go to this thing tomorrow night?*

Something fluttered in my stomach, and I put it down to a lack of dinner. My cheeks were burning and my palms were sweating.

I was coming down with something.

Jun didn't say what the thing was or if there'd be anybody else there.

But I didn't care.

I said, *Yes!* And then I wished I hadn't been so emphatic. It didn't call for an exclamation mark.

Did it?

CHAPTER 10

I stood in front of the mirror with my arms crossed and my heart thudding as if I'd been filling my veins with caffeine all day. It was just a coffee night. When Jun had messaged me back saying he was looking forward to it, I had to ask, *What's the thing?*

He said, *A Deaf coffee night. There'll be hearing people too. It's just going to be chill.*

Just a coffee night. Not a date or anything stupid like that. But it wasn't anything not stupid like that, either.

I tried on another shirt. It was already after seven and he'd told me to be there for eight and I literally had nothing to wear. I was turning into a drama queen. Everything I owned felt like too much or not enough—trying too hard or as if I hadn't tried at all.

I pulled the shirt off again and turned back to my wardrobe. I thought about the day I first saw him, his oversized cream sweater that I hadn't seen him wearing since I accidentally spilled dirty paint-water all over it. I hoped it wasn't ruined. I remembered how his hands were half-swallowed by the sleeves. The loose fit, the soft fabric. Effortlessly chic.

Were all his clothes like that? Muted tones and long sleeves. Something vaguely soft about all of it. Something warm.

I touched the sleeve of one of my wool sweaters. It wasn't soft enough. Wasn't Jun enough. But there was another one in a drawer that I hadn't worn since winter. Mum had said it was too big for me, but big just meant oversized, right?

I pulled it on. Mottled maroon. It sat low on my hips and wide on the shoulder, and the sleeves covered just the right amount of finger. I pushed them up, let them fall.

And I smiled. It wasn't right, didn't scream, but it said enough. Even if I did have to hike up the hem to put my phone and wallet in my pockets.

I dashed downstairs and pulled my shoes on in the hallway, shouting into the living room, "I'm going out for a bit."

"Don't be late," Mum said. She didn't ask where I was going.

But when Mick came out of the kitchen, he pulled a face and said, "Christ. How much cologne are you wearing—the whole bottle?"

I stood up from the stairs when I finished tying my laces. "Is it too much?"

He sniffed the air. "Are you going on a—"

"No," I said hurriedly.

Mick turned his smile into a loud frown. "Do we need to have the talk?"

"Oh my God, no."

"Get out of here," he said, turning from me.

"But is it too much cologne?"

"Stand in the breeze for a bit," he said. "It might wear off before you get there."

So I stood in the garden for half a minute before I jogged down the road to catch the bus. Dads—I don't care if they're biological dads, stepdads or alien dads from Mars—are guaranteed to take the piss out of you at least once a week. I think it's in their contract.

When I got to town, I had to use the maps app on my phone to find the coffeeshop. It wasn't one I'd been to before. It was a fifteen-minute walk from where I got off the bus and I hoped I could figure out the way back at the end of the night.

The coffeeshop was tucked down a cobbled side street with fogged windows and golden light spilling out onto the pavement. I stood on the other side of the street, staring at the entrance, wondering if Jun was already inside or not. Wondering if I should wait out here for him or text him or go the hell home where I probably belonged.

But somebody opened the door and laughter fell out behind the young couple that were leaving. And in the quiet that was left behind when the door was closed again, I dug my hands into my jeans pockets and seriously considered turning around.

I couldn't tell who any of the silhouettes were through the glass, but I knew that I couldn't stand on the street all night. So I bit my lower lip, crossed the cobbles, and stumbled through the door like I'd never entered a room before in my life.

The smell of fresh coffee hit me hard—bitter and rich—and voices overlapped somewhere on my right. I didn't know where to look, so I looked at the floor, and then the coffee counter, and then at the large group of people that seemed to take up half the tables all at once.

When I saw Jun, I smiled and tried not to. He was mid-conversation with a girl across the small table from him, his hands forming words in the air, hers reciprocating. He wore a white button-down shirt with a tiny logo on the breast and I was suddenly second-guessing my oversized sweater when he noticed me and grinned, waving me over.

I picked my way through the throng of chatting people, lots of sign language, lots of voices to go along with it, and he stood up when I came near his table. He waved again, a greeting this time, not an order to come closer, and he signed something to the girl. She waved, casual, effortless, and I nodded. My hands were useless, too self-conscious to sign to either of them.

Jun stepped away from his chair and touched my arm like he was giving me the gift of his tingle. It jolted up my arm to twitch at my lips. He walked me to a table near the counter and signed a few words to a woman there. She had a sheet of labels in front of her and she smiled at me while asking a question with her hands.

Suddenly, I'd forgotten everything I learned at the ISL class. I'd even forgotten the instructor's name. Thankfully, Jun signed my name to her and I recognised the characters as he did it. She wrote my name on a label and, verbally, said, "Nice to meet you, Owen. Don't let him get you into any mischief."

Jun took the label from her and turned to me. He pressed it against my sweater, patted it, and grinned. Then he signed something to the woman.

"He says he likes your sweater," she told me.

I wasn't blushing. It was just warm in there.

The label on Jun's shirt said JUN-HO and I knew it was going to be awkward if I called him Jun all night. But he took my mind off my gawkiness by twisting his hand near his mouth—coffee?

I nodded and he walked with me to the counter where I ordered an Americano and a caramel macchiato, because that's what he drank when we sat by the kiosk in the park. But Jun waved his hand and signed "no" to the guy behind the counter. He pointed at his table to tell me he already had a drink.

"Are you sure?" I asked. I'd never bought coffee for somebody before. Not even Ryan.

He smiled and I knew he was telling me it was okay, that he already had one and didn't need another. How could his face be so expressive? Then he led me back through the group to his table and he pulled out his phone to type on it. *This is Becca. Say hello.*

I smiled and raised my hand in a greeting, settling into the wooden chair beside Jun. I blew air at my fringe, nervous, and Becca said something. I looked at Jun and he typed, *She wants to know how tall you are*, and Becca blushed.

I pointed my thumb towards Jun and said, slowly, clearly, "I'm taller than him."

Becca laughed and Jun questioned what I'd said because the angle of my head was turned away from him when I spoke to her. But Becca refused to tell him in her glee.

I sipped from my coffee cup and glanced sideways, catching the curve of Jun's jaw as he told her off with words that I couldn't understand but knew perfectly well. Becca gave me a thumbs up and a wink, and then she said something to Jun, as if they'd picked up their conversation from before I'd interrupted it.

After a couple of minutes, Jun put her on hold, shifting towards me slightly, and typed, *I'm glad you came.*

I smiled. "Me, too."

It's not too awkward?

"I'm one hundred percent comfortable being surrounded by people I can't even speak to," I laughed.

You'll be fine. How was your day?

"Normal," I said. "Just school. Then dinner with my mum and Mick before coming here."

Mick? he typed.

"Stepdad."

He nodded. Smiled. And I took another sip from my coffee to fill the silence.

There was laughter behind us. And then somebody slapped Jun's back and mine, as if we were old buddies. I looked up and saw a tall guy with short hair, a couple of years older than us. He smiled at me, crouching and checking out my nametag, then signed something to Jun, speaking verbally as he did. "How's it hanging?" When Jun told him, he said, "No shit. I haven't played that in years. Who's your friend?"

Jun signed and the guy turned to me. "Hi, friend Owen,"

he said. He offered me his hand and I shook it, registering the word friend in seventeen different ways—none of which were *potential date*. "I'm Callum," he said. "Looks like you met my baby sister." He pointed at Becca who rolled her eyes. She swotted the air in front of me and signed something with one hand. "Oi," Callum said. And she laughed.

Callum's arm went around Jun's neck as he signed something else, not verbalising it this time, and I looked at my half-drunk coffee because it felt like eavesdropping.

Jun replied to him and I wondered who he was, how he knew Jun, and just how close were they? Their signing was animated and casual, too quick for me to even dream of studying it.

When Callum turned to me again, still crouched between our chairs, he said, "What school do you go to?"

"St Malachy's. You?"

Callum said something to Jun and he winked. Then he stood up without answering my question. When he smiled at me, his lips were wide and flat. "See you around, friend Owen."

"Yeah," I said, as he walked away. "See you."

Jun touched the back of my hand to get my attention and it shocked me like static. He typed, *He's only funny when he wants to be.*

"It's cool," I said and I melted a little when he smiled.

Jun looked in his cup before picking it up, but it was empty. That was my chance to finally buy somebody a coffee.

"Want another?" I asked, pointing.

His eyes softened and he nodded, but as I stood up, somebody—I think it was Callum—shouted, "Head's up!"

and a muffin (undoubtedly blueberry) sailed past my head. I ducked, spun, and my leg caught on the chair behind me.

I stumbled.

Fell.

But instead of hitting the floor, somebody caught me. My body rocked against him, his hand at the back of my head, the other one around my waist.

Jun.

And his face was just there. Those dark eyes. I felt his breath on my cheeks. Coffee breath with a hint of mint. I couldn't move. Couldn't breathe. It took all my effort to swallow down my panic at falling. My horror at falling into his arms.

Jun.

He eased back, pulling me upright. Straightened my sweater. And then he reached for his phone.

But I stopped him before he could type. I knew what he was going to ask. "I'm okay," I said, my voice tight, my heart dancing behind my ribs. He narrowed his eyes in a question. "I'm fine," I said. "Thank you. For, you know, catching me."

Jun smiled. And before I went to the counter to order coffees, he typed something and pressed the phone into my hand. He turned away while I read it.

I never caught a shooting star before.

Was he calling me a shooting star? What did that mean?

I went to the counter with his words in my head and I looked back at him when I'd ordered. He was talking to Becca again, but he glanced at me. Twice.

Because I was his shooting star?

Oh, God, my stomach.

"You all right?" the guy behind the counter said, putting the coffees in front of me.

I nodded and paid. I couldn't have spoken words even if I'd wanted to.

When I got back to the table, I slid Jun's coffee across to him and he signed, *Thank you.* But Callum was in my seat and somebody else had dragged a table closer, turning their conversation into a group chat. Jun pointed at the empty chair beside Becca and, reluctantly, I sat in it. I smiled at him when he grinned, and I watched him move his hands, the curl of his fingers and the tilt of his head.

Who's the loser? Callum was probably saying.

He's my shooting star, Jun will have replied.

Where'd you meet him? Callum's movements were exaggerated in my mind.

I just felt sorry for him, Jun likely said.

I sipped my coffee.

Becca interrupted their conversation, throwing in her own thoughts, verbalising her words as well as signing, and somebody at the second table interjected. Everyone laughed, so I did, too. A small one, because I didn't know what we were laughing at.

When I caught Jun's eye again, he tilted his head and raised an eyebrow. It said, *You okay?*

I nodded. Smiled.

Jun didn't push for more. But that was the hardest part. Nobody pushed. No one forced me to speak or leaned in to ask me a question, who I was or what I was doing there.

Which meant I had no role to play. Just an observer. Like somebody watching all the shooting stars skimming through the night sky and not knowing what they were.

I wasn't being excluded, I don't think. Not deliberately. But I wasn't being included, either. And that made something coil tighter in my chest.

I looked at Jun's hands, flying through fluent conversation with strangers and friends alike. Looked at my own, folded around my coffee cup on the table.

"Hang on," Callum said loudly, and I looked up. There wasn't any warmth in his eyes, but he said, "Sorry, mate, what was your name again?"

I looked down. The label was still stuck to my sweater where he could see it. But I said, "Owen."

Callum nodded. "You came to see Jun-ho, didn't you? And we totally got in your way."

"It's fine," I said. But it wasn't. It was as if they'd forgotten I was a stranger.

Jun looked at me with an apology in his eyes, and I wanted to feel miserable but I couldn't.

Callum stood up, scooped his arm around Jun's neck and knuckled his head, then he slapped his shoulder and said, "Come on, guys."

They left. And Jun remained opposite me, blinking like he didn't know what to say. Blinking like Morse code.

And I said, "I should probably get going anyway."

Jun tilted his head. *Do you have to?*

I shrugged. "It's getting late," I said.

CHAPTER 11

"You're leaving?" Callum asked when I stood up and gave Jun a wave, small, scared, tired.

"I've got school in the morning," I said.

Callum checked the time on his phone as Jun stood beside me. "It's not even late," he said.

Jun signed something, quick and sharp, and Callum shrugged. He walked away.

I turned to him but didn't say anything.

He typed, showed me. *I'm sorry, we were being rude.*

"No, you weren't. You're all friends."

You can stay.

"Nah," I said. I was feeling awkward enough as it was. "I've got school. Thanks for inviting me," I added, signing the motion. Thank you. Maybe it was the only sign I'd ever truly remember.

Jun held a hand out, hesitated, then widened his arms.

Was I comfortable with that? I'm not sure. Not after being ignored. But I leaned in, stiff and awkward, and we hugged. Casual. Friendly. Not at all how I wanted to hold him.

"Bye," I said, pulling away from his arms, searching his eyes for words he wasn't offering me.

And then I pulled open the door of the coffeeshop and stepped into the night.

It was raining. Gullies of rainwater crisscrossed along the cobbled street and I hadn't brought a coat. Just an oversized wool sweater that was getting wet. An oversized sweater that made me feel like a kid in his dad's clothing. And I still had a fifteen-minute walk to catch my bus.

I went down the street, drawing my shoulders up against my neck for protection, trying to shield my eyes from the rain with my hand, but my sweater was getting heavy and my trainers were beginning to squelch.

Perfect.

As I got to the corner, feeling drained more than anything else, a hand stopped me. Long, slender fingers at my elbow.

I turned just as Jun held an umbrella over my head.

He raised his other hand. *Hi.*

And I wiped rain from my forehead. "Hi," I replied.

He fumbled in his pocket, his shoulder knocking against me, the toe of his shoe touching the side of my foot. He pulled out his phone but couldn't unlock it with one hand so I took the umbrella from him, making sure it covered his dry head.

He said, *It's raining.*

I said, "I know."

He typed again and held the screen up, and I spent half the time looking at his words and the other half staring at his face that was just there. The rain drummed on the umbrella and the cold air crawled under it to join us.

Take my umbrella.

"I can't. You'll need it."

I have a coat.

"No," I said. Then I added, "Jun."

He looked at me. He put his hand around mine, on the stalk of the umbrella, his fingers warming my skin.

You can give it back to me later.

"You'll get wet," I said.

And Jun let go of my hand. He stepped back, away from the umbrella and into the rain. And he stared at me with a smile as the rain clung to his golden skin.

"Jun," I said.

He signed, *Thank you.* And then, *See you.*

He stood there for a second longer, holding his smile as I held his umbrella.

And then he turned and dashed back down the street and into the coffeeshop. At the doorway, he turned. Waved. And then he was gone.

I stood there for another awkward moment, and when I knew he wasn't coming back out to reclaim the umbrella, I looked up at the red and green fabric above my head, and then I went home, my shoes soaked but my hair almost dry by the time I got there. Protected by Jun's kindness.

Protected by Jun.

I propped the umbrella on the floor of the laundry room, open so it could dry, and I kicked my shoes off. My socks were damp. When I stood in the doorway of the living room, Mum was stretched across the couch, her head on Mick's lap. She was asleep.

Mick put a finger to his lips. More sign language. He said, "Is it raining?"

I looked at my sweater, soaked at the hem, sleeves hanging loose at the cuffs. The nametag label was still there, curled and peeling away from the wool, and the ink had run.

"No," I said, quietly so as not to wake Mum. "I decided to go swimming."

"How was your night?" he asked, ignoring my sarcasm.

I remembered the umbrella. And Jun's eyes. The hint of his breath when he caught me. The touch of his hand against mine.

"Fine," I said. And that was enough.

Upstairs, I peeled my socks off and pulled my sweater over my head. The T-shirt underneath was damp but I didn't care. I picked up my sketchbook and a pencil. And I don't know why, but I went to Grandad Tommy's room. I stood outside his door for a second, listening to the quiet noise of the TV downstairs, and then I went in and closed it behind me.

Tommy's essence was everywhere. His body was gone, but the smells lingered.

I climbed onto his high bed, my back against his pillows, and I closed my eyes for a moment, sitting in Tommy's quiet. In the gap that was left behind. On an easel, there was a half-finished painting of the family. Nobody had taken it down yet. Maybe they never would.

Grandad Tommy stood on one side, followed by me, Mum, Mick and Tommy Two, lined up like we were posing for a photograph, but he'd painted it from memory. And only half of it was coloured, the rest just faint pencil outlines, never to be finished.

I opened my sketchbook and I began to draw. An umbrella, opened and upside down, catching the falling rain, creating a pool of water inside. I sketched a little fish in it. And then I gave him a friend. Because everybody needs a friend.

I slid down the bed when I was finished, leaning my head against the pillows that still, even now, smelled like Tommy.

I twisted onto my side. I didn't mean to fall asleep.

But we always do things we don't mean.

The next day, Ryan pointed out how quiet I was, but I shrugged him off. "Just looking forward to the weekend," I told him. I didn't know how I was feeling any more. I still had Tommy's absence filling up the emptiness in my head, but also Jun, who was crawling under my skin even if he didn't know it.

On Saturday morning, Mum made a pot of coffee and I couldn't look at it without thinking about Jun's dark eyes. I'd folded up his umbrella and it was propped in the corner of my room, but I had no idea when I'd see him again. Our text messages were casual now because I didn't know what to say to him any more.

How is Callum? Who is Callum? Do you want to hold my hand the way I want to hold yours? I put all of those things into my texts without actually saying them. Because those were things I didn't want to know the answers to.

I'd forgotten what day it was when my phone reminded me about the ISL class at five p.m. Was it Tuesday already?

I wasn't sure if I wanted to go back there and learn more

ways for Jun to reject me. But because it was raining and because I'd brought Jun's umbrella to school with me, I walked the half mile to the community centre after class and stood outside the red-brick building feeling as grey as the sky.

And then Ella insinuated herself under the umbrella with me. I thought her fringe looked even shorter today than last time. She linked her arm through mine. "Jesus," she said. "Don't you hate the Irish weather?"

I actually liked standing in the rain. But I said, "Rain, rain, go away."

"Come again another day," she said, completing the kids' rhyme. "You coming in or just going to stand there like a wally?"

"Do I have a choice?"

"Nope."

She dragged me towards the entrance and when we were in room 1C, she shucked her wool coat off and patted the seat next to her. And even if there had been a hundred chairs in the room, I still couldn't have sat anywhere else, because when someone indicates the seat beside them, you sit.

Thanks for making me polite, Mum.

I was glad Sean's name was written on the whiteboard because I still couldn't remember it even when he came in and greeted us in sign language.

Hi, Sean, we signed, and I was glad to see I wasn't the only one struggling.

He took us through some of the basics again and we fingerspelled the alphabet a few times before he quizzed us, pointing and asking us to sign a letter. "K," he told me, and I got it right, but my fingers were all over the place. In ISL, a

K is like making a circle with your thumb and middle finger. Like a broken a-okay.

"P," he told Ella.

She held up three fingers and said, "Dib, dib, dib," like a boy scout.

We laughed, but Sean said, "Maybe don't say it aloud next time, but mnemonics is a great way to remember signs."

When we'd performed the entire alphabet twice, he left the room for a few minutes and said we could take five.

Ella tapped on her phone while she sat beside me and for some reason I expected her to hold the screen up to show me what she'd typed. Was I too used to having conversations with Jun, despite having only been with him a few times? But she put her phone away when she was finished texting, and said, "At least you came back."

"Why wouldn't I?"

Her face said all the words she didn't vocalise. "Things are good?" she asked.

I knew what she meant but played dumb. "Nothing is bad."

"Uh-oh," she said.

"What?"

"Trouble in paradise?"

But Sean came back and I didn't get a chance to respond. He sat a heavy cardboard box on the table in the corner of the room and said, "These belong to the centre, so you'll have to give them back. But you can hold on to them for a few weeks." He opened the box and pulled something out. "Noise-cancelling headphones," he said. "I know it's unconventional, but I've been watching you over the last few weeks and you're all relying on verbal cues more than the visual signs. And that's perfectly fine, while you're learning. But one day you're going to have a conversation with somebody who doesn't speak English. And at that point, you'll be saying, 'I wish I'd paid more attention in Sean's class,' but it'll be too late."

He handed them out.

"This isn't about letting you feel what it's like to be Deaf, but if that happens regardless, then so be it. Sometimes it helps to understand the person you're trying to communicate with in a way that makes it clear."

The over-ear headphones that looked like something you'd wear while using a pneumatic drill had the community centre's name written on the side in Tippex. We tried them on and adjusted the head straps to get them comfortable, and Sean signed something. He mouthed the words, too, just to make it easier, but I still missed half of what he said.

I draped the headphones around my neck after that so we could get on with the lesson, and Sean wrote a word on the board—*emotions*.

Tonight, we learned how to feel. Or rather, how to express our feelings without speaking. Happy. Tired. Sad. Frustrated. Signs that were partially made with the hands and partially with the face. Then he taught us some less obvious ones like proud and shy.

Ella leaned into me and said, "Don't get 'confused' mixed up with 'constipated' or you'll get really strange reactions."

I replied with the sign for tired and she understood the subtext.

And my shoulder still smarted from her thump by the end

of the class.

When she was leaving, she signed that she was frustrated with me, but then she stuck out her tongue.

"Child!" I called after her, laughing.

Her voice echoed back from the far end of the hallway. "But you love me anyway."

Outside, it had stopped raining, and I stood by the exit and signed, *I'm happy. I'm sad.* And then I wanted to go back inside and ask Sean what the sign was for, *I think I'm feeling all the emotions.*

When I got to the corner of the high street, the noise of rush-hour traffic and the beeping of pedestrian crossings swallowed me. Footsteps. People talking. Somebody shouting. Cars honking. And after the quiet of the community centre, it was overwhelming.

I stood near the crossing, with a busy Chinese takeaway behind me, and I put the noise-cancelling headphones over my ears. There was a switch on the side to turn on the ANC, and when I did, the sounds drained away, leaving me in the quiet of my own life.

It wasn't perfect. I could still hear things. But they were far away, just the gentle buzz of noise, a soft thrum that was actually pleasant.

I looked around. Two dogs barking as their owners passed by one another. A man shouting at somebody who'd bumped into him. The dull ache of a car horn that was distant even as it sped by. People walking. People talking. People living.

I saw a shop owner throw sudsy water on the pavement outside their store and scrub it with a hard-bristled broom. And somebody on a motorbike. Noises that were diluted.

Distant.

And then I took the headphones off and everything rushed in at me all at once.

I put them on again.

Hearing. Not hearing.

And I realised we all read sign language every day, even if we don't know it, or don't think of it that way. The sneer on a disgruntled face. The wave of a hand. The angry point of a finger. A head down so no one will talk to you. A look. A glance. We say more with our bodies than we ever intend.

Or maybe we do intend it. Maybe that's what language is. Motion over emotion.

I crossed the road with the headphones on.

And I walked the rest of the way home in silence.

I wasn't learning sign language. It was already part of me.

CHAPTER 12

I clung a little closer to Ryan that week even if I didn't want to tell him what was going on in my head. He was happy to sit with me, down by the river while I sketched, or in his bedroom after school while he beat me at Mario Kart.

Jun continued to message me. *How was school? What'd you learn today?*

And I couldn't figure him out. I knew the coffee night wasn't a date—honestly, I did—but I was still disappointed with how it ended, even if he did offer me his umbrella. When he talked to Callum and his friends, I was nothing. When he gave me the umbrella, I was everything. And I didn't know how I could be both.

"Out with it," Ryan said on Friday night, with a mouthful of pizza and Diet Coke. "You told me about some boy and

109

then never mentioned him again. What's going on?"

"Nothing," I said. "We're just friends."

"And yet every time your phone lights up, your face lights up with it."

"No, it doesn't," I said. And Ryan rolled his eyes. I guess he was right. Jun became this thing at the end of the phone that gave me something to care about beyond school, beyond homework and sketching. If I wasn't wallowing in Grandad Tommy's absence, I was falling into Jun's texts.

My phone lit up while Ryan reached for another slice of pepperoni pizza. "See?" he said.

I'd snatched my phone up from his bed the second it glowed, but when he called me on it, I sat it down again, unread.

"Read it," he said.

"No, I'm all right." I swapped out my character in the game.

"Read it. I know you want to."

"Piss off."

Ryan laughed. "Give me your phone. I'll ask him on a date." He grabbed it before I could stop him. And when I tried to pull it from his fingers, he said, "Holy shit."

"What? Give it back."

"Oh, man," he said.

"What?"

"You don't need to ask him on a date. Because he's asking you."

"Shut up," I told him, peeling my phone from his grip. I didn't look at it immediately. I was trying not to be eager. "Eat your pizza. And don't talk with your mouth full."

Ryan picked up another slice. "Will you answer his damn text already?"

I kept the phone facedown. Ryan was just messing with me like he always did. But when I flipped the phone over and looked, Jun had said, *We should go to the coast tomorrow. What do you think?*

I thought: marry me.

I thought: can I stare into your eyes the whole day?

I thought: will Callum be there?

"Told you," Ryan said.

"Shut up," I complained as I tapped my reply. *Sounds fun. What should I bring?* I wanted to add, *Who's going to be there?* But I didn't want to seem stand-offish to his opening request. "It's not a date," I told Ryan. "It'll be a group thing."

"He still invited you," Ryan said. "We really should have ordered two pizzas. I'm still hungry."

"You're always hungry." I gripped my phone, waiting for Jun's reply. When it came, Ryan rolled his eyes again. Jun said, *Don't bring anything. Just your walking shoes and your sketchbook.*

I had to ask, because maybe I'd suddenly have the flu if Callum was going, but I framed it in a way that I hoped Jun didn't catch on to. *Won't the others get bored if I stop to sketch all day? LOL.*

And Jun said, *What others? I meant just us.*

Us.

"What'd he say?" Ryan asked.

"Nothing," I grinned. "He said absolutely nothing."

"Yeah," Ryan said. He went back to the game, the empty pizza box discarded on the floor. And ten minutes later, he hit pause and said, "If you get a boyfriend and stop being friends with me, I'm going to put a horse's head in your bed."

"Crazy much?" I asked. "Why would I stop being friends with you?"

"That's true. I'm a delight to be around."

"Sure," I said. "You're as delicious as Angel Delight." I poked my fingers in my mouth like I was going to barf and he nudged me with his elbow. And then he won another round of Mario Kart because my head was elsewhere.

My brain was already at the coast.

In the morning, I stood on the southbound platform of the train station, letting the cold wind barrel along the concrete to push against me, and I waited for Jun, half-expecting him to turn up with a gang of his friends, all signing to each other and laughing around me. But when he got there, he was alone. His backpack was slung low and his hair was catching in the wind that stole along the platform, and the oatmeal-coloured jumper he was wearing seemed baggier than usual. When he waved, my brain refused to operate, and so I just stood there as he came along the platform.

He asked how I was and I replied with my stock answer from Sean's ISL class. *I'm good, and you?*

Then he typed, *Ready to go?*

And I signed, *Excited.*

Jun's eyes widened. *You're getting good.*

I didn't want to tell him I was taking a class, but I said, "I learn quickly. Anyway, where are we going?"

He gripped my sleeve and walked me to the station list on the wall, scanning it before pointing at Bray.

"Are you sixteen or sixty?" I laughed, and I had to say it

twice so he could understand me. Bray was a small coastal village, the kind you'd retire to, not visit on a day trip.

It's nice, apparently.

"We'll see," I said. In truth, I'd never been there.

When we got on the train, it was half-empty. We got a block of seats with a table and when Jun sat down, I hesitated. Should I sit beside him or opposite? But the train whistle blew and as it moved, I jerked forward, stumbling into the seat opposite. But that was fine; I could stare at him better from there.

Jun unzipped his backpack and pulled out two cans of Coke and a share-sized pack of crispy snacks with Korean script on the front. *They're from home*, he typed. *You'll love them.*

They were shaped like seashells. I asked, "What do they taste like?"

Jun pointed at the text above the brand name then typed on his phone, *Crispy and delicious*.

And you know what? They were. The packet was empty before we got to the next stop.

As we moved further out of the town and into the countryside, we were met with rolling hills and green fields, and Jun stared out of the window. He blinked and jumped when a train sped past in the opposite direction, and then he settled back again to watch the world go by.

I opened my sketchbook on the table and shaded in a quick outline of him, chin on his hand, eyes buzzing with a reflection of the entire world outside. And when he saw what I was doing, he blushed and covered his face.

"You asked me to draw you before," I said.

That was different, he typed.

"It's your fault," I said. "You told me to bring my sketchbook."

He laughed, posed for me, but his embarrassment won over and I closed the book before long. And as we inched closer to Bray, the coastline opened up and it looked like we were floating on the sea, trapped between the waves and the mountainside.

When we got off the train at the station, I heard the sea and the gulls. They engulfed me. And when Jun asked why I looked shocked, I realised for the first time that day that I was paying attention to something Jun had no experience of. I said, "I hear the waves."

He made a motion, a sign that I knew meant the sea, and then we raced along the platform to the stairs and the exit.

We dashed down the road and when we hit the corner, we saw the water, murky blue and cold. Jun pointed and we ran the rest of the way, his backpack bouncing behind him, until we reached the stone wall that separated land from beach, normality from fun.

It wasn't a race, but Jun leaned against the wall, catching his breath, and then typed, *I won.*

I frowned and signed my frustration at him, and he knew I was joking.

We can go back and race again. I'll let you win this time.

We walked along the wall, watching the waves as they foamed in over the dark, pebble-dusted sand. It was mid-spring and a sharp wind cut in across the beach, but the sun was shining and the seagulls were calling.

Jun took a couple of photos on his phone of the coastline, a close-up of some pebbles, and then he turned, snapped a shot of me, and set it as my profile photo in his contacts app. It was an awful picture, but when I held my own phone up for payback, Jun stuck out his tongue and wouldn't put it away until I'd taken the photo. So that was the face I saw every time he sent me a text. Eyes screwed up and tongue out.

Cute without meaning it.

It was too cold to take our shoes and socks off as we walked south along the line of sand near the water's edge, and as the wind stabbed me, I pulled my hood up against it. Jun squinted and walked backwards for a while, until I held my hand up to his face and shielded his eyes from the wind and swirling sand grains. We walked that way, side by side, my hand against his skin, until my feet stuttered in the wet pebbles and Jun smiled. Said thanks.

He blinked.

And there was sand grit in his eyelashes.

I stepped closer. Reached out. Eased my thumb over his eye.

He blinked again, expressionless, and I stepped back from him in case my lips were about to do something stupid.

Jun turned. Typed, *This way. Let's walk along the cliffs.*

And I suddenly wished I'd brought a picnic blanket.

We left the beach before it turned into a rocky outcropping and followed a narrow path that cut along the grass into the low hills. At the top, we stopped to look down and take some photos, and Jun swayed in the wind, holding his arms out, exaggerating how precarious it felt, as if he could be blown away by it.

I gripped the collar of his jumper, under his chin, and said, "Don't fly away."

He folded his arms in, gripping my wrist for safety, and shook his head.

We walked further up the path, kicking a stone between us like a football, and when the path veered in two directions, we stuck to the left and onto the jagged terrain. At a lookout point with a bench, we sat and I opened my sketchbook. Jun pulled his from his backpack and we drew the horizon in quiet togetherness. After a while, I realised he wasn't drawing any more and when I looked, he was watching my page, the lines leaking out of the pencil lead, giving birth to the scene. I tapped his half-finished sketch and he looked up.

"Stop watching me," I said, smiling.

He wrote on the corner of his page, *Yours is better. I like watching you.* His handwriting was small and neat.

I felt the heat of his arm beside me and, for a moment, I didn't move. I stared at the words on his page and then at his face. And Jun's hand reached up and turned my head back to the sea. He tapped my sketchbook, telling me to continue.

And I shaded in the dark coastline with the memory of his fingers tingling under my cheek.

When I glanced at him again, he was staring at my face, not the book. And so I nudged my shoulder against him. "Stop staring," I said.

And he covered his eyes with a hand until I tapped his fingers and said, "Fine. Stare all you want. But stop distracting me."

I watched the smirk spread across his lips before he wiped it away, and then he shuffled closer, his arm against mine, while he closed his sketchbook and watched me work.

When I was done, Jun pointed at it and made a bird

motion with his hands, so I handed him the pencil and he drew in two loose M-shapes for seagulls. Then I signed it, *Owen Kelly and Lee Jun-ho.*

I felt like a kid writing *Owen + Jun* in the margin of a workbook. K-I-S-S-I-N-G.

I looked at him and his face was alive with joy. Did he want to kiss me, too? I had no idea.

But he checked the time, then typed, *Lunch?*

We got a table on the veranda of a small restaurant that overlooked the beach. The sun was on the far side of the building now and we were in the shade, but I was warmed by his company, by the look on his face as he stared across the ocean. He slid his phone towards me. *Just imagine if you swam out there and kept going. You'd reach England.*

"Probably Wales," I said, but the idea was nice. Just keep swimming until you got to a whole other country. A whole other world. And maybe over there, there'd be no sadness. No school, no dead grandads. Just existing in a tiny cottage somewhere in the Welsh valleys.

That'd be nice.

When the woman came to take our order, she said, "Just so you're aware, there's no plaice," and it took me a second to realise she meant the fish, not that there was no room for us in her half-empty restaurant. Jun studied the menu and pointed.

"With chips?" she asked.

Jun nodded and bowed his head to her.

When I said I'd have the same—having no idea what he'd pointed at and hoping it didn't come with mushrooms—the woman left and I said, "You bow your head. I've seen you do it before."

Habit, he typed. *In South Korea, we show respect to elders and strangers. And even friends, but to different degrees.*

I tilted my head in a bow and he waved his hands beside his head—applause.

Then I signed, *Hungry*, and he nodded emphatically.

When the food arrived I was grateful he'd ordered cod, and Jun wouldn't eat until I'd tasted my meal first. I said, "It's nice. Is that another one of your customs?"

No, he typed, laughing. *If it was terrible, the joke is on you.*

I threw a chip at him and his shocked face made me laugh. Then I suppressed it into a shoulder-shaking snicker because the waitress walked by and asked how the food was. Jun gave her a thumbs up.

We ate mostly in silence. And sometimes, when I looked up, he was watching me. And sometimes, when I was watching him, he looked up and caught me. Every time he did, I turned my head to look at the sea and I chewed my food around the smile that I couldn't get rid of.

We argued over the bill when it came, but in the end, we split it. But the fact that he wanted to pay—and so did I— meant only one thing.

The day was starting to feel like a date.

CHAPTER 13

We walked along the strand and then into Bray, getting lost among the narrow residential streets, admiring the houses, the stone walls, and the quiet of everything. Jun took photos of flowers that grew over the tops of tall walls and of interesting cracks in the pavements. He coaxed a stray cat over with his fingers outstretched and stroked behind its ear, and I took a photo of him that he didn't know I was taking.

Maybe I'd sketch it later. Maybe I wouldn't. But it was nice to have the memory.

We didn't know where we were going, just following the roads, turning at random corners to walk in another direction, and when Ryan sent me a message asking if I'd snogged him on the beach yet, I sent him a parasol emoji and then said, *Go away.*

He replied, *I need the gossip. I'm dying of boredom.*

I sent him a heart and then put my phone away.

Jun saw another cat but it wouldn't come near him. I said, "You like cats?"

He nodded, shrugged, and then stretched his hands wide. More than cats.

"All animals?" I asked.

He smiled, and then, because he couldn't express it with his face and I was still a novice at sign language, he got his phone and said, *Animals don't lie. They don't hide things from you.*

"Dogs hide bones all the time," I said.

He turned his back on me and I laughed, taking his shoulder and spinning him back to face me.

"It was a joke."

He narrowed his eyes and stabbed his fingers on the keyboard, then he thrust the phone in front of my face. *Not funny!!!*

I didn't know what to say. I stared at the words and then looked at his face.

And I could have punched him. He was cracking up, silently laughing at my inability to catch his humour.

I scowled through my smile and said, "What's the sign for 'dickhead'?"

He showed me—and yeah, it's what you think it is—and then he leapt out of my reach when I pretended to take a swing at him.

Then he tapped my shoulder and pointed. He wanted to go that way.

We found a small row of shops, a convenience store, an

estate agent and a salon. And tucked among them was a used bookstore. Jun pointed and I nodded, and when we went in, there was a bell above the door that tinkled and the floorboards creaked beneath our feet. It had that musty, old book smell that Jun inhaled with his eyes closed, and he bowed to the man behind the counter before veering off to scan the shelves.

I followed him, touching the spines, feeling their stories, and I watched when he took down a book, read the back cover, and slid it neatly back into place, flush against the shelf. Something told me even his bedroom would be neat. And I blushed when I realised I wanted to mess it up with him.

Jun turned and traced his way along the shelves at the other side of the aisle and then ducked down the next. He sneezed, a quiet sound, and I mouthed, "Bless you." He made a sign that I thought meant dusty. I didn't ask. Didn't really need to.

There was a shelf of oversized art books, coffee table books that were filled with paintings by van Gogh and Munch and Rembrandt. When Jun found it, he came back to me, gripped my wrist, and dragged me to them. He pointed at them and then at me.

"I'll never be that good," I said.

But that's not what he meant. He pointed again and then touched my chest with both of his hands.

"I don't… You want to buy one for me?"

He nodded.

"No," I said, grinning. "You don't have to do that."

He touched my chest again. He wasn't using ISL now. He was just talking to me.

"Okay," I said, and when he smiled, I smiled too. I scanned the shelf, pulled down a book, flipped through the old pages, and then put it back. In the end, I found a book of prints from Edgar Degas that included his paintings as well as photos of his sculptures, dancing girls and men lounging on sofas. The price was handwritten inside the cover—twelve euros which, even though it was second hand, was a steal. "Are you sure?" I asked.

And he pressed the book against my chest where earlier he had pressed his fingers.

When he paid for it, the man said, "Have a beautiful day."

I said, "We are."

Next, we went into the convenience store and bought some snacks, and then we found a narrow row of concrete steps that lead down from one street to another. We sat near the bottom and ate crisps and chocolate, and Jun opened everything in a way that meant we could share.

He looked at me, then reached up to brush the corner of my mouth with his thumb. Crumbs. He didn't have to type it. And I watched him when I didn't pull away from his touch. Was he just being nice? Was he being more than nice?

And then I asked him a question that I didn't anticipate asking. The words fell out and I couldn't put them back in. He stared at my lips as I said them. "Have you always been Deaf?"

Jun didn't reply at once. His gaze skimmed from my lips to my eyes, held them for a second, and then he looked away.

He dusted his hands together like he was finished eating, and he stared across the street. But before I could say I was sorry, that I shouldn't have pried, he shook his head. Made the sign for no.

I waited. I knew he wasn't finished, wasn't going to leave it there. And I clasped my hands in my lap before he answered me.

He pulled out his phone. Typed. Deleted it. Typed again. He passed the phone to me and then he looked away as I read it.

Not always. I was born hearing. Lost it when I was seven. Meningitis. I got ill, had a fever, went to the hospital, and then there was only silence. I can still recall what things sound like. Or I think I can. I don't know. But I learned KSL and even though it was sort of lonely, my brother learned too. I could talk with him the way I couldn't talk with my parents. Mum learned KSL and ISL and taught me both. Dad tried. I guess. Anyway. I wasn't always Deaf. I used to hear but I'm better now.

I read it again. I knew he'd ended it with a joke, a jibe, but I didn't laugh. When I looked up, he was still facing away from me. I touched his shoulder. Squeezed. When he looked at me, I said, "I'm sorry."

He shook his head. It meant, *Don't feel sorry for me.*

I said, "I'm sorry that you got sick." He watched my lips as I spoke. "But I'm glad I met you."

He nodded and took his phone back. He didn't type anything now. He'd said enough. He nudged the half-empty crisp packet towards me.

And as I scooped some broken crisps into my hand, I said, "I didn't know you had a brother. Where is he?"

He blinked. I was full of awful questions today. Then he typed, *In Korea. Mandatory military service.*

"Mandatory? Will you have to do it, too?"

He shook his head, tapped one ear. And then he put his phone away. I knew the questioning was done. I just hoped I hadn't offended him.

He stood up and offered me his hand. When I took it, he hauled me to my feet and we gathered up our snack wrappers. And then we walked back down along the beach while I hugged my Degas art book and Jun stared at the seagulls as if maybe he was remembering what they sounded like.

We sat on the pebbles for over an hour, watching the waves and the birds in perpetual motion. There was a weight beside me, the heat of him, and for a while I watched his face instead of the sea. His jaw muscles were clenching. Memories do that—grip you and tighten you up.

I don't know what he was thinking. But when he looked at me, he smiled, and the warmth of it entered his eyes as well as his lips.

He signed something that I took to mean, *I love it here.*

And I nodded. So did I.

I rifled through the pebbles beside me and found one that was rounded and two-tone, the crack of a pale colour running through it like a lightning bolt. A different kind of rock, maybe? Ryan would know. The rest of the stone was grey except for that cream-coloured middle, and it reminded me of an Oreo or a custard cream. I rubbed it on my jeans to clean the sand from it, and then I covered it with my hands and presented it to him.

Jun closed his eyes and held his hands out like he was receiving a gift, and I dropped it into his palms. When he opened his eyes, his mouth made a *wow* shape—wide and exaggerated—and then he held it against his chest like he'd cherish it forever.

I stared at the sea for a second and then said, "I can't tell if you're being funny."

He questioned me with his eyes, then got his phone. *I'm always funny.*

"Ha ha," I said flatly.

He said, *It's a stone of two halves. Like friends. Held together with… whatever the pale bit is.*

"Cream," I said, and he dropped his eyes from me but I knew he was smiling.

When the sun had started to go down, we walked back to the train station, slowly, reluctant to leave. I didn't say it, but I wondered if Bray would be "our place". Somewhere I would always find him.

Somewhere we could come back to together and never be alone.

The train was busier this time, but we managed to find forward-facing seats together. I let Jun have the window seat and we ate more snacks while we waited for the rest of the passengers to board and the whistle to blow.

We chugged out of the station under the dull clank of the lines and the burr of motors, the grind of metal on metal tracks. And we sat there, the sky turning golden at the edges, and rattled beside each other, our shoulders touching, leaning into the motion of the train.

Jun pointed at some sheep in a field, and when he looked at me, his skin—framed by the wide window—was glowing. This was what I wanted to draw, but I didn't have the space to open my sketchbook here and Jun would refuse to pose for me anyway. So for the brief second he grinned at me, I studied his face to remember it for later. And I snapped a photo before he turned away.

The train stopped for a minute between stations, in the middle of a hilly field, and Jun settled back against his seat. He yawned, covering his mouth with a hand, and I wondered what those fingers would feel like if they were linked between mine.

When the train started moving again, somebody walked up the aisle, bumping against the seats as if they couldn't maintain their balance. "Sorry," he said.

I gave him a smile, knowing even as I did it, that it wasn't the same kind of smile I gave to Jun.

And then I felt the press of Jun's head against my shoulder. I looked. I could smell his hair—coconut shampoo—and feel the weight of him. His eyes were closed and his face was full of peace. And instead of nudging him awake, I let him lie there. Against me.

I tilted my head onto his and closed my eyes.

And in the distance, a train whistle called out my name.

CHAPTER 14

I slumped into my seat beside Ella on Tuesday evening, gripping my backpack on my lap, and I wasn't smiling. I wasn't.

She said, "What are you smiling about?"

I said, "I'm not," but I heard it in my voice even as I felt it in my facial muscles.

Ella cocked her head and leaned back to study me.

"What?" I said. Okay, I was totally smiling.

She folded her arms and chewed her lip, nodding as though I'd just confirmed her assessment. "If I didn't know any better, I'd say you got some."

"Some what?"

She laughed. "If I have to tell you, you clearly didn't get any. But you're different," she said. "Where's Mr Grumpy?"

"I was never grumpy."

"No," she said, stretching it out like the word had no end. "I checked with your mum about your birth certificate and apparently Grumpy is your middle name."

"Shut up," I laughed, pulling out my notebook and a pen.

"You're taking notes now?"

I shrugged. "How else are we going to learn?"

When Sean came in, Ella said, "Sean, how do you say 'I love you' in sign?" When he signed it, she repeated it to me, over again until I threatened to stab my pen into her leg.

"What's all this?" Sean asked.

"Nothing," I said.

"It's far from nothing," Ella said. Sean began the lesson, and Ella leaned into me. She whispered, "I'm happy for you."

"I don't know what you're talking about."

She beamed and nodded and signed *What time is the bus to Dublin?* when Sean illustrated it for us.

At the end of the class, while she was packing up her things and shrugging into her denim jacket, I said, "Can I ask you something?"

Ella sat down again. She said, "If it's about the birds and the bees, ask your father."

I blushed. "Why would I do that when I can just ask Google? Anyway. I've been invited to dinner."

"A date?"

"No," I said. "At his home. With his mum. He texted me this morning. It's tomorrow night."

"Okay," she said. "Start with the cutlery on the outside first. I think that's how dinner parties go."

"No, it's not that. I just—I don't know what to do."

Ella crossed her arms and her bangles clinked. "You go.

You smile. You be polite. And don't ravage him in front of his mother. That one's important."

I tutted. "Are you going to help me or not?"

"I just did," she smiled. "Seriously. You're sixteen. Go. Eat. And be yourself. How hard can it be?" When she stood up, I walked with her to the exit, and we stood in the carpark where somebody in a car honked and she waved. She said, "You'll be fine." Then, "Oh, hey. We're having a party next month. It's my boyfriend's birthday. You should come. Bring the boy. I'll get to practice my signing." She handed me her phone. "Give me your number. And if you text me tomorrow while you're stuffing your face full of food or full of your fella's tongue, I'll come over there and smack you."

She kissed me on the cheek before getting into her boyfriend's car, and she waved at me as they left.

Ryan came over on Wednesday evening after school and helped me choose an outfit. He said, "Have you got something to bring with you?"

"Like what?"

"A gift. For his mum."

"You mean like flowers or something?"

"Jesus, Owen, do I have to think of everything?" He pulled a fancy box of chocolate biscuits out of his bag and said, "You're welcome. And don't wear that unless you're going to iron it."

I checked myself in the mirror. I liked the shirt I'd picked, but he was right, and I didn't have time to iron it. So I yanked it off and pulled on a thin hoodie instead. It had a narrow cut, almost T-shirt material, and Ryan said it was better than a shirt anyway. "A shirt would make you feel uncomfortable, and also look like you're trying too hard."

I jumped in a taxi, and he waved from the pavement like I was going off to war.

When I got to Jun's house, in an area of town I'd never been to before, with tall but narrow houses and blocks of purpose-built flats, Jun was waiting for me. He stood in the open doorway with the sleeves of his hoodie pushed halfway up his arms and the steam from a mug in both hands clouding around his soft features.

I waved and he smiled, sipped from his drink, and then stepped aside to let me in.

In the small hallway, he pointed at the row of shoes just inside the doorway and he didn't have to explain. I kicked mine off and lined them up with the others, conscious that I'd worn socks with little fox faces all over them. I wriggled my toes on the cool tiles as Jun laughed.

He made a calming motion with his hand, telling me not to worry, and then he tapped the box of biscuits in my hands. I grinned and realised I hadn't spoken a word since I arrived, but we'd already had a whole conversation.

He led me into the narrow living room with a kitchenette at the back wall, a breakfast bar island separating his mum from us. Smoke rose from the griddle to the cooker hood and as we came in, she turned with a smile. I had known she was Irish—Jun had told me ages ago—so I don't know why I was expecting her to be Korean. Her smile was warm and wide, and she came around the island to greet me.

"Owen. It's lovely to meet you." She pulled me into a hug that I think surprised Jun almost as much as it did me. "I hope you're hungry. I'm making bulgogi." When she released me, she signed and spoke at the same time. "You're not allergic to anything, are you? I told Jun-ho to ask you, but I wanted to make sure."

"No, Mrs Lee," I said.

She slapped my shoulder. "Call me Eileen."

I glanced at Jun who was watching us with intent. "My mum would murder me if I did," I laughed. I don't know if my nerves were making my palms sweaty or my sweaty palms were making me nervous.

Jun's mum leaned into me again. "Your mother isn't here, and I insist. I miss the Irish warmth. And it's been a long time since we had anyone for dinner."

Jun tapped his mum's shoulder and signed something, and she stepped back from me.

"I'm just being polite," she told him with her voice and her hands. "Take a seat, it's almost ready."

She went back to the stove and Jun grinned at me. He pointed to my hands, and only then did I remember I was still holding the box of biscuits. I silently offered them to him, too embarrassed to speak to his mum again.

We sat on the couch, two feet apart, and Jun reached for his phone. *Are you hungry?*

I nodded. "Smells delicious."

It is, he typed.

I had no idea what bulgogi was, but it smelled like meat.

Relax, Jun said.

And I signed, *I'm okay*. I could still feel the press of his head against my shoulder from the train ride on Saturday evening. He'd woken as we pulled into our station and sat up, stretching his arms. He didn't apologise for falling asleep against me, he just smiled a crooked, shy curl of his lips, and blinked like he was trying to rid himself of a mirage. And when the train doors opened, the cold night air tumbled in and made him shiver.

His mum said, "Dinner's ready. Come to the table, please." And Jun brought his phone for conversation, a change from most families that say no phones at the table.

Bulgogi, by the way, is amazing. It's thinly sliced steak marinated in some sort of garlicky, gingery oil. And it tastes even better than it smells.

Eileen said, "Owen, I don't know what you're like with chopsticks, so I've given you a knife and fork as well. Just in case."

And I'm not sure why I did it, because my history with chopsticks was less than a dozen times, but I ignored the cutlery and opted for the chopsticks instead. I fought with them to pick up some of the meat from the platter in the centre of the table, and got flustered when I was no good with them, but Jun reached across the table and lifted some of the steak pieces onto my plate for me. His fingers, long and elegant as always, made it look easy. And that was enough embarrassment for one night, so I grabbed the fork instead.

Eileen laughed.

And Jun just grinned at me.

I signed, *Thank you,* and then I tasted the food. And now bulgogi has replaced steak, egg and chips as my favourite meal. There were more flavours in my mouth than I'd ever had in my life.

"This is amazing," I said. Then made the sign for beautiful because it was as close as I could get to what I wanted to say.

Eileen signed to Jun while looking at me as she said, "You can bring him more often, he's a delight."

While we ate, she quizzed me about my life, my family, my interests, and after her sixth question, Jun signed something and typed, *You're not a murder suspect on trial. You don't have to answer.*

I said, "I think a murder suspect wouldn't be grilled even half as much."

Eileen laughed so hard she had to put down her chopsticks. When she brought her laughter into check, she reached across, covered my hand with hers, and said, "This is why I longed to come back to Ireland. The banter."

"It's not like this in South Korea?" I asked.

"Stuffy," she said, and Jun made a hey-watch-what-you're-saying gesture. Eileen said, "I'm kidding. But there's a lot more formality and tradition. You should probably bow to me from the waist before you leave." She winked.

When the meal was done and I used my fork to scoop up some stray grains of rice, Jun stood, stacking the plates, and signed something over his shoulder. I caught the quick curl of his hand but missed the meaning.

She responded in Korean while signing something I couldn't decipher, and then Jun took my wrist and pulled me towards the door. He pointed up the stairs and nudged me to go ahead of him. At the top, Jun pushed open a door and I followed him inside.

It was bright, neat, the bed made and the floor tidied of any teenage mess. He eased the door closed and smiled, and I noticed the posters on the walls weren't of musicians but motivational quotes written over the top of mountain ranges and forests. "It always seems impossible until it's done," and, "Change your thoughts and you can change your world."

Jun offered me the chair at his desk while he sat neatly on the edge of his bed, as if even he didn't want to be out of place, and he signed, *Are you okay?*

I smiled. "You don't have to ask me that all the time," I said, then signed, *I'm happy.*

He showed me his shelf of comic books and when I pulled one out to skim through, it was in Korean. There was a muscular superhero on the front, saving a woman from a burning building. Jun took the book from me, pulled out a drawer under his bed, found what he was looking for, and handed it to me—the same book, written in English.

"Why do you have two copies?" I asked.

Why not? he typed.

We settled on the rug on the floor, lying on our backs, and we read the same book, his copy in Korean, mine in English, and I realised he understood at least four languages: Korean, English, KSL and ISL. I wouldn't be surprised if he could sign in Spanish, too.

He held the book above his face, his hair falling back, and I tried not to glance at him while he turned the pages and read about the hero who fell in love with the rescued woman.

Rescue me, I wanted to say to Jun. But I didn't.

I sat up after a while and closed my copy of the book. I was enjoying the story, but I preferred Jun's company. He remained on the floor beside me as I looked around his room. There was a framed photo on his desk of him, Eileen, and his father and brother. I didn't ask where his dad was because I'd already made that assumption. Was Eileen wearing a wedding ring? I hadn't noticed.

I spun around, leaning my back against his bed and pulling my knees up to curl my arms around them, and when I did, Jun sat up too. He moved opposite me, his back against his desk, and his toes were half an inch from my foxes. His socks were black with green trim and when he caught me staring at them, he wriggled his toes.

I looked up.

He didn't say anything. Didn't sign anything.

And so, this time, instead of him asking me, I signed, *Are you okay?*

Jun blinked and nodded, slowly. Then he reached out and gave my leg a light punch.

"Hey," I said. "What's that for?"

The corner of his mouth twitched and he punched me again.

"What?" I asked, smiling not because he was punching me but because he was touching me. He tried again and I slapped his hand away.

And then he leapt on me. He wrestled me down onto the rug, his arm around my neck, and his breath on my face as he laughed.

I turned, curled a leg, tried to round him over my shoulder but couldn't. He was small but strong. And at one point—I'm not sure how—he was sitting behind me, my body between his legs, one arm around my neck and the other around my waist, and his cheek was pressed against mine. I heard the puff of his laughter. And I submitted to him.

I held my hands up, leaning my back against him, pressing my head into his neck. "I give up," I said. "I give up."

Jun knuckled my head, but he didn't release me. We sat there, for a second or an hour, and I felt the pant of his chest against my back.

And then he slipped away from me. When I turned, his hair was tousled and his hoodie was ruffled, one sleeve up, one sleeve down. He held his arms in the air like a champion, and while he was gloating, I leapt, wrapping my arms around him, and pinned him to the floor.

I lay over him, grinning, and when he stopped struggling, I kept my weight there, holding him down.

Jun closed his eyes and flopped his arms down at either side of my body like he was playing dead. And I lifted one of his hands, let go and watched it fall back down. I playfully tapped his cheek. "Wake up," I whispered.

His face was under mine.

His eyes were still closed.

And his lips were full and shiny and loosely parted.

I breathed. I swallowed.

And then I heard his mum on the stairs, so I sat up.

She went past his room without entering and Jun opened his eyes, slow and deliberate in the absence of my weight on top of him. He didn't sit up, just lay there. He turned his head. Looked at me.

And when he put his hand on his chest, feeling the beat of his heart, I felt it too, sitting beside him, aware of my own heartbeat.

Aware of the world.

CHAPTER 15

I walked down the hallway at school with my head in my phone and a grin on my face. I'd sent Jun a message when I got home on Wednesday night, thanking him for inviting me, and his reply had been instantaneous. He said, *Thanks for coming. Mum likes you.*

Somebody has to, I told him.

And he didn't reply with *I like you too.* He just sent me a smiley face with hearts around it, which said more than the words could have done.

We'd been texting ever since. I sent him a photograph of my physics homework and he didn't tell me the answer but he told me how to figure it out. And he sent me a photo of his maths homework and I told him he'd be better off asking a rock for the answer than asking me. Jun replied with a photo of the two-tone stone I'd given him on the beach at Bray. He'd stuck a small Post-It note on top that said *1 + 1 = 8?*

That rock must be defective, I told him. *We'll have to get you another one.*

I had walked clean past my locker without realising it when Ryan yanked my sketchbook out from under my arm and said, "I always knew love was dangerous."

I looked up, my thumbs primed over the keyboard on my phone, mid-reply. "Huh?"

Ryan thrust the sketchbook back at me. "If you'd kept walking, you'd have fallen out of a window or smacked into Mrs McGregor." He pulled a face like the idea gave him chills. "Put your phone away," he said.

"Yeah. Two secs." I finished my message, hit send, and then tapped out a second text. *Gotta get to class. Physics now. You? Chat later.*

"Owen Kelly," Ryan said.

"Present," I said, like I was responding to the roll call.

"Do you want to maybe put that on silent before it's confiscated?"

"Yeah," I said, as my phone vibrated. *English Lit. Wherefore art thou? See ya.* I put my phone away.

"You'll get yourself in trouble," Ryan said as we walked back to my locker.

I stuffed my sketchbook inside and pulled out my physics and maths books because I wouldn't have time to make it back to my locker after my first class. "What play is 'wherefore art thou' from?" I asked.

"Romeo and Owen," Ryan said. We walked down the hallway together and before he went into the tech wing, he said, "See you at lunch?"

"What's on the menu?"

"Tomato and vegetable pasta with baked cheese," he said. "Which means ninety-nine percent pasta, one percent cheese."

I rubbed my stomach like it sounded tasty, and I managed to get through my classes without pulling out my phone to speak to Jun. At least until the lunch bell rang.

Jun went to a school across town that catered closer to his needs than a mainstream school would, and he sent me a photo of himself in his uniform the other day. White shirt, forest-green V-neck jumper with the knot of a black-and-green tie visible, and grey trousers. I set the photo as my wallpaper and stared at it when we weren't texting. Today, he told me, when I couldn't stop myself from messaging him again, he was having teriyaki chicken and rice made by his mum.

Ryan and I stood in the lunch queue, trapped in the thick smell of pasta and cheese, and when we got a table, I spooned some into my mouth and tapped my phone screen awake to check if Jun had messaged me yet.

"How does your battery survive?" Ryan asked.

"I have a power bank in my bag."

"You're apocalypse-ready," he said. "You're coming to the match after school, right?"

I was texting.

Ryan said, "Owen. The match. You're coming, aren't you?"

"Of course," I said, distracted.

He nudged my food tray. "I'm happy you're happy, but the rest of us are miserable here."

So I put my phone away and the nervous energy in my leg made the table shake. I looked at him, clasped my hands together like a therapist, and said, "What's troubling you? Tell Dr Kelly."

"My best friend's gone missing," Ryan said, stabbing his pasta with his fork.

"He's not missing."

"But he's not here. He's in la-la land with some boy I haven't even met yet. I cry myself to sleep every night, tears on my pillow, until my room is flooded and I drown. And then for some reason I wake up in the morning and get to do it all over again." He slumped on the table, exaggerated and exhausted.

"And how does that make you feel?" I asked.

"Empty," Ryan told me. "No, lonely." He looked up. "Does he have a cute sister? A cousin? Hell, I'd be happy with his teddy bear at this point."

My phone vibrated in my pocket. "I'll ask him," I said.

And Ryan groaned. "Go on. Answer it." He was smiling. And I knew he was letting me fade back into my conversation with Jun. I texted him, *I'm going to my friend's football match after school. Don't let me forget.*

And at the end of the day, he said, *Don't forget the match.*

When I sat on the grass, Jun was with me even if he wasn't present. The sun was warm and I squinted against the glare, looking up and cheering when everyone else did, not really paying attention but trying to be there for Ryan all the same. I snapped a photo of him dribbling across the pitch and sent it to Jun.

Way to go, Ryan, he said.

The whistle blew at halftime and Ryan sat beside me for a minute, elbows on his knees, chomping on an apple. He said, "Tell him I said hi."

I said, "I already did."

And then one of his teammates came over and crouched in front of us. "Keep an eye on number seven down the wing. He's getting handsy." Then he snatched my phone out of my hands and stood up. "Who're you talking to? A girlfriend?"

"Give that back," I said, panicked, jumping to my feet. I reached for it but he held it out of my way.

He scrolled back and saw the picture of Jun in his uniform. "Who the fuck is this?"

"Mason, give it back," Ryan said.

"Who is he?" Mason asked. "A boyfriend?"

"Just give it back," Ryan said.

And I stepped up to Mason and gripped his wrist. "He's not my boyfriend. But so what if he was?"

He glowered at my fingers on his arm and made like he was about to throw my phone across the grass, but Ryan said, "Mate," and Mason thrust the phone against my chest.

"Whatever," he said. He walked away. I glanced at the screen, just to make sure the photo was still there and hadn't been deleted under Mason's thumb.

Ryan said, "You all right?"

I stared at Mason's retreating back, my heart thumping. Outing myself wasn't the issue, I wasn't shy about that, but it was an invasion of privacy. I hadn't even shown Ryan the photo of Jun and now a random stranger had seen it.

"I'm fine," I said, my jaw tight.

He gripped my shoulders. "You sure?"

When I looked at him, I knew what he was thinking. "Leave it, Ryan." But he tripped Mason up on the pitch five minutes later and got a yellow card. He held his hands up to show that it was an innocent accident.

And Jun asked, *How's the match?*

Brilliant, I told him.

On Saturday morning, Jun asked me what my plans were for the day and I half expected him to invite me to Bray again or to his house. But I'd already promised I'd hang out with Ryan today. I knew I'd been slipping away from him—because he'd hinted at it enough—and I knew it was entirely my fault, not Ryan's and not Jun's.

So when I told him we were going to the shopping mall, he casually dropped into the conversation, *Which one?* while he was asking me about something else.

And I casually told him the name of it. Casually hoping I'd see him there.

Mick dropped us off and said if we needed a lift back later we should let him know. Ryan said, "How much taxi fare does he owe you now?"

"Don't worry, I'm keeping a tally," Mick said.

On the ground floor, Ryan dragged me into a perfume shop and asked the girl about the scents of fifty different colognes but didn't buy a single one. When we left, we smelled like we'd taken a bath in bergamot and lemon and orange, with a hint of old-man's cedarwood.

There was a blood drive booth on the top floor, across from the food court, and Ryan said, "They give you biscuits, don't they?"

"How would I know?"

He spoke to the woman at the booth where people were being taken into a closed-off area, and she took one look at us and asked what age we were. Then she said, "It's admirable. We need all the blood we can get. But you'll have to come back when you're seventeen. Sorry, boys."

"So, no free biscuits?" Ryan asked.

He had this way of making you feel sorry for him when he pulled out the puppy-dog face, so the woman gave us each a single-serve packet of digestive biscuits, two per pack. So it wasn't even worth it.

But Ryan said, "Unless I'm bled dry by a vampire between now and then, I'll come back on my seventeenth birthday."

She gave him a card with some details on it and said, "Eat some garlic. Vampires hate that. See you soon."

We queued for baked potatoes in the food court, a line that was somehow messier than the school lunch queue, and before we got to the counter, somebody tapped on my shoulder. I turned from Ryan, grinning because I knew who it was.

But it wasn't Jun.

"Callum," I said.

"Good memory," he said, inclining his head. "Graham, wasn't it?"

"Owen."

"I was close."

Ryan leaned close to me. I think he could sense my unease, and his chest against my back became a strengthening barrier so that I couldn't fall away. He said, "Who's this?"

"Callum," I said, and I couldn't help the flatness of my voice. "What are you doing here?" I asked him.

"I bumped into Jun-ho downstairs, so we're getting lunch."

I bit the inside of my cheek to stop myself from grinning. I was neither a cat nor from Cheshire. But Jun wasn't with him. "Where is he?" I asked. I wasn't looking desperate, I don't think.

And the guy behind Callum said, "There's no skipping, kid."

"I'm with my friends," Callum said. "They were holding my place."

"Were we?" Ryan asked.

I looked around but still couldn't see Jun.

"Were we?" Ryan asked again.

"Yeah," I said. "Sorry," I told the man.

Callum grinned and slipped into the queue, and he rocked on his feet for a few seconds before leaning in and saying, "He's at Red Dragon. But that shite's too spicy for me."

I scanned the food court. Red Dragon was at the far side, opposite the tables, but I could just about make him out at the counter, holding his phone up for the server to read, the cuff of his hoodie sleeve locked around his fist the way it always was.

"We should sit together," I told Callum.

And I felt Ryan's finger poking into my back. "Should we?" he whispered.

I eyeballed him. It's Jun, I was trying to say. Jun is here.

When we carried our trays through the court, weaving among the busy tables, Jun had already been served and was seated at a table for two. He was looking around, head oscillating more than it should be. It made me wonder if he was looking for me.

Callum dropped into the seat opposite him and signed

something, and when Jun looked up, he caught my eye and grinned. He stood and waved. And Callum tore open a salt packet.

Hi, I said. *How are you?* And then, because I'd just learned it, I added, *When's the next bus to Dublin station?*

He cracked up and then he looked around, but Ryan was already sliding a table closer. When he'd grabbed two chairs, he dropped one beside Jun, said, "Hello,"—loud and slow—and then patted the chair. "You sit here, O."

He never called me O. I think he was trying to be overly familiar. Or he was nervous.

When I sat beside Jun, I knew my cheeks were burning. I said, "What brings you here?"

He shrugged and signed a word I didn't know, and while he pulled out his phone to type it instead, Callum said, "Shopping."

Ryan said, "I'm Ryan."

"Shit," I said. "Yeah. Sorry. Ryan, this is Jun. Jun-ho," I added. And I pointed. "You've already met Callum."

"Good to meet you," Callum said, signing it as well. "What are you boys doing here on a Saturday afternoon?"

I didn't have an answer, and when Ryan said something about needing to buy new football boots, Jun bumped his shoulder against me, softly, to get my attention. He looked down, and when I followed his gaze, he was discreetly passing me his phone. I took it, keeping it under the table, and read. *Sorry. Didn't know he'd be here. We won't stay. But it was nice to see you.*

I typed, *It's OK. Stay,* and passed it back.

Ryan said, "So, you're the famous Jun."

Jun signed and Callum responded for him. "Famous?"

I blushed.

"Maybe infamous is more appropriate," Ryan said and I wanted to stab him under the table with my fork. I wanted to stab Callum, too, but if I did that I'd have no cutlery left.

I breathed and remembered I was not John Wick.

Callum reached for the ketchup bottle and there was a small plaster at the crook of his arm. Ryan saw it too, and he pulled out his packet of digestives. He said, "I'll have these for dessert."

Callum smirked and didn't mention them.

And then Jun flicked his fingers at Callum to get his attention, and signed something, far too quickly for me to decipher. Callum watched him, then picked up a napkin from his tray and handed it to him.

Jun signed again.

"More?" Callum asked. Then he glanced at me. At Jun. At me again. He nodded, wiping his fingers. "Sure, I'll get you some more napkins. I serve your every command." He stood up. "Give me a hand," he said to Ryan.

"Eh?"

"You need some napkins, too?" Callum asked me.

"No," I said, and then figured it out. "Actually, I could use some pepper. They never give you enough."

"Pepper?" Ryan asked, confused.

And Callum flicked the side of Ryan's arm. "Come on, kid, you've had your orders."

Under protest, Ryan stood up and followed Callum, and when we were alone, I looked down, toyed with the food on my tray, and then looked at Jun.

His smile was soft. Barely visible. Then he curled his lips around his drinking straw and I copied him. There was more ice in my cup than Sprite. Fountain-drinks were just a rip-off.

You're buying football boots? Jun typed.

"Not for me," I said. "I don't look good in shorts."

He smiled but didn't reply. He indicated his food and held his disposable chopsticks towards me.

"Not a chance," I said. "I'll practice in private before using chopsticks around you again." But I speared some of the meat from his plate onto my fork and tasted it, and after a second it burned in my throat.

He laughed and nudged me with his shoulder. Then I nudged him back.

This was awkward. Why was it so damn awkward?

"Did you see that?" Callum said. When I looked up, he and Ryan were hovering over us, standing beside each other like they were old friends.

"No," Ryan said, "I didn't see anything. Did you?"

"There was nothing to see," Callum said. They sat down and he dropped a stack of paper napkins in front of Jun.

Ryan released his hands above my tray, sprinkling a handful of pepper packets on top of my food. "Pepper for m'lord," he said.

He nudged his chair closer to Callum.

"Children," he said. And Callum agreed.

CHAPTER 16

"I don't know," I said.

"What do you mean, you don't know?"

Mr Madden was leaning back in his chair, his feet up on the desk the way I'd never seen any other teacher do. The room smelled like paint thinner, and his fingers were dusted with white chalk powder like the grey flecks in his beard.

"We've got two and a half months until the end of term, Owen. I really need you to pick something already." He slid a sheet of paper across the desk to me. We'd been sliding it back and forward for ten minutes.

"None of the options speak to me," I complained. But we'd already been over this. I had to choose a topic for my end-of-year art project and the list he'd handed out had only three options left.

Home Away from Home.

Highways of the Heart.

The Things We Carry.

You can see why I was having problems. Jun was away from the home he knew in Korea. Jun was mapping his way to my heart. Jun was something I carried with me. But I couldn't wrap him up in a bow and hand him in to the examiner.

Mr Madden tapped the sheet with a chalky finger. "Make one of them speak to you. Where's your sketchbook? Maybe there's something in there that'll spark an idea. The brief is just a title—what you do with it is up to you. I'm not asking you to Sellotape your wallet and phone to a backboard and call it 'The Things We Carry'."

"You'd give me an F if I did that."

"Damn right I would," he said. He dropped his feet to the floor and leaned his elbows on the desk. "Let's flip through your sketchbook. You're bound to have something."

I handed the spiralbound book over, reluctant, wondering how many pages were filled with Jun. Sketchbooks didn't count towards our final grade, but we could submit them if we wanted, to show progress over time.

Mr Madden opened it. Birds. Trees. The park. Shadows of Grandad Tommy. A missing page where I'd torn out Jun's first portrait. An old man at a kitchen table, paintbrush in hand. The pond at the park. An upturned umbrella with fish in it—Mr Madden chuckled at that. Jun on the train. The horizon over Bray. Jun. Jun. Jun.

He closed the book but didn't give it back.

"There are two things you're carrying, Owen, and they're not in your pockets."

I looked at him.

"Your grandfather. I'm guessing you started this sketchbook not long after he passed away?"

I nodded. "And the other thing?"

He opened the book again and went to the last sketch of Jun. He turned it around so I could see it, even though I already knew. "An Asian kid with sad eyes."

"They're not sad," I said.

He looked again. "Aren't they? Maybe not. My point is— the things we carry doesn't have to be literal. You're carrying grief. And you're carrying," he tapped Jun's face, "something more than grief."

My cheeks darkened and I shrugged.

Mr Madden pushed the topic sheet back to me, and I wrote my name beside The Things We Carry. I still didn't know what I was going to submit, but I knew what it was going to be about.

I sat at the back of the art room for the rest of the period, jotting down ideas. But no matter how hard I tried to steer it somewhere else, it all came back to one thing. It couldn't be Jun. I wouldn't do that to him. I wanted him to be my friend—more than that—not my final grade.

It was Tommy. And grief. And the weight we carry even after they're gone.

I sketched a coffin. Not to be morbid, I just needed to get the image out of my head. And beneath it, I sketched me. Or someone like me, doubled in pain.

Because grief wasn't just a word, it was the ache of pain that never went away.

I picked a topic at last, I messaged Jun.

Jun said, *Woohoo. Is it "Why is Sign Language the Best Language"?*

Sadly that wasn't an option, I said. *Maybe next year.*

"All set?" Mr Madden asked me as I put away my phone.

I said, "At least I know my topic. But I'm still not sure what the end product will be." He noticed the coffin on the page and when I saw him looking, I closed the book.

"Put your sketchbook in the bin."

"What?"

"Not literally," he smiled. "Come with me."

I followed him through the side door, into the storeroom that was lined with blank canvases, tubes of paint, packets of coloured chalk and tubs of paintbrushes. On a shelf on the far wall was a stack of old paintings that used to be on display in the foyer for visiting guests to see. A couple of mine were in that stack, forgotten about and gathering dust—a badly painted night scene with a purple sky and Darth Vader, ominous without his lightsaber.

On the floor below the shelves, a huge bin filled with chipped clay models and wireframe figures that were incomplete rose like a mountain of broken dreams. He pulled the bin into the middle of the small room and said, "Can you pick that up?"

"Where do you want it?"

"Nowhere," he said. "Just pick it up."

I tried, but it was too heavy.

Mr Madden said, "What about the things you're already carrying? You pick those up every day."

"If you're talking about grief and stuff, that's different. It's metaphorical weight."

"But it's still weight, right?"

I looked at him. "So?"

"So maybe you can carry more than you think."

"I thought you were going to help me with my project," I said. I didn't know where he was going with this.

Mr Madden folded his arms. "I am helping. You said you don't know what to make, but you're already making something. Or making sense of something. That coffin you didn't want me to see just now? That was raw. It was honest. And this"—he kicked the base of the large bin—"is what it looks like when people give up halfway. Don't make something neat and tidy for the examiner. Make something true. Forget about your grade. Forget about your sketchbook. Art isn't confined to the page, so why should you be?"

I listened to his words but I wasn't hearing him. I said, "What's that?" I pointed at a dark leather object in the far corner, tucked behind a stack of printer paper and a mess of dowel rods and bottles of PVA glue.

When he pulled it out, it was a large suitcase, one of those ancient wartime ones with no wheels, the kind you'd see covered in travel stickers in old movies. It was filled with newspapers and magazine cuttings that looked like somebody's failed 1990s fashion project.

Mr Madden wiped the dust from the corner and revealed the initials A.B., branded there by a hot iron. He said, "It's been here longer than I have."

"Can I use it?" I asked.

"What are you thinking?"

"I don't know yet," I said. "It's still germinating. But I might have the start of something."

"The start is a very good place to begin," Mr Madden said.

We emptied out the contents and stacked them back in the corner of the storeroom—yellowed pages that would get recycled eventually—and I carried the case into the art room. I took a photo of it and sent it to Jun.

He didn't reply until the end of the day—I guess he was busy with classes—but when he did, he just sent me a question mark. I knew he'd be confused, but that was okay. So was I.

And I sent him back a shrug.

I carried the case to the bus stop after school, banging against my leg with its emptiness. I still didn't know how I'd end up using it, but I knew I had to. Even if I just packed it full of my grief and stored it under my bed.

Ryan eyed me with suspicion while we waited for the bus to arrive and I said, "Don't ask. I literally have no clue."

"You're leaving me, aren't you?" he said. "Haven't I been good to you? Haven't I given you everything you ever desired? Twelve babies and a loving home. How could you do this to me just as Junior is about to go off to college? My life is ruined!"

I trapped the case on the ground between my legs. "How did we end up in a soap opera? And why aren't you in the drama club?"

He rolled his neck as the bus pulled in. "I have enough drama in my life. I don't need a club for it."

"You make most of that drama yourself," I laughed.

I clanged up the aisle of the bus behind Ryan with my case, and one of the girls from St Margaret's said, "Ryan, I saved you a seat."

He fell into the seat beside her, pushing his backpack down between his feet, and said, "Mia. I didn't see you last week. I thought you'd transferred." They'd been bantering against each other for the last few months, but she'd never kept him a seat before.

I wrestled my case into the row behind them and Mia looked at me over her shoulder. "What is that dirty old thing?"

"Hey," Ryan said. "He has a name."

I slapped the back of his head. "It's art," I told her.

"Doesn't look like art."

"It will," I said. I sat down, clinging to the case so it didn't rattle around while the bus chugged up the road. Trees and lampposts and people blurred by outside the way my thoughts were blurring in my head. I listened to Ryan and Mia's conversation for a while, studying how natural his flirtations were, rolling my eyes when he said something that dripped more cheese than melted Lunchables. But I grinned when she giggled at it despite how tacky his words were.

He made it look easy, and Mia tucked her hair behind an ear and batted her eyelashes and touched his arm and leaned into him as she laughed.

Ryan said, "We should hang on Friday."

Her bosom heaved. Or I'm sure it would have done if I'd looked, like one of those badly written porn stories on AO3. "Where should we go?"

"Bowling?" he asked. Then he turned to me. "We should all hang. What do you think?"

Mia said, "Are you dating someone?"

"No," I said. "We're just talking."

She shrugged. "They don't make you wear those God-awful

shoes any more, do they?"

Were we talking? I thought. Is that what we were doing? I should ask him.

If I was brave enough.

CHAPTER 17

We stood outside the bowling alley at the top of the steps, and even though the doors were closed we could hear the music, the bells and the almost violent whir of arcade machines. The sun had gone down and the flashing lights from inside gave me three shadows—each of them pointing for home.

"He's not coming," I said, defeated.

"He'll be here," Ryan told me. He'd already been inside to see how busy it was and to buy a bag of Haribo for Mia who had offered me one when she opened the packet, but I didn't take it.

"Anyway," she said. "I didn't know you were into boys."

"Yeah," I said. "I'm into people."

"No, you're not," Ryan said. "You're into one person. There's a difference."

"And it's a boy," Mia said.

Ryan put his arm around her neck and his other arm around mine. "He'll be here. Will the pair of you calm down? You like Jun. And you," he said to Mia, "you totally like me. So everyone's happy. Right?"

She shrugged out from under his arm. "Who says I like you?"

"Did I not just buy you Haribo?"

"Do you think that's all it takes?" she asked.

"I can buy you more."

"It had better be the stars," she said.

And Ryan kicked the edge of the step, then he grinned. "Be right back," he said, and disappeared inside.

I checked the time on my phone again. And even though he'd sent me a message thirteen minutes ago to say he was on his way, I was still convinced he'd fail to show up and I'd be the third wheel trapped between the axle of Ryan and Mia.

While we stood there, alone, she looked at me, one hand holding her bag of sweets, the other dipped inside it to fish out another one. She said, "You look nervous."

"No, I don't."

"You really like him, then?"

I didn't answer her, just checked my phone again. Then I said, "Listen, before he gets here—this isn't a date. I don't know if we're properly talking or not. I'm not even sure if he likes me."

"Want me to find out?"

"No," I said. "I can do it. I'm just taking it slow."

She smiled. "Maybe speed up a little."

And then Ryan came through the door, holding something

behind his back.

He said, "You asked for the stars? Your wish is my command." He held out a packet of Milky Way Magic Stars.

"Oh, God," she said. "How did I not know you were this cheesy?"

He put his arm around her again. "I think you mean delightful."

I checked my phone, stared across the carpark at the entrance, and then said, "Why don't you guys go on in. I can wait for him. I'm sure he won't be long."

Ryan wasn't convinced that I wouldn't just turn around and go home the second they went inside, but I assured him I'd see them in there as soon as Jun arrived, and when I was alone, I tugged at the hem of my shirt and scanned it for lint that wasn't there. When a car pulled up at the foot of the steps, I looked, but it wasn't him. Two girls rushed past me and went inside, and the noise washed over me to leave me dripping in its wake when the door fell closed behind them.

And then another car. Jun in the passenger seat. Eileen behind the wheel. She touched the horn and waved at me, then signed something to Jun before he got out. And the relief that flooded through my veins replaced every drop of blood I owned.

I stood at the top of the steps, watching Jun say something to his mum—won't be late; I'll call if I need you; probably all the things I said to my own mum. And when he got out, I tugged at my shirt again as if I was adjusting the wrapping paper on his gift. He was wearing a white sweater and a pair of dark chinos. Very warm. Very Jun.

At the bottom of the steps, he signed hello. And he was

already typing by the time he reached the top. *Sorry I'm late. Traffic was terrible.*

"You're here now," I said. Does anybody know how to get a smile off your face? Because I don't.

We stood there for an awkward moment, then he typed, *Are we waiting for someone? I thought Ryan was going to be here.*

"He's inside with Mia," I said, fingerspelling her name. "You can say hello if they're not already chewing each other's tonsils." Then, because I had no idea if he understood me, I fingerspelled *kissing*.

He smiled, his eyes scanning the ground instead of my face, and then I held the door for him, and we went in.

I was hit by the barrage of noise and lights, an air conditioning unit above the entrance that pushed me further inside, and the gruff scowl of a bouncer outside the door of the pub that adjoined the arcade. And although we couldn't see the lanes from here, I heard the clatter of pins and looked around. I wasn't sure if Ryan would be trying to win a cuddly toy for Mia from a claw machine or racing against her in the car games.

Jun walked beside me, close enough that I felt his jumper against my shirtsleeve, and his eyes were purple and pink and white from the lights. "This way," I said. "Have you ever bowled before?"

He typed, *I'm the king of bowling.*

"We'll see," I said.

Ryan and Mia weren't anywhere in the arcade area, so we walked across the top of the lanes, and I went past them when Ryan waved, and Jun tapped my arm to point to him.

"We're doing teams," Ryan said. "You and Jun against me and Mia."

Mia had a drink in her hand that looked alcoholic even if it wasn't. Dressed up and dusted in makeup, she looked six years older than us. She stepped into Jun's space and said, "Hi. I'm Mia. I wanted to be on your team because I bet you're better than Ryan, but he wouldn't allow it because he's a caveman."

I tapped his shoulder and signed, *This is Mia*. I twisted my pinkie finger between her and Ryan; it wasn't an ISL sign, but he knew what I meant.

And Mia leaned into Ryan to say something in his ear that was probably, "He's deaf? Nobody told me he was deaf."

Jun typed on his phone and passed it to her, and then he let me see it. *We definitely have to be on the same team. These cavemen are going down!*

I punched his shoulder. "Cavemen?"

And Jun offered the crook of his elbow to Mia, who slipped her hand into it so naturally that they looked like a couple.

"What's going on?" Ryan asked. He already had a bowling ball in his hands.

"New teams," Mia said.

We bowled horrendously. None of us—Jun included—was the king of bowling. But we had fun. Jun did get a few strikes, and every time he did, Mia wrapped him in her arms like they were the best of friends, and Ryan slumped into the seat beside me, his hands in his pockets, and said, "My girl-friend is stealing your boyfriend."

"He's not my boyfriend," I said. "And anyway, she's not

your girlfriend either."

"Not yet," he said.

"Such confidence," I laughed.

Ryan narrowed his eyes. "If you don't have confidence in yourself, nobody else can. Anyway, she's getting really handsy with him."

Mia and Jun were high-fiving. I said, "Probably because she doesn't see him as a threat. As far as she knows, he's here with me and has absolutely no interest in her."

Whatever conversation was going on between Jun and Mia on his phone, passing it back and forward as they took turns typing, they kept stealing glances at us.

"Do you think they're talking about us?"

"She's probably telling him how useless you are at bowling," I said.

"Or maybe they're comparing our bodies," Ryan said, puffing out his chest.

I stood up. "Never say that sentence again for as long as you live."

When I went to the conveyor belt that carried the balls back from the pit at the end of the lane, I reached down to pick up my size-nine ball, but Jun lifted it before I had it. I looked at him and his lips were bunched in thought. He blinked at me, then he held the ball out so I could take it. When my fingers touched his, I got an electric shock—and I don't mean in some clichéd romantic sense. I mean an actual static charge. Jun felt it too and we fumbled the ball.

And then we laughed.

"What happened?" Mia asked. She nudged Jun and said, "We're thirty points ahead, don't give him the ball he loves."

I'd picked it up again and gripped it against my stomach like I owned it, but when Mia said that, I offered it to him. "You did have it first," I said.

But he shook his head and pushed the ball towards me again. He typed on his phone and passed it to me while he picked up a different ball.

You still won't win, caveman!

We didn't win. He and Mia gloated for five minutes before somebody came along and said it was their turn on the lane, so we picked up our Cokes and skirted around the edge of the arcade room. There was a young couple strapped into a VR machine that was flopping them around on a rollercoaster and spitting air at them, and a couple of kids shooting miniature basketballs into miniature hoops. A man with a kid sitting on his shoulders was trying to win a toy from a claw machine while the girl pressed her hands and face against the glass above his head, saying, "Right a bit. Right a bit."

We took turns playing air hockey, winner stays on, and Ryan got his chance to act like more of a caveman around Mia while he danced around her as the air-hockey victor.

"If you're going to dance," Mia said, "why don't you bring your A-game?" She pointed at a Dance Dance Revolution game that a couple of girls had just stepped off.

"Not even if you paid me," Ryan said.

And Jun handed him a coin with a grin. It amazed me how well he could read lips even under those violent lights.

"Consider yourself paid," Mia laughed.

They stepped onto the dance squares and the music blared from the speakers at either side of them. Foot patterns lit up and I heard the clang of their feet as they moved.

Jun, beside me, had closed his eyes. He held his face up, and then he touched his chest, holding his hand against it like he was living in a moment, some quiet space where only he existed.

I nudged his arm and when he looked at me he was smiling. He pumped his hand against his chest, in time to the rhythm of the music. And I was surprised. I cocked my head and gave him a questioning look.

He took my wrist and drew me closer to the speakers. He held my hand up, palm towards the music, and I felt the intensity of the beat, the tingle of energy that came from it.

"You feel that?" I asked. I didn't shout. I didn't have to.

Jun nodded and closed his eyes again. Beside him, Ryan was panting as his legs moved, and Mia's hair was bouncing as her head turned.

Jun looked at me again, then put his fingers in front of my eyes. He was telling me to close them, so I did. And I tried not to listen to the music but to feel it. It thumped through me, sizzling into my body like it needed to be there, like I didn't exist without it.

Then I held Jun's arm. "Vibrations," I said.

He nodded.

I pulled him away from the speaker, into the dark corner beside the machine. His eyes were wide. It was still loud, but the music was vibrating in the other direction, away from us. I leaned into him, my hand on his cheek, thumb under his chin, and I tilted his head away from me. I pressed my lips against his face, between his ear and his jaw, and I said, loudly so that I could make my own vibrations, "Do you feel this? Can you feel me?"

As I pulled my lips away from his warm skin, his eyes were closed. I thought—panicked, actually—that maybe he'd been expecting a kiss. And then I thought: why the hell didn't I kiss him?

But he was smiling, his face still tilted away from me, eyes still closed. When I let go of his arm, he opened his eyes, faced me. And he nodded.

He got his phone, typed something even though he was looking into my eyes. And it took me a second to pull my gaze away from him to look at what he'd written. He said, *I feel you. I can feel the sound of you.*

Something fluttered inside me and it didn't feel like butterflies. It was dark and sordid and light and floaty all at once.

And then Mia bounced in front of us. "I won."

"I let you win," Ryan said. And then, "Did we interrupt something?"

I quickly shook my head. I was glad of the interruption because the thickness in my chest was getting heavier.

And Jun made an eating motion, nudging his shoulder against mine before he pointed at the diner-style seating area in the corner. We got hotdogs and chips and sat together around a small table while Mia sipped from a straw and stared at Ryan, and he held her gaze over the top of his glass.

I pushed the sleeves of my shirt up to eat, and Jun, in the seat beside me, tapped my forearm. He wrapped his hand around my wrist, where there was just enough room for him to touch his thumb to his middle finger, as if he was measuring me.

He smiled. And then he turned my arm over, and he traced something on the underside, his index finger making lines and curves. A circle, a dash. It wasn't English, but the way he did it, I knew it was a word. Korean, most likely.

When he was finished, he released my arm and picked up a chip as if he hadn't just been signing a contract on my skin.

I said, "What was that?" I glanced across at Ryan and Mia but they were locked in a staring competition.

Jun shrugged. He traced the word again, his finger tickling my forearm.

"What?" I said.

His smile was tiny, trapped like he didn't want it to escape. And he typed, *I'll tell you. One day.*

CHAPTER 18

The long sloping field gave way to a thick line of trees at the bottom where children were playing. I followed the curve of the path around a water fountain and past the bandstand where everyone had congregated with an explosion of picnic blankets, pop-up tables and at least four footballs being kicked in multiple directions.

Jun had invited me to another Deaf community event, a picnic in the park and, yesterday, after visiting the cemetery with Mum for a few minutes, where I'd brought one of Grandad Tommy's narrow paintbrushes and wedged it among the flowers, Mum said, "We should glue it to the headstone."

I smiled. Shrugged.

That evening, I pulled the suitcase out from under my bed,

the one Mr Madden had let me take from school.

I ran my hand over the cracked, textured blue-leather case, the stamped initials on the side, *A. B.*, and I wondered who it had belonged to. Then I unclasped the brass fasteners and lifted the lid. It was still empty, still just an idea. But I stared into that emptiness and wanted to climb inside and close the lid.

Mr Madden was right. We carry a lot more than the things in our pockets.

I went to Grandad Tommy's room, hovering outside his door, listening to the sounds of Mum and Mick downstairs, and then I went inside. I took one of his paintbrushes, a larger, flat, three-inch one that he always used to drench his canvases in liquid white.

I took it back to my room and placed it inside the case. And then I closed the lid.

Grandad Tommy was in my art project now.

Like I knew he would be.

Today, the plate of cocktail sausages—some pinned together with cheese, some with pineapple—that I'd made at home was still warm in my hands. Mum had offered to help, to turn it into one of our old cooking sessions like we did when I was six or seven, and while she ate as many chunks of pineapple as she pierced with cocktail sticks, she'd said, "What was his name again?"

"Jun-ho," I said, and it was weird saying both syllables.

"And he's Korean?"

"Half-Korean."

"Which half?" she asked.

"The left half" I joked, and she popped another square

of pineapple into her mouth. "I'll have none left if you keep doing that," I told her.

She leaned against the counter. "Is he cute?"

"Mum!"

"But is he?"

"No," I said. And then, after a breath, "He's more than that." When she didn't say anything—neither teasing nor supporting—I looked up and she was desperately trying to contain her smile, but it had a difficultly level of 100. "Stop that," I said.

"Never," she told me, stealing another chunk of pineapple before helping me lay everything out on a plate and wrap it in foil.

At the park, I carried it to the food tables and said hi to the woman who'd given me a name badge at the café all those weeks ago. "Is Jun-ho here yet?" I asked.

She shielded her eyes with a hand against the sun and scanned the park, then said, "He's definitely here, I saw him five minutes ago. Look for the biggest group of people and you'll no doubt find him in the middle of it."

I thanked her and walked across the grass to the path, following it through the throng of people that were dotted around on blankets. There was chatter and signing, noisy laughter and silent laughter. A group of girls were doing handstands to see who could stay up the longest, and some boys were chasing after a football.

"Hey, sexy," somebody said as I passed. When I looked, Ella was getting up from the ground, dusting off the shirt that was tied around her waist. She gave me a hug. "Come sit with us."

On the blanket were some people I didn't know. I nodded at them and said to Ella, "I definitely will, but I'm just looking for somebody right now."

"Loverboy?" she asked. She scanned the crowd. "What does he look like? Wait, don't tell me. Let me see if I can guess your type."

"You won't," I said.

She pointed, moving her arm from one teenager to another. "Nope; too tall. Too short. Too… what look would you call that? Hippie?" She shuddered. "Ah," she said. "Ding, ding, ding! Looks like we have a winner."

I followed the direction of her finger and Jun was standing in the centre of a group of kids, some our age, many younger. They were sitting on the grass around him as if he was their ruler.

"How did you know?" I asked Ella.

"Because he's staring at you the way I would be if you were my type. And a few years older."

"No, he's not. Is he?"

"Mate," she said, "if you don't cement that deal soon, somebody else will."

"That's helpful," I said, leaking sarcasm out of my pores. I put my hands in my pockets. "Wish me luck." And then I walked towards Jun with a smile that was as awkward as it was genuine.

Jun signed, *Hi, how are you?*

Good, and you? I asked.

He nodded, then to the group he said, *This is O-W-E-N. He is hearing but knows some sign.* Then he said something I didn't understand and the kids around him applauded me with their hands in the air. He motioned for me to sit and when I crossed my legs on the grass, Callum was suddenly beside me.

"He's in the middle of a story," he said, without any pleasantries, shuffling into position at my side.

I waved at Becca, Callum's younger sister, who sat in her wheelchair at the far side of the small group, and then Jun made a motion.

"Where was I?" Callum translated for me. "Oh yes, the tiger." Before he continued, Callum caught me up. "It's a Korean folktale. The mother left home, telling her son and daughter not to open the door to anyone but her. But she was eaten by a tiger on the road and now the tiger has disguised itself in her clothes and knocked on the door."

"Like the wolf in Red Riding Hood," I said.

Then Jun mimed the tiger pulling on the mother's clothes and signed as Callum voiced it for me. "He knocked on the door and said, 'Children, let me in. It's your mother.' But the boy and girl said, 'Mother, your voice sounds different.' The tiger scratches his throat against a thorny bush and returned to the door." He mimed knocking again and I watched the children with their wide eyes and blinking delight.

"He said, 'Let me in, children.' But the boy and girl looked under the door and instead of their mother's shoes, they saw the tiger's claws." Jun made a growling tiger motion and everyone laughed.

He looked at me and in his eyes I saw the joy that he was expressing in his hands.

He said, "The brother and sister were wise, so they slipped out the back door to escape. But the tiger saw them go and he chased after them through the forest. In a clearing, they knelt and prayed to the heavens, 'Save us!' and, suddenly, a magical rope appeared from the sky. The brother and sister climbed the rope," he signed, miming his way to the heavens. "But the tiger was right behind them. A second rope came down from the sky and the tiger began to climb it. He was gaining on them. But when he was halfway up, the rope snapped and he fell!"

He mimicked falling backwards with arms wide, and the kids gasped in silent awe. Becca put a hand over her face. And as I watched Jun pretend to fall, I pretended to catch him. He grinned and signed, *Thank you.*

He went on. Callum translated, "He fell all the way to the ground and smashed into the trees and he was pierced by the stalks which turned them red. And the heavens, seeing how brave the brother and sister were, transformed the brother into the sun and the sister into the moon."

Hurray, everyone signed.

"But," Jun added. "That's not the end of the story. The sister, who was afraid of the dark, said she was too scared to be awake at night. And so the brother switched places with her and now the sister shines brightly every day."

We applauded him and one of the girls signed something that I didn't catch. While everyone laughed, Callum told me, "She says she's not afraid of the dark."

I am, I signed and the girl giggled.

When the children dispersed, Jun offered me his hand and he pulled me to my feet.

"What am I? Chopped liver?" Callum said, and he reached up both hands, groaning as we took them and helped him up.

A football rolled by and he kicked it, running after it with a sign I didn't recognise. And then Jun stepped into the space between me and the sunlight. His head was haloed in gold. His eyes were as dark as they were warm.

Hungry? he asked.

We went to the food tables and then joined Ella and her friends on their blanket. Ella introduced herself to Jun, winking at me as she did, and then told us her friends' names, Laura and Rob. They were a couple, she said, both Deaf, and Ella met them at college. Rob verbalised his words while he signed, but Laura was a silent signer, like Jun.

Jun asked them something and their response was quick and animated. I thought I understood the words *book* and *weekend*, but that wasn't enough for me to decipher what they were talking about.

Ella offered me some of her crisps and said, with her head turned away from the others, "I feel lost in spoken conversations. Now we have a whole other language to feel lost in."

"I just like watching them," I said. "It's mesmerising. Will we ever be that fluent?"

"One day," she said. Then she lowered her voice even further. "He really likes you."

"Do you think?" I asked.

But Rob tapped her arm and said, "It's not polite to talk in company." But he was grinning.

"Sorry," she said. And as we turned back to face them, she winked at me again. "It's obvious," she said.

I watched Jun as he spoke in the air and remembered the smell of his skin when I'd touched my lips to his cheek in the corner of the arcade, when I wanted him to feel the vibrations of me, of my voice. It was the softest thing I'd ever felt and I could still, even now, feel the tingle of him on my lips. I wanted to get that close again, to press my lips into the softness under his jaw. I wanted to feel his vibrations.

I blushed for no reason.

And Jun pointed at me, mid-conversation, without taking his eyes away from Rob and Laura.

"What?" I asked, interrupting them. I signed it. *What?*

He put his finger to his lips for silence. And then he laughed.

"See?" Ella said, and she lay back on the blanket with her hands behind her head.

I joined her, letting the others have their conversation, and we talked to the sky while listening to each other.

Ella said, "I invited my boyfriend, but he didn't want to come. He doesn't know any sign language at all, except for 'more', which I taught him. And now I wish I hadn't."

I signed the word in the air. More. I didn't ask what he wanted more of.

Ella said, "You're still coming to the party, aren't you? Don't tell me you've forgotten."

"I'll be there," I said. "But you haven't given me the address yet. Will there be booze?"

"I won't tell your mother. Unless you want me to. I don't know what kind of masochist you are."

"I'm not any kind of masochist."

"Sure you are," she said. She turned onto her side, head propped in her hand. "If you weren't, you'd have done something about your friend already. So I can only assume you get off on your own suffering."

"What am I supposed to do?" I asked, turning to match her pose. I glanced at Jun before continuing. "I can't just ask him out on a date. Hand him a bunch of flowers and say, 'Kiss me till the cows come home.'" My cheeks were burning even before the words came out.

"That'd certainly be the most unromantic way anybody has ever declared their undying love."

"See?" I said. "I'm hopeless."

She lay down again as the clouds scudded across the sky, and when the sun came back out, she put her sunglasses on. "Maybe he wants to kiss you, too."

"I may never know," I said.

"Take him into the trees."

"Pervert!" I said, nudging her.

She laughed. "I mean go somewhere private. If it's going to happen, it'll happen." And then she slapped my chest and sat up. "Rob, Laura, I heard one of the guys over there has a cooler full of beers. Come on." When she stood, she said, "You boys don't mind, do you? Why don't you take a walk. See the sights. I'm sure there are some interesting things to see over that way."

"What things?" I challenged her, wishing the earth would open up and take me.

She leaned down and ruffled my hair like I was a cute little kid. "You won't know until you find out."

And then they were gone.

Jun looked at me, a smile on his lips that was half tender, half confused.

I studied the curve of his jaw between his earlobe and his neck because I couldn't look him in the eye.

"Fuck it," I said. And I signed, *Walk?*

We moved slowly along the path, away from the bustle of the others. I looked over my shoulder once and Ella waved at me. I don't know what she signed to Rob and Laura, but they watched us walking away.

Jun got his phone out and typed, *They seem nice. But I enjoy the "quiet" too.*

"Quiet?" I asked. Was he messing with me?

He puffed a tiny laugh through his nose, then typed, *I just mean crowds are tiring. Sometimes less is more.*

I kicked a stone at my feet. The noise was receding behind us and the trees loomed tall and thick on our right. I said, "You always seem to be at the centre of a crowd. Don't you like it?"

He thought about it before typing, *People flock to me because of how I look. My face isn't like everyone else's. I'm foreign and I stand out.*

I said, "I like your face." Then, because he looked embarrassed, I added, "I guess people want to know more about you. Where you come from and what your life was like there."

He nodded. *I enjoy telling them. But I'm saying the same thing every time.* He showed me, then typed something else. *You never asked me about Korea.*

"Asking you about Korea doesn't tell me who you are," I said. "Did you want me to?"

Jun shook his head. *I'm glad you didn't*, he typed. *But I'd tell you if you wanted to know.*

I did. I wanted to know everything. But only when he wanted to tell me.

We veered off the path, onto the grass, and it wasn't my

doing. Green shadows speckled his skin under the shade of leafy branches.

I had a video call with my brother last night, Jun typed. *He's finished his military service.*

"That's excellent," I said, but it didn't look like excellent news on his face. "Isn't it?"

His smile was flat, but he nodded.

And then I felt a spark of rain on my skin. Another one.

Jun held his hand out like he wanted to catch it. It wasn't heavy, just a sun shower. I wondered if we should head back to the others, but Jun pointed towards the trees and we stood underneath one as the rain got thicker and more urgent.

Then Jun crossed his legs and sat on the dry earth where the grass didn't grow, and he reached up, took my hand, and pulled me down beside him.

When I sat, Jun's hand lingered on mine, his fingers still, his eyes turned towards it.

I moved my pinkie. Just a touch. Enough to curl it around his. And I looked up.

Jun's eyes came up to meet mine. They were wide and brown and warm and endless. His lips parted. Closed again.

I swallowed, and the noise of it in my head shocked me.

I looked at his lips. At his eyes.

He blinked. And his head tilted. Leaned close.

I closed my eyes.

Softly.

Quietly.

Waiting.

And Callum said, "Oi, lovebirds." He ducked under the branches and sat beside us. His hair was mussed and his

T-shirt was damp around the shoulders.
I pulled my hand away from Jun's.
And I cursed myself for doing so.

CHAPTER 19

If I hadn't pulled my hand away, were we about to kiss? Or was I just imagining it?

I sat in my room that night, playing it over in my head. Sometimes, Callum didn't interrupt us and Jun's lips met mine. Sometimes, Jun turned his head away from me, refusing my kiss. And, sometimes, the tree branches came down around us to give us the privacy we had earned and we kissed softly under the sound of a summer storm.

But mostly, it played out exactly as it had done—or hadn't. Callum and his perfect timing.

On Monday, teachers said things that made no sense, and boys shouted and laughed and fought and burped in the corridors. Somebody smashed a window with a golf ball—thrown by hand, it transpired—and there was a fuss about getting out of the way until the janitor swept up the shards of glass and covered the window with plywood.

Ryan had a friendly football match at lunchtime and I ate alone in the canteen, sitting at a table with some other boys from the year below us. I didn't talk to them and they didn't look at me. And when I was done, I slouched towards the football pitch but the match was already over. I didn't know where Ryan was, and my brain was too muddled, too tired to figure anything out. Jun's fingers on my hand, his dark eyes, his lips—they swirled around inside me, not just my brain, and they got knotted in my stomach with my tormented anguish. If my therapist tells you I'm prone to exaggerating situations in my mind, don't listen to her.

I slipped into the art block and sat at the back of Mr Madden's empty classroom, and when my pencil met a blank sheet of paper in my sketchbook, it made dark strokes, thick and heavy, to mask the grating mess of my life.

He was going to kiss me, wasn't he?

I'm sure he was—as much as I was sure he wasn't.

I wasn't shading in Jun's face today. It wasn't any face, just a page of darkness, like thick fog at night unfolding across the page. And somebody's shadow fell over the desk.

"There you are," Ryan said. He dropped onto a stool beside me. "You're brooding."

"I'm drawing."

"You're drawing while you're brooding," he said. He lifted my hand off the page so he could see the dark scratches clearly. "Ah, yes. The Virgin Mother and Child," he said, tapping the scribbled page, "under cloak of night."

I put my pencil down. "You can have it," I said. "Seeing as

you appreciate it so much."

"I'm afraid there's no more room on the fridge."

"What are you doing on Thursday?" I asked, closing my sketchbook, trapping the darkness inside. If I could count on anyone to pull me out of myself, it would be Ryan.

"Why?" he asked. "Are you taking me on a date?"

"You wish. There's a party. This girl from my ISL class."

"Will there be cake?"

"How would I know?"

"You should ask," he said. "I need to know if it's a 'party' kind of party or a 'cake' kind of party."

"What's the difference?"

He shook his head. "One has cake. Dickhead."

I groaned. But I smiled. See? I hadn't thought about Jun for twenty-seven seconds.

"Can I bring Mia?" he asked. "Is Jun going to be there?"

"I guess so, and yes," I said, answering both of his questions.

As we walked back to class after lunch, I checked my phone. Jun had sent me two text messages. The first one said, *Wearing a tie can restrict blood flow to the brain by 7.5% (scientific fact). Is this why school kids can be stupid?*

The second said, *I'm kind of nervous. A bit.*

He didn't say what he was nervous about, and when I replied to ask him, the bell rang. I got to my class and the teacher said, "Phones away, or they'll end up in my drawer until Friday."

My phone vibrated a few minutes later, in my pocket, and when the teacher was facing the board, I pulled it out to check it.

The party, Jun said. *I haven't been to many. In Korea, it's all about karaoke, but what use am I with a microphone?*

Was he being funny? I couldn't tell. Maybe he really was nervous about parties—or was he nervous about seeing me again after our almost-whatever-it-was at the picnic?

I had never been more invested in figuring out the science behind keeping the party as far away from me as possible, while bringing it closer with equal force.

When Thursday finally breached the parapet of the week, I suffered through the school day like a snail on a bobsleigh. Classes seemed to go as fast as they did slow, in some weird anomaly of the space-time continuum. That evening, I stood in front of the mirror in my bedroom with two shirts in one hand and no idea why I was still undecided. It's not like either choice mattered. Not really.

I tried both—one made my shoulders look broader, the other had a softer, brushed texture. But then I pulled on a jumper instead. Dark grey, slightly baggy, the collar stretched from wear. If I was going to be anything tonight, it had to be comfortable.

"You ready?" Mick called from the bottom of the stairs.

"Hurry up," Ryan shouted from behind him. When I stood at the top of the stairs, Ryan wolf whistled with mock delight and Mick rolled his eyes. "He scrubs up well, doesn't he?" Ryan said.

"He was in the bathroom for over an hour," Mick said. "That's a heck of a lot of scrubbing."

I came down the stairs as Ryan said, "But at least he scrubbed."

"Shut up," I said. "Can we get a move on already?"

"Hold up," Mum said, coming into the hall from the

kitchen. "You know the rules, right?"

Ryan held up his fingers to count. "Drink lots of beer. Do all the drugs that are available. Kiss as many girls—or boys—as possible. Oh, and don't forget to put the toilet seat down."

Mum swished a tea towel at him. "I feel sorry for your mother," she said. She kissed my cheek. "Do the opposite of all those things, sweetheart. Except the toilet seat rule. Always do that."

Ryan said, "What's the wiggle room on kissing girls?"

"I thought you were taking somebody with you."

"I am."

Mum nodded. "Then you're allowed to kiss one girl. If I find out you've done anything else, I'll drag you by the ear to face your mum. Understood?" He saluted her, and she turned to me. "As for you," she said.

"Don't, Mum. I don't need any talks, lectures, birds, bees, or motherly advice."

"Then you can settle for a direct order," she said. "Just be yourself. If he likes you, he likes you."

I groaned. Outside, as we were getting in Mick's car, Ryan whispered, "Be yourself? That's all you get? We seriously need to swap mums."

We picked up Mia first. She came down her driveway in a short skirt and fluffy jacket, and Ryan, in the back seat, gripped the headrest in front of him and said, "Somebody pinch me."

"Not in my back seat," Mick said. When Mia slid into the car beside Ryan, Mick said, "All aboard the Party Express?"

Mia looked at me and my eye roll was loud. But Ryan said, "Onward, driver!"

"At least compliment my outfit first," Mia told him as she punched his arm.

When we got to Jun's, I stared up at his door and chewed the inside of my cheek.

"Should I honk?" Mick asked.

"No," I said. "I'll text him." I got my phone.

"You could walk up to the door, you know. Unless I'm mistaken, you do have a working pair of feet."

But I didn't think I did in that moment. When I messaged him, he said he'd be right out, and a few seconds later the door opened. I caught a glimpse of his mum behind him while he signed something rapidly and then closed the door. I didn't see what he was wearing because I couldn't take my eyes off his face. He was smiling and I was melting.

He got in the back seat as Ryan slid into the middle, and I turned, signing hello. Jun's smile widened. I caught the light scent of his cologne, something citrusy and clean.

And then Mick—did I ever tell you how much I love my stepdad?—turned to face him, and he signed, *Hello J-U-M*.

Jun and I laughed.

"What?" Ryan asked, confused.

"Mick, it's N," I said, showing him the sign. "Not M." And in that instant, I forgot all about my nerves.

The lights were on when we got to Ella's place, and other than the heavy bass of some far-away music, locked behind the closed door, you wouldn't know there was a party inside. This wasn't a college rager.

Mick wanted to come to the door with us, to make sure we weren't stepping into a cult or an orgy, but I convinced him we'd be fine and I'd call him if I needed anything, and we stood on the driveway until he drove off.

I looked at Jun, forgetting—I had to admit—that Ryan and Mia were even there. "Ready?" I asked. I didn't dare say anything more than that.

He nodded.

Ryan knocked on the door and somebody opened it, a girl I didn't recognise. She let the door swing wide and then stepped away, a wordless invitation.

Inside, the house was warm, the windows closed and the music loud. It had a distinct 90s or early 2000s flair, somewhere between prog rock and Brit pop.

In the living room, swallowed in a cloud of smoke, two people were slow dancing while others sat around on the couch or the floor.

Somebody said, "Either I'm stoned, or some children just walked in."

"Children," Ella said, peeling away from the man she'd been dancing with. She wrapped me in her arms, smooshing her cheek against mine. "You came!"

We did introductions. She'd already met Jun and signed a greeting before kissing his cheek, and then she took Ryan and Mia's hands and kissed them both. "You look stunning," she told Mia. Then she dragged her boyfriend over. He was tall, with long hair and a sleeveless denim jacket, and a cigarette in his hand. He waved a cloud of smoke away from his face before shaking our hands.

"Paulie," he said as an introduction. "Sit anywhere. Do anything. There's drink in the kitchen."

A single spotlight flickered in the corner of the room, turning from green to red to blue.

"Happy birthday," I said, shaking his hand again. He nodded before going back to the middle of the floor to sway by himself.

"He's normally a grump," Ella told us. "You got more words out of him in a minute than I usually do in a week." She led us to the kitchen and popped the lids off some beers, handing them to us. Her friends that we'd met in the park, Rob and Laura, were in the corner, kissing. Other guests milled around. It was the most informal party I'd ever been to. Not that I'd been to many. There's a time between eight and eighteen where parties shift from pass-the-parcel to pass-the-bong. And I was still trapped in the in-between.

Somebody knocked on the front door and Ella said, "I'll be back. Enjoy yourselves. Have fun."

I looked at Jun. He sniffed the neck of his beer bottle and pulled a face. I said, "Are you going to drink that?" He shook his head and sat his bottle on the counter. Kids always drink at house parties, it was the done thing, but because Jun didn't, I put mine down too. There was a row of vodka bottles and soft drinks, and a stack of plastic glasses nearby, so I filled two with Coke, then looked at Ryan and Mia. His bottle was already upturned at his lips.

I said, "Don't get drunk or you'll end up sleeping at my house and I'm tired of your snoring."

"He snores?" Mia asked, like maybe it was a dealbreaker. But then she put her hand on his arm and he grinned.

We sat on the floor of the living room, surrounded by strangers. By flashing lights and loud music and the thick fog of cigarettes. The room was dense with heat, heavy in a tired way. Mia sang along with whatever song was playing—something I didn't recognise—and Ryan bobbed his head to the chillness of it all.

Somebody handed us a pack of playing cards, but then took them back when we realised they were tarot cards. And we sat there, quietly, drinking our drinks and taking in the atmosphere. This wasn't a high school party. It was grown up. Lazy, almost. People were having conversations. Somebody else had joined Ella in the middle of the room to dance. Smoke curled across the ceiling. And Jun was glowing with the spotlight fading in and out behind him.

His dark eyes were black holes that pulled me in, time dilating the closer he felt.

He caught me staring at him. And he signed, *Hi*. His smile was perfect.

I signed it back.

And then he pointed.

Ryan and Mia were snogging.

CHAPTER 20

I scanned the snacks on the coffee table that had been pushed up against the wall so Ella could dance. Then I read the names on the spines of paperback novels on the floor, stacked in the chaos of a library explosion. There were crime novels—Larsson, Coben, Deaver—as well as fantasy novels—Terry Pratchett, which I loved—and an ISL guide next to a self-help book that promised to make you quit smoking in 30 days. To be fair, I hadn't seen Ella with a cigarette once, so maybe it worked. Or maybe it was Paulie's and he was yet to read it.

The walls were smoky white and the carpet was thin but clean, and apart from a collection of guitars displayed on the wall, there were few signs of decoration. No family photos, no wooden signs that said Love or Home. An incense stick that smelled earthy, with something sweet under the heavier notes, smouldered on the mantelpiece.

And then I studied the dust on the edge of the skirting board because when I looked at Jun, all I wanted to do was pull him towards me and study his mouth. I'd avoided looking at his face for so long that I could describe, in great detail, the tan-coloured shirt he was wearing, or the navy-blue chinos with the turned-up hems and the pristine creases on the legs. The white Nikes that looked almost new, and the colourful socks beneath them that were visible when he adjusted his position on the floor, crossing his legs like he was meditating.

Movement beside me—I'd been avoiding looking at Ryan, too, because nobody wants to see their make-out session—made me bring my attention back. Ryan grabbed a bowl of cheese balls from the coffee table and carried it to the corner of the floor, away from us, where Mia joined him with the tarot cards. She laid them out in a cross like she knew what she was doing.

And Jun tapped my knee. When I looked, he signed, *You okay?*

I smiled—smiling was becoming my thing. His drink was empty, so I nodded towards the kitchen and we stood up.

When we hovered by the collection of drinks, I asked, "Are you having a good time?"

He got his phone. *It's not what I was expecting*, he said. *Are all parties like this?*

I shrugged. "I have no idea. I don't think so. Nobody has vomited yet and nobody's broken a vase. And, clearly, there's no karaoke. So that's a bonus."

Jun said, *If you ever host a party, I promise to break one of your expensive vases.*

"Thank you," I said, pouring fresh drinks. "That's very kind of you."

He typed, then showed me his phone with a grin on his face. *I aim to please.* He'd added a geek emoji to the end.

I handed him his plastic glass and his fingers took it from me with a gentle stroke of my skin. I was convinced of it. He brought it to his lips and I watched the dark liquid quench him the way I wanted to.

I turned away from him, blushing, and almost knocked over somebody else's drink. Rob signed and spoke, "Careful, kiddo." His eyes were droopy, like he'd had one glass too many, and then he signed something to Jun that I didn't catch.

Laura came back from the bathroom and joined us, and when she saw Jun, she kissed his cheek and asked him something that made him smile as he replied.

When Ella bounced into the kitchen, I was relieved. Jun, Rob and Laura weren't excluding me, but because two of them were silent, I couldn't follow their full conversation.

Ella threw herself against me. "I just had a ten-minute nap," she said.

I laughed. "Aren't you the host? You're supposed to be filling glasses and making sure the canapes never run out."

"I'm a terrible host," she said. "Are you having fun?"

We stepped away from the others just as Rob said the word "Korea", and I glanced at Jun, wondering if he was having the same old conversation he always had with strangers. But there was no indication on his face that he might be bored. His eyebrows were as animated as his hands.

"Ryan and Mia surprised me," I told her.

"She's gorgeous," Ella said. "But why are you surprised? Aren't they a couple?"

"I mean, they went from chatting on the school bus to going to the bowling alley once, to playing tonsil hockey on your living room floor."

"Isn't that how it always goes?" she asked, taking my arm, throwing a small wave to Jun, and walking me back into the living room where the music had been turned down and Mia was explaining one of the tarot cards to Ryan and how he was going to have at least seven babies one day. I'm pretty sure that's not how tarot cards work, but what do I know?

Ella flopped onto the couch and pulled me down beside her. I said, "Maybe it goes like that for you."

"Please," she said. "I had to chase Paulie down with a baseball bat just to get him to go to the student bar with me." She looked at Ryan and Mia who were flirty and touchy. "You don't have it so easy, do you?" she asked me, quietly, so nobody else could hear.

"I can't read the cues," I said. "And it's not like I can just walk up to a random boy and say, 'Let's get coffee and by the way can I kiss you?'"

Ella nudged me. "But it's not a random boy, is it?"

"That doesn't make it any less awkward," I said.

"It should," she told me. "Do you want my advice?"

"No," I said, only half serious.

"Okay. Sheesh." She pulled a scatter cushion into her arms to sulk.

"Fine. Tell me."

"Nope," she said. I could tell she was trying not to smile. I looked around to see if Jun had come into the room yet, but he was still in the kitchen with Rob and Laura.

"Tell me."

"Fine," she said. She leaned in, cupped my ear to whisper, and said, "Let's consult the cards." She dragged me off the couch and onto the floor with Ryan and Mia. "Shuffle them up, it's Owen's turn."

Mia handed the cards to her and Ella shuffled them, dropping a couple and picking them up. "It's good luck to drop a shuffle," she said. "It means the reading's going to be clear." She pushed the half-empty bowl of cheese balls out of the way and sat the deck down between us. "Cut it."

I cut it somewhere near the middle, and she put the bottom half on top. Then she laid out a grid of cards on the carpet. She took my hands, stared into my eyes with more intent than anyone ever had, and then she took a deep breath to centre herself.

She turned the first card. "The Fool."

"Thanks," I said.

"Called it," Ryan laughed.

"Shush," Ella said. She pointed. "This is you. Standing on a cliff, about to throw yourself at the mercy of the universe."

"Don't jump," Ryan whispered.

Ella shook her head. "That's his choice. But if you jump, you're probably going without a parachute. Make sure you land feet first."

She turned the second card. "Two of Cups. This one's obvious."

"It is?"

"Quiet," she said. "It means connection."

Ryan touched my leg. "I didn't know you cared."

"Hey!" Mia said.

And Ella closed her eyes, her hand hovering over another card. But she changed her mind and turned the next one first. "The Hanged Man."

"I knew it," Ryan said. "You jumped off the universe like the fool and accidentally hanged yourself."

Ella slapped his leg.

"I thought you were giving me advice," I said.

"Not me. The universe." She tapped the hanging man card. "You're stuck. Hanging upside down like a clown in a trapeze act. It's time to get off your arse—not literally; wait till I'm finished first."

She flipped the last card in the row, ignoring the one in the middle that was still face down. "The Chariot," she said. "But it's reversed."

"What does that mean?"

"You don't know where you're going."

"Does anyone?"

"I do," Mia said.

"Straight to my heart," Ryan told her. She pretended to vomit.

"Okay," I said. "So I'm upside down, jumping off the universe, with a connection to something but no idea where I'm going. Why does my life sound like it's screwed?"

Mia said, "You should probably just lock yourself in your room forever and throw away the key."

"But there's still one more card," Ryan said, like he was actually buying into it.

Ella nodded. She pointed at it and said, "Turn it over."

"Me?" I asked.

"No, the man on the moon." So I flipped it. "The Wheel of Fortune," she said. She grinned.

"What?" I asked. Maybe I was buying into it too.

"It's fate," she said. "And it's inevitable."

"What is?"

She gathered up the cards. "Everything," she told me. "It's all inevitable. It always has been."

Our circle widened when Paulie nudged himself into our group with one of his acoustic guitars, and then a few others joined us. Paulie strummed dramatically, something flirty and Spanish-sounding. Then he said, "Any requests?"

"Lady Gaga," Mia said, and he actually knocked out a few chords from *Alejandro*.

Then his fingers drifted into a softer, slower piece that sounded dreamy and ethereal. Somebody turned the music off and joined us, and Jun, Rob and Laura came in from the kitchen.

Jun picked carefully over the people and put his hand on my shoulder as he sat beside me, pressed into my side where I could feel his warmth.

At my other side, Paulie nodded at Jun, then stopped playing for a second. He indicated for Jun's hand, and when Jun held it out, Paulie pressed it against the body of his guitar so that Jun could feel it when he played.

And all I could feel was Jun's arm stretched across me, his shoulder leaning into me, his face near mine.

Paulie played. And Jun smiled.

And then we applauded. Jun leaned back, pulling his arm away from me, and shook his hands by his head in appreciation. *Encore*, he signed, and Rob told us what he'd said.

"Later," Paulie said. "I need a smoke."

And the impromptu recital dispersed. But Jun was still leaning into me.

I looked at him. At his face. At his eyes.

And then he signed, *Air?*

I tugged the loose collar of my jumper. It really was getting hot in there. And air was exactly what I needed. I nodded and we went to the kitchen, leaving Ryan and Mia fighting over the bowl of cheese balls, and Ella testing her signing skills with Laura.

Some people were still deep in conversation in the kitchen, and Jun tested the back door. It was unlocked, and we stepped into the night, where small solar-powered spotlights dotted the grassy garden and a wrought-iron bench was barely illuminated beside a tall hedgerow.

Jun filled his lungs with cool night air and he pointed at the bench. When we sat, it was cold and unforgiving. It tightened the muscles in my back and stomach. Or maybe being there with Jun did that.

In the darkness, he took out his phone. Its light splashed across his face and made his eyes glow. He typed, *Everybody's being so nice.*

"Good," I said. "Are you glad you came?"

He turned his phone, shining it on me, and asked me to say it again. In the darkness, I guess my words were lost to him. He said, *Of course I am. Are you?*

"Am I glad you came? Absolutely." I grinned, trying to make it sound jokey.

Jun's eyes flicked down. Up again. He didn't type. He signed, *Happy.*

And I signed it too.

When his thumbs went back to his phone to say something else, I stopped him. I put my hand on top of his and he looked at me.

"Don't," I said. "You don't need it. Not right now."

He turned the screen off and his face fell into darkness. We sat there, knees touching, facing each other.

I took his hands again, and he didn't object. His fingers were warm. When I found his eyes, with the light from the garden spotlights dotted inside them, my heart was thumping. And something in his eyes told me his was doing the same. Maybe I could feel it in the touch of his fingers.

I opened my mouth to say something, but Jun raised his hand. Touched my lips. Silenced me. I inhaled him, and I whispered against the soft pads of his fingers. "I want to kiss you."

I don't know if he could feel me. If he understood. But he lowered his hand. Found mine.

And he leaned in.

No words.

No interruptions.

Just him. Me. Us.

And we kissed.

CHAPTER 21

He grinned against my mouth, lips twitching and wide. Beautiful even though I couldn't see it.

I lifted my hand to his cheek, needing to know him with more than taste. The warmth of his skin. The quiet of his presence.

When we pulled apart, barely, our foreheads touching, eyes blinking out of focus, I breathed him in. The cool air he stirred, the gentle essence of his cologne that I recognised from the car earlier. And my eyes closed against the dizziness of Jun-ho Lee.

The night was quiet, trapping us in its embrace, a love song of stars above us and the cool rush of a breeze over the grass and the dandelions. I sighed, slowly, easing out the relief that had filled me, and we kept our foreheads together for a while, saying nothing, doing nothing. Being nothing.

I found his hand, twined my fingers through his, brought it to my chest and pressed it there, letting him feel the frantic thudding of my heart.

He smiled again, pulled his head back and looked at me. In his eyes, the universe spoke my name. And he lifted my hand, placing it against his own heart.

It was the loudest thing about him.

I kissed him again, because I needed to. Words would ruin it. Language—English, ISL, Korean—was nothing in this moment. There was nothing in words that my lips couldn't say, so I let them speak for me.

His hands came to my face, pulling me into him, cradling me against his tender touch, and my heart slammed against my ribs like it needed out. Needed release.

The world fell away from us—the smells of smoke and evening grass, the quiet hum of the party—until there was nothing but us. His breath against my lips. His heartbeat under my hand. His mouth soft and urgent against mine.

And then he pulled me to him, arms tight around my neck, and I fed into the warmth of his touch, the softness of our motion.

When he pulled back, blinking blindly, he moved his hand. Signed, *Thank you.*

And I laughed, giddy with the taste of him. "You're welcome," I said.

Jun turned his head, looked at the house, the garden, the sky.

I touched his chin, drew him back to me. And I signed, *Thank you, too.* Because I couldn't take all the credit for our energy.

And then the door opened. Ryan and Mia stumbled into the garden, hand in hand. "Oh," Ryan said, like he didn't know we were here. And then, "Oh!" when his brain caught up with his eyes. He spun Mia around. "Inside. Now."

"What? Why?"

He pushed her through the door, closed it behind him, and he pressed his back to it on the inside, stopping anyone else from coming out. I could see him against the glass.

Jun put his hand over his mouth, hiding his laughter.

And I took his fingers because I wanted to see his smile. Wanted to feel his joy.

"Well," I said. "I guess I don't have to tell Ryan that we kissed now. I think he just figured it out."

Jun covered his face with his hands and leaned into me, his head against my chest. I wrapped my arms around him, and then tilted his face so he could see me. I said, "Embarrassed?"

Jun shook his head, lifted his phone, typed, and showed me. *I'm too happy to be embarrassed.*

When I looked at the house again, half of the party were staring through the kitchen window at us. Ella was grinning like a loon.

I pulled Jun back into my arms to shield my own face from embarrassment.

And when Mick came to pick us up, a little after eleven—my curfew extended just this once, even though it was a school night—he took one look at us as we stood on Ella's driveway, my fingers linked with Jun's, and he said, "Good night, was it?"

"No," Ryan said, getting into the back with Mia.

"Somebody ate all the cheese balls and now they feel sick."

"It was you," Mia said. And to Mick she added, "If he hurls in your car, you have my permission to kick him into next Friday."

Mick laughed. "A good night all round, then."

Reluctantly, I let go of Jun's hand and slid into the front seat as he got in the back. And before he set off, Mick stared at me. "What?" I asked, trying to keep the smile off my cheeks.

"Nothing," Mick grinned.

"Can we go then?"

"Absolutely," he said, still staring. And then he gave up, popped the handbrake, and we headed out of Ella's street under the silence of his smile. I knew what kind of conversation he'd have with Mum in bed tonight. And my ears were already burning.

Jun texted good night and then good morning. And the four hours of broken sleep I got between those two messages were filled with swirling dreams of kissing and touching and holding and laughing. Jun crossed his heart with a finger and crossed mine with the same hand, and dawn folded over me with its glorious weight, shattering the colourful rubble of my dreams.

I reached for my phone, replied to his message, and then pulled the duvet over my head. It wasn't a dream. It couldn't be. It better not be.

Jun sent me another message, a video. He was sitting up in bed, loose T-shirt, holding his phone at arm's length, and he signed, *Hello*.

I didn't sit up. I took a video where I lay, hair a mess, face shadowed from the duvet, and signed, *K-I-S-S me*. I didn't know the word for "kiss" in ISL so I had to fingerspell it.

Jun replied with a string of hearts and kissing emojis.

But I couldn't kiss him yet. In case no kid has ever said it before, school is a curse. It is the ruination of teenage-kind.

At school, Ryan came into my business studies class, even though he was in a different set, even though he didn't belong there, and he flopped into the empty seat beside me, his bag on the desk, elbow on top of it, and he nudged my arm until I looked up.

"Well?" he said.

"Well what?" I turned back to my workbook, highlighting another sentence that probably didn't need highlighting, the yellow ink fading from overuse.

"How was it?"

"I don't know what you're talking about," I said. "Don't you have calculus or something?"

"Probably. But tell me. How was it?"

"You know how it was. You and half the world were watching us through the window."

"Nobody saw what you were doing," he said. "You'd already stopped. But you guys looked pretty close out there. Was it all smooshy and soft and warm?"

I didn't look up. "What was it like kissing Mia?"

"Smooshy and soft and warm," he said.

I laughed. "Yeah." And then I looked at him. I think he was grinning as much as I was. "You can go back to your class now."

"We should compare notes," Ryan said.

"That's disgusting. Get out of here," I told him.

He stood up, weaved around the tables, and hovered in

the doorway. And, loud enough for everyone to hear—I'm just thankful the teacher hadn't arrived yet—he said, "Big kisses! Love you!"

"Love you more," a gruff voice from the back of the room said, and everybody laughed.

I kept my head down. This was mother-in-your-changing-room levels of embarrassment. But for the rest of the day, I couldn't flush the smile off my face. Not even at the dinner table that night.

Mum sat my plate in front of me, and although she didn't mention it, she'd formed the mashed potatoes into a heart shape. "What's this?" I said, avoiding her eyes.

"Dinner," Mum said. She touched the back of my neck, lightly, a quiet brush of her fingers. "Eat your spuds," she said. The juices from my steak were bleeding into the edge of the potatoes and turning them love-heart red.

And Mick said, "Where's my heart-shaped potatoes? I've just got a lump."

Mum pretended to box his nose. "I'll give you a lump to complain about."

Tommy Two, still dressed in his work suit—Mum had forced him to come for Friday dinner tonight like he used to—said, "Am I missing something?" He guzzled from his beer bottle and sat it back on the table.

"Owen can catch you up," Mick said.

I dragged my fork through the mashed potatoes, disguising the shape of them, and then filled my mouth with broad beans so I couldn't talk.

"Leave him alone," Mum said, sitting down and handing Mick the jug of peppercorn sauce. "Let's just eat dinner in peace, shall we?"

Grandad Tommy's seat was still empty, no place setting, no cutlery. Just the stain of his glass on the worn polish of the table. Mum used to pick his glass up and sit a coaster under it, and when Tommy lifted it to drink, he'd sit it down beside the coaster instead of on top. It drove her mad.

And while I sliced into my steak, I wished he was here, one last time. Just so I could tell him. So he could see the smile on my face and know it was real.

"So," Mick said. "How was everyone's night last night? Everybody have a good time? Do anything fun?"

I glared at him.

Tommy Two said, "I started watching that show you mentioned. The one about the serial killer. But I fell asleep during the first episode. God, it was boring."

If my steak wasn't already dead, the way I cut into it would have been the killing blow.

"Is that so?" Mick asked. "Very interesting." I could tell from his voice, without looking up, that he was having the most fun he'd ever had in his life. "And what about you, Maggie? Did you get up to anything fun last night?"

"No, Mick," she said. "Did you?"

Mick chewed before answering. "I can't quite recall, if I'm honest. Let's circle back to me. What about you, Owen? How was your Thursday night?"

Steak. Mashed potatoes. Beans. Sip of water.

"No?" Mick said. "Nothing?"

I put my cutlery down, politely. Cleared my throat. "I went to a party, Mick. When's the last time you were invited to one?"

"Probably the day I married your mother," he said, beaming. "And how was your party? Was it good?"

"It was fine," I grumbled, returning my attention to the plate.

"Fine, he says. Do you hear that, Tommy Two? The party he went to was fine."

"Come on, now," Mum said at last. "Quit teasing him. He's clearly not going to *kiss and tell*."

"Oh my God," I moaned.

"Uh-oh," Tommy Two said. "He's gone red in the face."

"No, I haven't." But I had. Bring me your eggs, I'll cook them for you on my cheeks.

Later, when I was clearing the plates into the dishwasher, Mum rubbed my back for a second. She said, "They're only teasing."

"I know," I told her.

"We're just happy for you. You deserve it."

"Deserve what?" I asked. "Don't rush things. It's too new."

And Mum said, "A new penny isn't new once it's in your pocket."

CHAPTER 22

Friday, Saturday, Junday.

Jun said he had things to do with his mum on Saturday, going to see a solicitor—he didn't explain why and I didn't pry—and then to buy new clothes for the coming summer. But he assured me he wasn't trying to get out of seeing me, which had been the one thought going through my head when he said we couldn't meet up on Saturday.

Mum says my Irish blood means I haven't finished growing yet >_<, he said. *How will you ever cope without me until Sunday?*

I'll probably just slip into a coma for the day, I told him.

I moped around the house on Saturday morning until Mum said, "Get in the car."

"Where are we going?"

"I'm going to drive you to the edge of town and leave you

there," she joked. "You can come to the supermarket with me. I'll let you push the trolley."

"I'm not a kid."

"No, but you're obliged to do as I say until you get married and become somebody else's problem."

I followed her around the supermarket—pushing the trolley, of course, because it turns out I was a kid after all—listening to her ramble about the amount of sugar in cereals and the rising price of kiwis. We stopped at the butcher's counter and I stared at the trays of raw meat. There were two sausages that sat apart from all the others, linked together like they were holding hands. And I wondered what Jun was up to.

Then I suggested stopping for a coffee and because we hadn't eaten since breakfast, it became lunch. I could tell she wanted to ask me about Jun while she ate a club sandwich, but she held back. Part of me wanted to tell her about him, but I also wanted to keep it a secret—something that was just between us, not for public consumption.

The most she said, after last night's teasing, was, "Is that him?" when my phone buzzed and I smiled at the message.

I nodded and didn't say anything as I tapped my reply.

When we got home, I helped put the groceries away and ate a small yoghurt with a big spoon, staring at Grandad Tommy's chair at the table.

Mum said, "Put the spoon in the dishwasher when you're done."

She went upstairs to run a bath and I forgot all about her instructions. I threw the empty yoghurt pot into the recycle bin and tossed the spoon into the sink, ever the model son.

When Sunday arrived, the morning was slow and deliberate. I texted Jun, ate breakfast, texted Jun, had a shower, texted Jun, got dressed.

Texted Jun.

He arranged to meet me at the park, by the bench where we first met. He didn't say, "where you threw dirty water all over me," but I'm sure that's what he was thinking.

He was already there when I arrived—and I was ten minutes early, hoping to be there before him. He stood up as I walked down the path with my sketchbook under my arm. He was wearing a new pair of loose-fit jeans and a light sweater with a single, solid stripe across the chest and arms. He said, *Hello*.

I said, *K-I-S-S me*.

And Jun blushed. He showed me the sign for kiss—touching his lips, and I wanted to kiss him right there in the park. Instead, we settled for a hug, brief but tight, and I was reminded of holding him in my arms on Thursday night. As we parted now, our fingers lingered in each other's hands before we sat down.

He pointed at my sketchbook. *Will you draw?* he signed.

"No," I said. I wasn't sure why I'd brought it. It's not like I wanted him to pose for me, draped across the bench, butt naked and smiling. "I don't have to."

Do it, he signed. *I'll watch*.

"Won't that be boring?"

He shook his head, and I realised our conversations were getting more fluid, more fluent. He hadn't taken his phone out to type on yet.

I looked around, then brought my face back to him.

"What should I draw?"

Jun searched the park. There were no ducks on the pond, no kids playing with toy boats. A jogger went by, and a man was stooping on the grass to clean up after his dog. Two kids on bicycles. Jun shrugged. *Use your imagination*, I assumed his sign meant.

"Think of something," I said as I opened my sketchbook to a blank page.

My hand moved, started sketching the outline of him, and when he realised, he said, *No*. He covered his face as if he was embarrassed.

I said, "I can draw you without even looking." And I did. I turned from him, made rough marks, sweeping strokes, light shadows. And then I held it up for him to see.

You're very good, he signed.

I turned my pencil over and erased the strokes of his mouth, then shaded it back in as puckered lips. He slapped my arm. And he kept his fingers there a second longer.

I closed the book, shuffled closer to him, my shoulder pressed against him, legs touching. I rested my hands on the sketchbook in my lap and Jun stroked a finger across the back of my hand. I grabbed his finger in my other fist. Wouldn't let go. He wrestled against me for a few seconds, grinning, then gave up, letting me keep the finger. But it wasn't enough, so I rearranged our hands, threading my fingers through his. And we sat like that, linked together like sausages, watching the wind ripples spread out across the pond. Feeling something ripple in my stomach in the same way.

Coffee? Jun signed with his free hand.

I nodded, pointing over my shoulder at the kiosk where

we'd first had a macchiato.

But he signed, *No. Further away.*

Okay, I signed. Jun stood up, but I refused to let go of his hand. I pulled him back down onto the bench.

Coffee, he signed again.

"In a minute," I said. I squeezed his hand. And then I made the sign for kiss.

Jun looked around.

I squeezed again to get his attention. *Kiss*, I signed.

And he grinned. He leaned in, kissed me, and it was smooshy and soft and warm. Just like Ryan had said.

We walked through the park and onto the street, not holding hands but holding the space between us, our arms brushing together as we moved. He kept looking at me and smiling. How did I know that? Because I was looking at him, too. At one point, near the corner of the high street, he put his hand on my chest to stop me. There was dog poo on the pavement.

Thanks, I said. We stepped around it and walked on.

He took me to a small café that I'd never been to. It was narrow and long, and the AC kept the customers icy. We ordered at the counter, getting a couple of enormous cookies as well as coffees, and then I looked around for somewhere to sit, but Jun pointed to a set of narrow stairs that went up. We passed another floor of seating, warmer here, large windows letting in late-spring light, and Jun pointed up again.

At the top, he pushed through a door and we came out onto a roof terrace with a wrought-iron safety rail and long planters of vividly coloured flowers like one of Grandad Tommy's artist palettes. There were four two-seater tables and because the space was so limited, only two of them had parasols.

A middle-aged couple sipped coffee at one of the tables. They wore hiking boots and had bandanas tied around their necks, a large rucksack propped against the guardrail with camping pans dangling from the side of it.

Jun indicated the table furthest from them, and when we sat, I shuffled my chair closer to him so we weren't sitting opposite each other, then I stared across the horizon like I was on top of the world. I had to twist my head to see along the street between the high buildings, but looking east, it seemed like I could see for hazy miles.

It's beautiful, I signed.

He grinned and sipped his coffee, and I moved my sketch-book because I was afraid of spilling all over it. But Jun held the edge of it before I could put it on the ground.

May I? he asked.

I nodded and he took a bite of his double-choc cookie, dusting the crumbs off his fingers before opening the book. He stopped as he came to the fourth sketch of him, went back and looked through the pages again, and then studied my face.

Why me? he asked.

"Because."

But why?

"Because I like you."

He put his hand on my arm for a second, warm fingers against my skin. And then he skimmed through the rest of the pages. When he came to the darkly shaded page, just thick scratches of pencil strokes that Ryan had pretended to admire, he ran his finger across the darkness of it, and some of the lead transferred to his fingertip. He said, *What's this?*

I didn't really know. But I said, "My soul?"

He poked my arm.

Hard.

"I was lost when I did that," I said. "I have an end of year art project to complete and I just started shading. I didn't really mean to fill the whole page."

Jun looked at it, held it out so he could see it better. And then, for the first time today, he got his phone out. He typed, *It feels dark and stormy. Almost like it's hiding something.*

"It's hiding my inability to come up with anything good for my art project."

You still don't know what to make? he asked.

"I have a plan. But I don't know how to execute it."

You will, he said. And he put his phone away.

When the campers finished their drinks and left, we were alone on the rooftop. Jun tapped my hand, and when I turned, his face was close, leaning into me. He kissed me by surprise. And when he pulled away, I pulled him back. Kissed him again.

Kissing is fun. Why does nobody talk about that?

I put my arm around him, and then he typed, *Finish your cookie. I want to show you something.*

We walked back down the street we'd just come up, turned into a narrow alleyway between the backs of two rows of tall buildings, and then onto an overgrown area where the grass was filled with weeds. A wide field gave way to a construction site that was old, unfinished, and abandoned.

"Where are we?" I asked.

He pointed. There was a large sign facing onto a road at the far side that said, CEDAR HILL: LUXURY APARTMENTS COMING 2021. But 2021 was years ago, and even the sign showed its age.

Jun typed, *I guess they ran out of money or something.*

"How did you find this place?"

I went exploring a few weeks after we came to Ireland. I had an argument with Mum—I don't remember why—so I walked off on my own. I shouldn't have, but then I found this.

He took my hand, led me across the grass and onto the loose gravel of the abandoned site. There were holes in the ground that had been covered with sheets of metal for safety, and the foundations of at least a dozen buildings had been laid and then forgotten about. And next to the struts of a gable wall, beside what should have been somebody's kitchen or bathroom, there was a large concrete culvert, a tube tall enough to stand inside if you didn't mind stooping. It was like a skatepark's halfpipe if the halfpipe had never been cut open.

He walked inside and stomped his feet, holding his hands out like he was catching the vibrations of his echoes.

When I followed him, I clapped my hands and hollered, and the sound of me warbled back through the concrete tube.

Jun's smile was enormous.

"You can feel it," I said, and he held his hands up as if he was showing me his ears. How he felt. How he heard.

The sunlight fractured into the tube behind him and I was so desperate to kiss him that I didn't ask. Didn't give him a chance to say no. I took his hands, then wrapped my arms around his waist. And when my lips met his, in the privacy of the culvert, his mouth was just as hungry as mine.

We stood that way, stooped under the low ceiling of the pipe, kissing until our necks hurt, and then we laughed, giddy with perfect passion. We sat near the mouth of the pipe, facing each other, leaning against the curved sides, feet touching as the sunlight draped across us like a warm blanket. He tapped my foot with his and I nudged him in reply.

He smiled, rested his head against the wall of the culvert, and closed his eyes. I could see why he liked it here. Not for the vibrations of stomping echoes, which he could get anywhere, or the crude graffiti that stretched across the inside of the pipe, but for the solitude. The peace of being alive in a dead construction site, hidden from a world that didn't know we even existed.

When his phone vibrated in his hand and the camera flash blinked maddeningly to alert him to it, he opened his eyes, read his message, and then something clouded over his face that soured his mood.

I tapped my leg against his. "What's up?"

He shook his head, then showed me his phone. A text exchange—mostly one-sided—and entirely in Korean.

"Your brother?" I asked. I signed it, too, because I'd been learning family words. I butted four fingers against my side. *Brother.*

Jun breathed. Said, *No. Father.* He made an F sign with each hand and knocked them together.

Are you okay? I asked.

Jun opened his notes app and typed, *Translated directly, he says, "It's not too late to fix all things."*

"What things?" I asked.

Everything, Jun signed.

CHAPTER 23

Clouds scuttled across the sky and the culvert went dark. Jun stepped out, stretching his back and then dusting off the seat of his jeans.

When I stood up beside him, I touched his arm. He still had his phone in his hand but the soft smile that had been on his face all day—the one that made his eyes shine—was gone.

"Do you want to talk about it?" I asked.

He shook his head. Then he shrugged and nodded. He typed, *It'll only bore you.*

"You could never."

Not me, he said. *My father.*

We walked away from the concrete pipe, because the mood had shifted, or because he didn't want to be near it when he spoke about his dad. He stepped onto the foundations of a luxury apartment that never came about, balancing on the corner, and I waited for him to sign or type.

He looked at his phone. Then he typed, *I wasn't to blame for their divorce. But it was still about me.*

He cleared the screen and typed again. *My father wants me to get a cochlear implant. There have been many success stories, even years after hearing loss. Mum says it should be my choice. And I chose no.*

It was telling that he said *father* not dad, but *mum* not mother. Like there'd always been an imbalance between them. His mum's Irish ways, the constant casualness of her demeanour, versus his father's Korean values.

"Of course it's your choice," I said. But he put his fingertips against my lips to stop me.

I nodded, turned from him, and found a section of the wall that was high enough to lean against if I sat down. When I was on the ground, I patted the area between my legs, asking him to sit with me. He came down in front of me, leaning his back against my chest, and I looked over his shoulder at his phone while he typed.

They argued a lot. Not just about being Deaf. About everything. When Woo-sung packed his things for military training, I knew he was relieved to be leaving, to get away from the arguments. And when he left, the house was hollow for a while, as if my father felt the loss of his eldest son.

But because I was the only son left, he redirected all his attention to me. Mum screamed. Father screamed. And now we're here.

I put my arms around him and he pressed back against me. I didn't feel any sadness coming from him, but there was something in his body language that looked weary and confused.

He said, *In Korea, everybody watches. Everybody talks. Mum said we needed a place where nobody cared if I signed or stayed Deaf. Father's family disapproved of the divorce.*

I kissed his temple, then I tilted his head so he could see my lips. "I don't understand. He wants to fix you? Your hearing? Or the divorce?"

Everything, Jun signed again. He typed, *He wants to restore his family as well as restore my hearing.*

I pulled him tighter. Kissed him.

I didn't know what words to say, so I didn't say any.

His phone screen dimmed and turned off, and we sat that way for a while, my arms around him, feeling the sun dip in and out among the clouds. And even when the gravel under my butt was beginning to hurt, I didn't move. I would have stayed there as long as he needed.

Jun took my hand, turned it palm up, and traced a circle around it. Then he kissed it and folded my fingers closed.

"What was that word?" I asked. "The one you traced on my arm at the bowling alley?"

Jun dropped his head back to my shoulder and kissed my chin. He peeled my fingers open again and drew the word, the same one from before.

He typed it in Korean for me, the way he'd written it on my arm, then showed me the pronunciation. *Goyo.*

"What does it mean?"

Silence, he typed. And I know he was saying more than the fact that he was Deaf. That maybe he wanted me to share in it. To be in it with him.

I nodded, though he didn't ask me anything. "Silence," I

said.

And I held him against me, in our silence, his shoulder under my chin, cheek against cheek, in the abandoned bones of a future that never came true.

I wondered how many people would have lived here if the apartments had been finished as planned. If, in 2021, a minor celebrity had cut a red ribbon with giant scissors and declared Cedar Hill officially open, would there be families? Couples? Children playing in the streets? Would another couple of queer teens be sitting right here, leaning against this wall, sharing impossible secrets?

I felt Jun sigh beneath my arms, not with exasperation, but with contentment.

I kissed his neck.

Then he typed, *If we go into town, there's a Korean restaurant called Dalbit. It means "Moonlight." Do you want dinner?*

I checked the time in the corner of his screen. "It's two p.m.," I said.

Later, he signed. And he settled back into my arms.

"Later," I agreed.

When we left the construction site, squeezing through a narrow gap in the tall fencing instead of walking back across the field and through the alleyway, there was a bus stop on the other side of the road that would take us into town. I sent Mum a text message, telling her I was going to have dinner with Jun, and Mum's reply made me cringe.

Send a photo of you both, I want to show Samantha.

Samantha McDonald was a neighbour and one of Mum's oldest friends. I sent a selfie of me with my tongue out instead. Jun was mine, not hers.

He held my hand while we rode the bus, and then he led me past a row of Chinese and Indian takeaways, down a cobbled side street, and right onto a square of older buildings whose paintwork had seen better days. A convenience store, a Turkish barbershop, a few more nondescript buildings, and in the far corner, tucked away where you'd never find it unless you knew it was there, was Dalbit.

It was cool and dim inside, with faint notes of steamed rice and sesame oil. When we entered, a Korean man in a white shirt smiled. He saw Jun and bowed, speaking rapidly in Korean. And then he signed hello. They'd obviously met before.

"Come, friend," he said to me, and he led us to a booth near the back with a white tabletop and a small, battery-operated candle that flickered in the centre. Intimate. Quiet.

Perfect.

Jun pushed me into the booth and slid in beside me, holding my hand under the table while we studied the menu that was written in Korean and English. There were knives and forks in a pot on the table, but Jun opened a secret drawer at the side of the table and produced two pairs of metal chopsticks and some long-handled spoons. When he offered the chopsticks to me, I said, "Okay. But you'll have to show me."

We ordered japchae and tteokbokki, words I had no idea how to pronounce, but with English descriptions in the menu that made them sound delicious. And we sipped fiery ginger beer until the food came.

As he held my hand, his thumb casually stroked mine, as if he wasn't even aware he was doing it, and although he wanted to keep that contact alive while he ate with his other hand, chopsticks moving deftly from one dish to another, I said, "I'm going to need both hands or I'll starve."

Jun pincered some beef and glass noodles and fed them to me, which was messy and playful and—for some reason—arousing.

I concentrated on using my own chopsticks until my brain had control of my blood flow again, and I let Jun teach me how to hold them correctly. It was awkward at first, but I quickly got the hang of it.

Before we were finished, locked in the quiet sound of clinking chopsticks from other patrons and the sweet-caramel smell of somebody's grilled meat, Jun pulled out his phone and typed, *You have soy sauce on your chin and I don't think the owner would appreciate it if I licked it from you.*

"He probably wouldn't," I said, reaching for a napkin, "but I might."

Jun's eyes widened as if I'd shocked him. And then, when he made sure nobody was watching—and only after I'd wiped my chin by myself—he leaned in and kissed me, quickly, before filling his mouth with more tteokbokki so that I couldn't kiss him back.

We shared a thick pancake for dessert that was filled with brown sugar syrup, and this time, I refused to let Jun pay. He'd brought me into his world, shown me how tasty these dishes were, and—best of all—had spent half the day kissing me. The least I could do was pay for dinner.

When we left the restaurant, the sun was low, tucked behind the buildings, and we sat at a bus stop, watching the traffic float by, shoulders pressed together, sharing our silence.

He looked at me. Smiled.

I closed my eyes, snapshotting his face into my brain. And when the bus arrived, I almost left my sketchbook at the stop and had to ask the driver to open the doors so I could grab it.

We rode out of town quieter than we came in, and when Jun had to get off a few stops before me, he squeezed my hand. *School tomorrow*, he signed.

I yawned because I forgot how to sign the word for boring.

Then he hugged me and stood on the pavement, waving while the bus rolled by. I smiled the whole way home, and even though the sky was still a rich blue, the moon was there every time we passed a junction.

When I got off the bus, I made sure I had my sketchbook with me, and I walked the few streets home without even realising I was walking. My mind was everywhere.

Mum and Samantha were sitting at the kitchen table sharing a bottle of wine when I got in, and Samantha said, "There he is."

"Here I am," I said.

"Good day?" Mum asked.

I made a noncommittal noise and looked in the fridge even though I wasn't hungry. It was better than watching them stare at me.

"Were you on a date?" Samantha asked.

I closed the fridge, lifted an apple from the fruit bowl and rubbed it against my shirt. "Something like that," I said, and then I went upstairs before she could quiz me. I heard their quiet laughter as I closed my bedroom door.

I flopped onto my bed, full of delicious food and delicious memories, and bit into the apple as I opened my sketchbook. I looked at Jun's face, the one I drew this morning in the park, and smiled. Then flipped back through the other pages.

I stopped at the page of dark shading, the block of nothingness, and I could see the faint smudge in the pencil lead where Jun had touched it. I ran my finger across it. Dark and stormy, Jun had said. Like it's hiding something.

Maybe it was. Maybe the darkness was hiding everything. Jun's quiet anger at his father. My grief at losing Grandad Tommy long before he had the right to die.

Maybe—above everything, above words and sounds and feelings and pain—the only thing left was darkness.

Like a black hole, where not even light escapes.

I sat up. Something in the scratches on the page, in the way Jun had said "hiding", made me slip off the bed and pull the old case out from under it.

I unclasped it. Opened it.

One lonely paintbrush inside.

I picked it up, turned it over in my hands, and then I went to Tommy's room, gently easing the door open. The bedding still hadn't been changed, tucked neatly except for that bottom corner that I'd pulled out for him so long ago. There was no dust. Maybe mum had been in to clean, or maybe it just hadn't been long enough—used enough—for the dust to gather.

I searched his drawers, pushing my fingers through his tubes of paint, looking for the larger squeeze-bottles in the bottom drawer. Acrylic. Carbon black.

The bottle was half-empty, but there was enough. At least enough for now.

Back in my room, I laid down some sheets of scrap paper to protect my desk and I coated the three-inch paintbrush in the black paint, from the tip of the handle to the end of the bristles. I let it dry before turning it over to coat the other side.

And when it was done, still tacky, smelling faintly of the acrylic paint, I held it up. The matt black finish dulled the brush, coating it. Covering it.

Hiding it.

The brush was still there, just like my feelings. But it was masked, the way people always do. Hidden. And I knew what my art project was going to be.

It would be ugly. And beautiful. And real.

Just like everything else worth clinging to.

CHAPTER 24

Room 1C of the community centre buzzed with noise. Chairs scraped against the floor as everyone stood up and somebody screamed when a wasp dashed around their head before flying into the corridor beyond the door. Sean shut the door to lock it out and we closed the windows even though it was too warm. My shirt clung to my back and I was desperate to get out of my school uniform the minute I got home. I'd already loosened my tie and untucked my shirt, but it wasn't enough to combat the torture of late spring in a building with weak air conditioning.

"Find a partner," Sean said, and Ella linked arms with me, as if I had any choice in the matter.

"You and me, kiddo," she said.

"Could it ever be any other way?"

"Never," she said.

I hadn't seen her since Paulie's party, and when we arrived today, I thanked her for the invite.

She said, "Any time. If you ever need a place to chill with your fella, you're welcome to come over. Just give me some notice first—you do not want to see Paulie in his Underoos."

"Noted," I laughed.

When we were standing up, Sean made everybody face each other so that one person from each team was able to see him at the front of the room, and the other team member couldn't. He was going to hold up a phrase on a sheet of paper and we had to sign it to the other person. They'd write down what we said and find out later if we got it right.

"Having a Deaf boyfriend is going to come in handy," Ella told me.

"I don't have a Deaf boyfriend," I said. "We haven't had that conversation yet."

"Well, hurry up and have it."

Sean held up the first phrase and I gave it some thought. He was using words we'd already learned, but this time if felt different. Staged, almost. I signed, and Ella made me sign it again before she wrote her answer down.

"Did you get it?" I asked.

"I hope so."

Sean held up another phrase, longer this time, stringing eight words together as a sentence, and I was certain I forgot how to say bicycle, so I formed the letters instead and when Ella wrote her answer down, she showed me the correct sign. So much for Jun giving me the upper hand.

After five phrases, we switched places and Sean told us

not to talk.

He held up the next card and Ella said, "Oh, God, I know this one." Sean must have reminded her to be silent because she signed, *Sorry*, and then signed what I thought was, *Please buy a loaf of bread at the store*.

The next phrase was, *This bus doesn't go to Dublin*, and honestly, I only remembered the sign for Dublin because Jun had used it on our return from Bray, touching his thumb and fingertip to his chin, followed by the flat of his finger against the same spot.

At the end of the round, we waved our hands in applause and took our seats again.

Sean signed, *Well done, everybody*. He read out the answers, and Ella got four of the five sentences correct. "Did I sign it wrong?" I asked.

Ella said, "I thought you said juice, not milk. I wondered why the baby was drinking OJ!"

"As long as there wasn't vodka in it," I said. I signed milk again and then juice, making sure I knew the difference as well as showing Ella. They were visually similar if you didn't know what you were doing, but so far in ISL, there weren't any signs as similar as *their*, *there* and *they're* in English. Although, sometimes it came close.

Sean said, "Hold on to your noise-cancelling headphones for now, but you'll need to return them before the end of the month. Please don't forget them, or the management will come down hard on me."

I put a reminder in my phone to bring them with me, and when we were packing up at the end of class, Ella said, "How's it going with cutie-pie, anyway?"

"Good," I said.

She waited, as if I was going to elaborate, and then she said, "Is that all I'm getting?"

I said, "What more do you want? You're not my therapist."

"Friends are cheaper than therapy," Ella laughed. "Seriously, though. You like him?"

"Of course."

"And?"

"And what?"

"Oh my God, it's like pulling teeth," she said. "Do you love him?"

"I just met him," I told her.

She bumped her shoulder against me as we walked out of the room and down the corridor. "You're sixteen. If you haven't fallen in love twice a week by Wednesday, are you even a teenager?"

"Is that how easy you fall in love?" I asked.

"At your age, I was in love with anybody who'd look at me."

"That's healthy," I laughed.

Outside, Ella said, "You should fall in love often. And you're allowed to do it with the same person, over and over again."

"How many times have you fallen in love with Paulie?" I asked.

She waved at him as his car pulled into the carpark to pick her up. She kissed my cheek before walking away, and she said, "Every time I look at him."

I rode the bus home, tuning out the sounds of people and engines and all the world around me. Love was one of those words that you treated differently as you got older. When you're a kid, you love your favourite toy. In primary school, you love your best friend. In high school, maybe you love the idea of love. I knew Jun made the bubbles in my stomach pop. Was that love? Probably. But I knew it became something different as we got older. You love one person, not many. Love gets a new meaning.

I'm not sure why, or how, but you start by loving everything, and then one day you love very little. And that seemed wrong to me. Shouldn't we have more love as we got older?

I could fall in love every day—especially, as Ella had said, if it was with the same person on repeat.

When I got home, we ate dinner in the living room with the TV on, and Mum said something about maybe painting Grandad Tommy's room one day soon.

Mick and I exchanged a look. We knew what she was really saying, even if she didn't say it out loud. And then, instead of forcing her to open up about the idea, he simply asked, "What colour were you thinking?"

She put her cutlery on her plate and looked up, as if she could see through the ceiling and into Tommy's room. "Something bright," she said. "A soft yellow, maybe? Or a really pale orange?"

"That'd be nice," Mick said.

"One day," Mum whispered, and it was enough that she was thinking about it. We hadn't spoken about Tommy's things, what would happen to them or where they would go, but those words would come, too. I knew the room didn't need to be a shrine—we had our memories of him that we'd carry everywhere—but the fact that Mum could acknowledge the very idea of doing something with Grandad Tommy's bedroom was a huge step. She picked up her cutlery again, and Mick put his hand on her arm for just a second, a look passing between them that showed me that people—even Mum and Mick—were still falling in love every time they looked at each other.

I hadn't heard from my biological father in so long that I seldom thought about him any more. And watching Mum with Mick made me realise that she was better off. We were all better off.

Mick winked at me, and I nodded. I was smiling a lot recently. But today, it wasn't just because of Jun.

In the kitchen, ten minutes later, while Mum was filling the dishwasher and I was rooting in the freezer for the ice cream, she hugged me, wrapping her arms around my neck while she stood behind me, just as I had done with Jun at the construction site.

I leaned into her because I knew she needed it, and then I said, "What's this for?"

"Am I not allowed to hold my only son?" she asked.

"If you keep it up, I'll start charging you," I said.

"It'll be worth it," Mum told me, tightening her arms. And I let her have that one for free.

While I sat in my room later, poring over my physics textbook and realising how little I knew about wave-particle duality, my phone buzzed alive. It was a video call from Jun, and before I answered it, I checked myself in the screen, ruffled my hair, straightened my collar, and swiped to answer.

He waved hello, a smile spreading across his face, and he repositioned himself because a patch of evening sunlight had kissed his eyes. He blinked and asked how I was.

"I missed you," I told him.

No, you didn't.

"Yes, I did."

He put his finger to his lips, the simplest way to tell me to stop. *Homework?* he asked.

"Physics," I said.

Physics, he signed for me.

I copied him, adding it to my bank of knowledge, then said, "Did you know Einstein had a theory about space?"

Yes? he asked, dubious. I could see on his face that he knew where I was going with this.

I said, "It was about time, too!"

Jun rolled his eyes but he was smiling. He held up the rock I'd given him in Bray. It still had his Post-It note attached. He signed, *Does one plus one still equal eight?*

Eleven, I signed.

Ah, he said, and slapped his forehead. Then he grinned. *Meet me?* he asked.

"For kisses? God, yes," I said, far too eager. Light played over his face again. And maybe my eagerness jinxed it, because Jun looked away from his phone, his face twisting into a question, and he signed something to somebody that I didn't catch. He paused, watching, then signed again.

And his mum leaned over his shoulder, waving at me. "Hi, Owen. Are you well?"

"Lots of homework," I said, "but otherwise I'm perfect, thanks."

I didn't get to be polite and ask how she was. She barrelled in with, "I'm sorry, but Jun-ho is going to have to hang up now. He'll talk to you tomorrow, okay?"

She signed while she spoke, and Jun signed, *Mum*, adding a visible exclamation mark with his face.

I'm sorry, she told him. *Say goodbye.*

Jun shook his head, looked at me, his eyes dark and angry through the screen. He didn't move for a second. And then, reluctantly, like it was hurting him to do so, he signed, *Goodbye*.

The call ended before I could respond. And something about that word—goodbye—made my chest hurt. It had never felt so final.

I closed my physics book and leaned back in the swivel chair, spinning slowly to face the window, staring at the evening-blue sky. No answers there—physics or otherwise. I knew I couldn't spend every waking hour with Jun, but that short phone call—cut off before I could make him laugh— hollowed me out. I picked up my yellow highlighter, sat it down, turned in the chair, kicked the old suitcase under my bed—one lonely black paintbrush inside—and realised I was going to be useless for the rest of the evening. And there was no point in being useless with my homework.

I pulled on my trainers in the front hall and slipped out of the house while Mum and Mick were in the kitchen, and I walked up the street to Ryan's house. But he wasn't there.

His mum said, "He's gone somewhere with that nice girl of his. I forget her name."

"Mia."

"That's it. She seems nice."

"She is," I said.

"Do you want to come in and wait for him?"

"No, thanks. I'll probably bump into him later." I signed thank you without even thinking about it and then walked back down his driveway. But I turned before she closed the door. "By the way," I said. "What's for lunch at school tomorrow?"

She smiled. "Mac and cheese, but you didn't hear it from me."

"I'll bring a packed lunch," I told her, tapping the side of my nose for secrecy. And she laughed.

I stood at the top of the street and, for the first time in ages, I was at a loss for something to do. Something to take my mind off how ominous Eileen's demand that Jun hang up the phone had been. To take my mind off my art project and my homework and the looming crisis of my end-of-year exams.

Jun had been my distraction for weeks now. Longer than that, because he'd flitted around inside my head long before we kissed, ever since I spilled paint-water on him and dropped my soul into his dark eyes.

I shoved my hands in my pockets and crested the hill, walked down the far side, away from home, and turned onto Chambers' Row, across the old playground with its rusted swings and monkeyless monkey bars, and down the grassy hill to the river where Ryan and I used to hang out. Before Jun and Mia. Before falling in love with every look.

I walked along the bare ground where years of feet had compacted the earth so that grass refused to grow there any more, and I skipped a stone across the shallow water before following it upstream to the rocks we would sit on, where I'd sketch Ryan's face, a lifetime ago.

Somebody else's lifetime ago—because it no longer felt like mine.

But as I got closer, I heard laughter, high and light, a girl's voice.

Mia.

Ryan looked up when I stepped onto the flat rock near the edge of our base.

"Oh," he said.

"Yeah," I said.

They weren't doing anything—which I was glad about—just sitting beside each other, a plastic bag of snacks in front of them the way Ryan and I would sit in that distant past.

"I didn't know you were here," I said.

"Where's Jun?" Mia asked, looking behind me.

"Not here."

"You're alone?"

I shrugged. Was I alone? They were here. But they weren't with me, so I guess I was. "Why are you guys here?" I asked. I didn't mean it to sound aggressive. They had a right to be here, as much as I did. But Mia's name wasn't carved into the rocks like ours were. She didn't know which stones to step on to get to the other side without getting your shoes wet. Didn't know about the loose rock that Ryan had hidden a bottle of beer under once, when we were twelve.

"We were just checking out the old haunt," Ryan said. "Where we grew up."

"Yeah," I said again, my voice as flat as the stone I was standing on.

Ryan said, "Remember that time we threw our shoes to the other side but one of yours fell in the water and went down stream?"

"It didn't," Mia said, as if it was the most amazing thing she'd ever heard.

"It did," Ryan told her. "We had to chase after it for a mile."

"It wasn't a mile," I said. "It was, like, twenty feet."

"It was almost a mile," Ryan said.

Mia rattled in the bag of goodies and sucked one end of a strawberry lace into her mouth. She twirled the other end in front of Ryan, like Lady and the Tramp, but he didn't bite.

Ryan said, "Is something wrong?"

"Why would there be something wrong?" I asked.

He stood up. "Wait here," he told Mia, and he came to me, took my elbow, and led me away from her, through the tall grass. "What's wrong?" he asked.

"Nothing."

"Owen."

"Nothing."

"O when the saints," he said. "Something's wrong. Where's Jun?"

I turned from him, pulled on the long reeds until one of them tore free from the ground, and I twisted it around my finger—a finger I could have used to sign the word Dublin. Or friend. Or boyfriend.

"I don't know what's going on with him," I said at last. "He called me earlier, but his mum cut the call short."

"How come?"

"I don't know."

"I'm sure it's nothing," he said. "Come and sit with us."

I shook my head. "I'm all right. I'll see you at school

tomorrow."

"Wait," Ryan said. "You're not angry, are you? That I brought Mia here?"

"Of course not."

"You're sure?"

I smiled, but there wasn't any warmth in it. Not because I didn't mean it, but because my head was somewhere else. "It's fine," I said. And before I left, I said, "It's mac and cheese tomorrow."

Ryan made a puking noise. "How do you know?"

"Your mum told me."

"Oi," he laughed. "Get your own informant."

I left him there with Mia, accepting the fact that everything was different now. Friends grow up. And even if they don't grow apart, they still grow separately.

I went home. Mia was filling the spots in Ryan's life that I had vacated. And it wasn't anybody's fault but time.

CHAPTER 25

On Thursday, I managed to snatch thirty minutes with Jun. We sat in the park, on our favourite bench, and he held my hand while he studied the still surface of the pond. A dog splashed into the water on the far side, chasing after a ball, breaking the stillness for a minute, and then the ripples folded across the pond until they couldn't be seen any more.

I hadn't brought my sketchbook; there wasn't a lot to draw. Spring was giving way to summer and the trees were full, the path along the way was darkened from the overhanging branches, and the grass had been cut since the last time we were here. There were people and dogs, and I saw the faint flash of a squirrel among the thickness of the trees, but the sky was overcast, dulled by distant rain, glowing on top even as it darkened underneath.

But still there was nothing worth drawing.

"Is something wrong?" I asked.

No, Jun signed.

He smiled and squeezed my hand, and even though his fingers were warm, I felt the chill of the north-westerly wind. I leaned into him, touched his chin, and when he kissed me, it wasn't any different than before. He wanted it as much as I did. So why did everything feel different?

"Are you sure?" I asked, and I wondered how many times somebody had ever answered the question, "Are you sure?" with a different answer than the one they'd just given.

It's, Jun signed, then he dropped his hands into his lap. A sign-language ellipsis. *It's nothing*, he said at last. *Family*, he added.

I nodded, and he squeezed my hand again. He made the sign for kiss and I didn't have to be told twice.

When his phone vibrated and he looked at his messages, he said, *Sorry. I have to go.*

Already? I signed.

Sorry, he said.

We stood up and hugged. And when I held him, it felt like he didn't want to let go. So I held him tighter. I pressed my lips against the corner of his jaw and kissed him loudly, so he could feel the vibrations.

He smiled.

Waved.

And I watched him walk away. Today, he didn't look back.

On Friday, I carried my loneliness into Mr Madden's art room along with the leather-bound suitcase. I lifted it to a paint-spattered desk, onto a turntable so I could spin it, and lined up the two bottles of black acrylic paint that was in the storeroom, along with a small paint roller and a couple of narrow brushes.

It wasn't enough. I'd have to stop in town to buy more, because I had a lot to cover. I was able to give the case one coat, but as I watched it dry, it turned patchy and the blue of the leather shone through the brush strokes.

I thinned down what was left and gave the case a second coat of paint. And, while it dried, I took some thick sheets of card from the storeroom in a mix of bright colours and used the guillotine to cut them into three-inch squares.

On each card, I wrote a word, an emotion, all the things we carry with us. Anger. Pain. Sorrow. Happiness. Joy. Love. By the time I'd run out of emotions and feelings, I'd amassed over thirty cards.

I punched a hole in the base of each one, below the word, so that I could affix them to wire stands later, and then I used a clear varnish to coat each card, protecting the word.

"That looks interesting," Mr Madden said.

"I'm not finished," I told him.

"What are you going to do with them?" he asked.

"You'll see."

He nodded, scanned over the emotions where they were laid out for the varnish to dry—shame, envy, surprise, gratitude—and then he turned to Jared, one of the other kids in my art class. Jared was building a wire frame that he said was going to be a showstopper.

"You've got some competition, it seems," Mr Madden told me.

I studied Jared's frame and couldn't tell what it was meant

to be, something flat and wide, tapered at the back. "Good luck," I said.

Jared looked at my cards and the blackened suitcase. "Are you going to lock your emotions away?"

"Not quite," I said.

He nodded. "I hope you're happy with second place."

"It's not a competition," I told him. But it was. We'd be given a grade for our end-of-year project, but each piece from the class would also be displayed in the school before being judged by Mr Madden and Mrs O'Connor, the principal.

Jared turned away from me, twisting his wire frame, and then holding it up to check the weight of it.

When the varnished cards were dry, I used what was left of the acrylic paint to coat them black, blocking out the words that I'd written there—annoyance, boredom, awe, fascination—and I asked Jared if I could cut two meters of wire from his roll. He couldn't really object because it belonged to the school, but he grumbled about it as I measured out the length I needed and used the wire cutters to bite through it.

I cut it down into foot-long strips and used some needle-nosed pliers to loop the ends, attaching the blackened cards to them and fixing the other ends to the open case with a glue gun. For the next twenty minutes, I stood there, holding the wires aloft so that the glue set without the cards leaning into each other. They stood up like the silhouettes of tall sentinels around the lip of the case.

It wasn't complete, but it was all I could do for today.

There was a long way to go.

"What happened to your words?" Mr Madden asked when he saw the cards had been painted black.

"They're hidden," I said.

"So, how do we know which one is which?"

"You don't." I covered the project with a dust sheet. "Not yet."

On my way out of the art room, I looked at the list of project titles that Mr Madden had tacked to the wall. Jared's name was written beside the theme *Nature vs Nurture*. I looked back at him and his wire mess. I still had no idea what he was making.

I sat with Ryan during lunch and he spent the time messaging Mia, laughing at whatever she'd said, showing me the silly memes she'd forwarded to him.

I sent Jun a text. *Ryan and Mia are practically joined at the hip now. It's a good job we go to an all-boys school or they'd be snogging in the canteen.*

He replied, *Come to my school. I kiss missing you.*

*Miss kissing**, he corrected.

I sent him a grinning emoji and said, *You can kiss-miss me as much as you like. How long until I can see you again?*

He typed. Stopped typing. And Ryan had three messages from Mia before his reply came.

Soon. I hope.

I locked that hope in my chest for the rest of the day, failing to pay attention to the teacher in physics class, even though Mr Byrne had written *2 weeks until exams* on the board. I wrote the same thing in my workbook, in block letters, and I underlined it three times, each in a different colour. He said something about forces and equilibrium, about balance and stillness, but it didn't make any sense to me. There wasn't any equilibrium in my brain, and whatever forces propelled me, they did it with dulled momentum.

I didn't get the bus home with Ryan. Instead, I walked. I put my noise-cancelling headphones on and looked both ways before crossing the road. Then I gripped both straps of my backpack to stop it from bouncing on my back and weaved through the streets, into town, away from the Chinese take-away that Ryan loved—I'd have to tell him about Dalbit one day—and I crossed at the traffic lights and kicked a crushed Coke can for a while until it got trapped in the gutter.

I passed the park and kept walking, cut through the car-park outside the church, and only when I was standing in the cemetery did I take the headphones off. A new quiet entered my mind, one filled with the hum of distance: traffic, birds, wind. Everything that was far away, trapped outside the cemetery like an invisible barrier had refused them entry.

Are the people buried in cemeteries deaf now? Would he hear me if I spoke to him?

Maybe it wouldn't even matter.

I reached out and touched the weather-smoothed stone of St Michael. His sword was copper and green, slotted through the loop of his hands, and his wings were coiled. The devil underfoot. His expression, despite the violence in his posture, was serene. Empty.

Like mine.

I knew where Grandad Tommy was buried now. Didn't have to think about it. I went right at Helen Ishicca, 1903-1981, and around the side of Benjamin H. H. Molloy, 1955-1967—and I wondered what had killed him at such a young age and what his middle names were.

Sandra and Tommy were on the next row, and when I

stood in front of the headstone, somebody—Mum or Tommy Two—had replaced the flowers and transferred the paintbrush that I'd left behind from the bouquet to the base of the stone where the wind wouldn't take it.

I adjusted the weight of my backpack, pulling on the straps, and I read the words on the headstone as if they were new to me. I was just a baby when Sandra passed away. If it hadn't been for the framed photographs on our walls at home, I probably wouldn't have been able to pick her out of a lineup.

But Tommy had tucked me in at night. Read bedtime stories. Encouraged me to draw when nobody else saw the glimmer of enjoyment at the end of my crayons. It was Tommy that put plasters on my skinned knees when I fell off my bike, holding my leg in the air for Mum to kiss it better. Tommy who gave me courage—always courage, never fear—when I was faced with something new, something scary.

Something bleak.

I leaned forward on my feet, my backpack full of weekend homework. I said, "I didn't bring any flowers. Sorry."

Grandad Tommy didn't say anything.

Maybe he *was* deaf now. Or I was. What if the dead scream and we just can't hear it?

The grass that formed the roof of his resting place was lengthening, a cluster of daisies in the corner. Does somebody mow it? Are we supposed to do that? I didn't know.

I plucked one of the daisies and twirled it between my thumb and finger. I didn't pull the petals from it—he loves me, he loves me not—but I sniffed it. I could only smell the faint tang of grass.

I sat it on top of the gravestone. I said, "I'm sorry I didn't know you, Granny. But I know Grandad Tommy loved you."

It was true. His eyes shone every time her name was mentioned. And his hands, wrinkled, blemished, would flutter to his mouth as if he was remembering her kisses.

I said, "Can you hear me?"

I said, "I can't even hear myself."

And then I turned and walked back past Benjamin H. H. Molloy, Helen Ishicca, and St Michael and the devil.

At the gate, I sent a message to Jun. *I miss you.*

And he replied just before nine p.m. that night.

I'm sorry, he said. *I wish I could see you. But I can't.*

CHAPTER 26

Friday night slipped into Saturday with the quiet of loneliness. Ordinarily, I'd have celebrated the end of a school week with Ryan, eating junk food and playing videogames, but he was doing those things with Mia now and I should have replaced Ryan's energy with Jun's.

Except Jun wasn't here.

I hope everything's okay, I messaged him. And I half-meant his family and half-meant us.

We're okay, he sent back. He even put a kissing emoji at the end. But emojis weren't lips. They weren't the real thing.

When I got into bed, I sent, *Good night*, and his reply was instant.

When I got up in the morning, I sent, *Good morning*, but I got no response.

I lay there, the duvet pulled around me, and I scrolled back through our messages, then through the photos I took in Bray. He looked so happy when he was stroking the stray cat. When he stood beside me for a selfie, eyes wet with laughter.

And when Ryan knocked on my bedroom door and opened it—I hadn't heard Mum at the front door—he said, "Are you dressed?"

I pulled the duvet over my head. "Who let the hounds of hell in?"

Ryan jumped on top of me, trapping me under the covers, and gave me a noogie. "Are you alive under there?" he asked, knocking my head with his knuckles.

"Get off."

He peeled the duvet away from my face. "Arise, Sir Swamp-Monster," he said.

I scowled. If Ryan was still Ryan, why was I not still me?

He pinned my arms down and I let go of my phone. For a second, I imagined Jun lying on top of me. And then I had to buck Ryan off before my brain went to places it didn't need to go.

"Why are you here?" I asked.

"Why are you still in bed?" he countered.

"Because I'm lazy."

He sat on my desk chair and swivelled. "Get up. We're going into town."

I pulled the duvet over me again. "Wake me in time for Christmas," I said.

"Get up or you'll get a lump of coal for Christmas. Mia's meeting us in forty minutes."

I groaned. I was destined to be their third wheel for the

day, but a day with Ryan and Mia was probably better than moping in bed. And if Jun was busy, I could be too. I left Ryan in my room while I showered and then told him to turn his back while I got changed—all the things we would have done on any other Saturday morning.

But it was different now.

"You're wearing that?" he asked.

"What's wrong with it?"

"Nothing," he said. "If you're aiming for virgin librarian, you're winning."

I changed my shirt. "I can't tell who you're insulting more, virgins or librarians."

And before we left the house, Ryan said, "Don't pretend you aren't both."

Mia was waiting for us outside the shopping centre, standing by the sapling trees that had been planted a couple of years ago but that refused to grow, as if they were made of plastic not photosynthesis. She took her earbuds out when we arrived and she kissed my cheek before Ryan pulled her into his arms.

"Where's my kiss?" he asked.

"You don't deserve one."

"What'd I do?"

She slipped out from his embrace and curled her arm around mine, sticking to me like Lego. "Where do you want to go first?" she asked me.

"Hey," Ryan said.

I shrugged. I needed the art supply shop, but I didn't think dragging her there would win me any favours.

"I need to buy a card for my mum," Mia said, ignoring

Ryan's protestations, and she led me through the automatic doors and into the noise of Saturday morning chaos. Crowds flooded in and out of shops, stood in groups near the benches, music blaring out of hidden speakers, smells of perfume and stale coffee and the leather of new shoes. A line of people at the only ATM that appeared to be working.

I went where Mia went because she wouldn't let go of my arm. I saw young couples and old couples holding hands. Mums with toddlers, boys with girls, security staff patrolling the wide concourse, and bright signs in shop windows that claimed fifty percent off already low-low prices.

"Guys," Ryan said, trailing behind us. "Mia."

"You've had me all week," she told him. "It's Owen's turn now."

"We're taking turns?" he asked.

I knew what she was doing. She wasn't annoyed with Ryan, she was annoyed with Jun. I had no idea what Ryan told her, but I got the feeling she knew there was something off about me, about Jun's absence, and was trying to make me feel better.

"I'm all right, you know," I said, as she walked me through the greetings card shop, one arm locked around mine, the other scrolling over the rack of birthday cards.

"I know," she said. She lowered her voice. "But it's making Ryan jealous and I love it."

"Isn't that mean?" I asked.

Her smile was wicked. "Not when he buys me something to make up for whatever he thinks he's done wrong."

"Your mother must be proud," I laughed. And I realised, feeling that laughter in my chest, that what she was doing was helping. I hadn't thought about Jun for a few minutes.

But I thought about him now, and that, in turn, made me think about grandad Tommy. The way you let the ache go for a minute before gripping it tightly again. This is what adults mean when they say it gets easier over time. Not that your loss is any less painful. Just that you forget about your loss for longer moments. It isn't easier, it's just less frequent.

"What do you think of this one?" Mia asked, squeezing my arm tighter.

On the front of the card, it said, *To a mum who has everything*, and on the inside, it read, *I decided to get you nothing*.

"You're not very good at this, are you?" I asked, and I helped her choose something better. "Parents don't want funny cards. They want something meaningful. They want poems that rhyme, something about how you can't live without them. Here," I said, handing her a card with a cute graphic on the front and a poem split across three pages inside.

"Nobody told me you were a parent whisperer," she said.

"It's a curse," I told her.

When she let go of my arm to pay for the card, I pulled out my phone and checked my messages. Still nothing from Jun. I wanted to text him again, but he hadn't even read my last text. Was his phone dead? Was he ignoring me?

I stuffed my phone back in my pocket, trying to push him out of my head. How could he open up to me at the construction site and then ghost me? That wasn't fair.

Outside the card shop, Ryan said, "I'm hungry."

"You're always hungry," Mia and I said together.

"The food court's right upstairs. I'm just saying."

But Mia's attention had already wandered. "Look at those

shoes," she said, pushing her arm under mine again. She was trying on shoes thirty seconds later.

Ryan did buy her something, just as she'd predicted—a teddy bear the size of his thumb. She kissed him at last and held the bear in her fist as we went to the craft shop where I bought four bottles of black paint for my art project.

"Going through his emo phase," Ryan said.

I pretended to squeeze one of the bottles at his face and he leapt out of the way, almost knocking over a display stand of crepe paper rolls, and then we stood outside the ladies' toilets on the second floor, waiting for Mia, like a dutiful boyfriend and their third wheel.

Ryan said, "You okay?"

I nodded.

"No, but seriously," he said. "Are you?"

"I'm fine."

"Do you want to punch him in the face?"

"No," I said. "He's just busy. There's nothing wrong."

Ryan said, "I could one-inch punch him in the chest, if you want."

I pushed him and he stumbled. "You couldn't punch your way out of a wet paper bag," I laughed. Then I said, "Can you just leave it now? I don't know what's going on with him—it's family stuff—but he and I are still all right."

Ryan put his arm around my neck. "But if you need me to throat-punch him, I will."

As Mia came back, I said, "I knew those three karate lessons you had when we were eleven was a bad idea."

"I still got the yellow belt," he said.

"You stole a yellow belt," I laughed, and he chased me

around the indoor water fountain before Mia intervened.

She stood in front of me like a bodyguard, arms wide, and said, "If you want him, you'll have to get through me."

Ryan tried to sidestep her, then he distracted her with a kiss. He clipped my ear while I wasn't looking.

"Food," he said.

"Fine," we told him.

We went upstairs and I quietly checked my phone again. Just in case.

Ryan and Mia went straight for fried chicken, but the last time we were here, Jun had been over at the Red Dragon counter. I said, "I'm getting noodles. Whoever gets served first can find a table." They didn't protest when I walked away, the plastic bag full of paint bottles swinging at my side.

Jun wasn't going to be there—I wasn't that stupid, even if I did scan the tables, pretending I was looking for an empty one instead of Jun's smiling face. Hopeful but not convinced. And I stood behind a group of teens in the Red Dragon queue, studying the menu on the lightbox instead of staring at my feet.

I couldn't remember what Jun was eating last time, but when I got to the front of the queue, I ordered a chicken chow mein. The guy behind the counter sat a tray in front of me and dropped a knife and fork onto it, but I said, "Do you have chopsticks?"

He took the cutlery away and replaced them with a paper-wrapped pair of disposable sticks and he didn't ask me why I could use chopsticks instead of a fork. Because he didn't care.

Jun would have smiled. Maybe he would have teased me.

Maybe I was missing him.

I walked through the crowded space of tables. Ryan and Mia were still in the queue for their fried chicken, and I waved at them when I found a table. Whoever had been sitting there before us left their trays and chicken bones, salt scattered across the tabletop and the floor. I stacked everything at the edge of the table and sat down. And I kept looking over at Ryan and Mia, just to let everyone know I wasn't alone.

That I wasn't a loner.

When they came to the table, I relaxed. Ryan sat their tray down and then pulled a chair out for Mia like they were at a fancy restaurant. She ate a French fry and then let him kiss her. Ate another and expected a second kiss.

I pinched my noodles with the chopsticks and slurped them into my mouth—loudly, trying to distract them from their food-based make-out session—and Mia said, "You're really good with those."

"Jun," Ryan said, as if that explained it. Which I guess it did. He held a corncob to his mouth and said, "Eat with me."

"Not a chance," Mia said, but she took a bite anyway, using a napkin to wipe melted butter from her lips.

And then Ryan buried his face in her neck where he whispered something that I didn't hear.

"Can you not?" I said.

He looked at me, his cheek pressed to her shoulder. "I can't help it," he said. "Doesn't she have a cute neck?"

"The cutest," I said.

"Shut up and eat your chicken," Mia told him.

"She's like my little dominatrix. I'll have her stepping on me in her high heels later."

I shuddered. "Thanks. My brain needs an acid bath now."

When they were finished feeding each other, I took my tray—and the one that had been left there before us—to the clean-up station, and then we took the escalators to the ground floor while Ryan and Mia shared a milkshake, passing it between them to drink from the same straw.

We stopped by the confectionery kiosk so Ryan could buy gum, and while I stepped out of the way of the human traffic, I saw Callum coming out of the bookshop opposite. I was going to wave, but he didn't see me.

He stopped in the doorway, turned, and said something to somebody who was still inside.

And then Jun came out behind him, followed by somebody else. A taller boy. Korean.

His brother? Why was he here?

"You coming?" Ryan asked.

I looked at him. Looked back at Jun. "Hang on," I said, and I crossed through the busy concourse. When I was close enough, I said, "Hi." I signed it too.

Callum looked up at the sound of my voice, and Jun's eyes followed.

He looked at me.

Blinked.

I said, "Hi," again. "How are you?"

Jun didn't sign back. He simply nodded. Once. Just an acknowledgement of my presence. Nothing more.

The other boy, tall, wide at the shoulders, shorter hair than Jun's but similar in features, stared at me. I signed, *I'm O-W-E-N*.

His eyes scanned down my body, back up again, and he looked at Jun. He signed something I didn't understand—it wasn't ISL—and he spoke verbally in Korean. Then he walked away, hands in his pockets.

"Jun?" I asked.

He shook his head. Signed, *Sorry*. And he touched Callum's arm, a soft, light touch—like a goodbye—and he followed after his brother.

"Jun!" I called. It didn't matter to me that he couldn't hear the word. I needed to shout it.

And Callum said, "Mate. Let him go."

"What? No."

"Stay," he said. "We should talk."

CHAPTER 27

"I'm not leaving," Ryan said. He gripped Mia's hand and stared at Callum.

"It's okay," I told him. "You guys go ahead. I'll catch up."

"What's going on?" Ryan said. Not to me. To Callum.

"It's private," Callum told him.

I handed Ryan my bag of paint bottles. "Please," I said. And I waited while he sized Callum up, as if he was figuring out the best way to take him down, but then decided against it. He nodded at me.

"We'll wait outside Game On," he said. "If you're not there in five minutes, I'm coming back for you."

"Better make it ten," Callum said.

"Just go," I told Ryan. "Please." I think he heard the exasperation in my voice. He tightened his grip on Mia's hand

and they walked away.

"He's a good friend," Callum said when they were gone.

"Like you'd know," I spat. I stomped away from him, and at that point, I didn't care if he followed me.

I went through the automatic doors, into the sunlight, past the smokers and over to a low wall that bordered a raised flowerbed, late-spring flowers coming into bloom, yellows and blues to punctuate the darkness that hovered around my face.

I sat on the wall and stared at my feet.

"He misses you," Callum said. I didn't look up as he sat beside me.

"Sure he does."

"He does."

I should have kept the bag of paint. At least I'd have something to occupy my hands with, something to smack him in the face with if I needed to.

"He'll meet up with you but not me?" I asked.

"Steady on," Callum said. "I bumped into him ten minutes ago. This wasn't some pre-arranged tryst."

"But he's still messaging you, isn't he?"

Callum didn't hesitate. "Yes," he said.

"But not me," I told him. "He's ignoring me."

Callum reached into his pocket, pulled out a packet of mints, and offered me one. I didn't even acknowledge him. He popped one into his mouth and said, "It's easier that way."

"What's easier?"

"He can talk to me," Callum said. "As a friend."

"Am I not his friend?"

"No," he said. "You're his boyfriend."

I looked at him at last. "He said that?" Something lit up in my chest, but it wasn't very strong. It didn't matter if Jun had said the word or not—why wasn't he saying it to me?

"You really are oblivious, aren't you?"

"I don't understand," I said.

"Exactly." Callum leaned back, holding his face to the sun for a second. Then he said, "You haven't asked me about the other guy. The one he was with."

"His brother," I said.

"But why's he here? Why is he in Ireland?"

"Just tell me," I said. I didn't care for guessing games.

"Woo-sung. He came with their father. I haven't met the dad, but from what Jun-ho says, he's not the happiest chap in the world."

"That still doesn't explain why he's avoiding me," I said.

"Because he doesn't know what to say to you."

"He can say anything."

"Can he? Can he tell you that his father wants him to go back to Korea to see a specialist about getting an implant?"

"He told me that ages ago," I said.

"Yeah," Callum said slowly. "But now his dad's here. To make sure that it happens." I looked at him again, but before I could speak, he said, "Do you see now? That look on your face. That's what he was trying to avoid. You're angry."

"I'm not angry," I said—angrily.

"Yeah," he snorted. He checked his watch, then said, "Jun-ho and his mum have been trying to convince his dad not to go through with it. That the choice should be Jun-ho's. But you try talking to a brick wall. It's not easy."

"I should call him," I said, pulling my phone out.

"He won't answer," Callum told me, standing up. "Not if the outcome is still going to be a disappointment."

He touched my shoulder, nodded, and then walked away. And when I looked up the street, Ryan and Mia were there, far enough away not to have heard our conversation, but close enough that he could have intervened if he needed to.

I covered my face with my hands, the sun warm on the top of my head. I remembered Jun's quiet look while he stood beside his brother in the doorway of the bookshop.

And the light in my chest went out again.

I didn't tell Ryan and Mia what was going on. Only that Jun's dad and brother had arrived and it wasn't exactly a happy reunion.

"I get it," Mia said. "My dad left when I was thirteen and for two years I wanted to murder him in his sleep."

"Why do families have to be so complicated?" Ryan said.

We walked back up to Game On so that Ryan could check out the new-release videogames, and I was quiet for the rest of the afternoon.

When I got home, Mum was preparing dinner, and she said, "How was Jun?"

"Huh?" I asked.

"Didn't you go out somewhere with him?"

"No," I said. "Just Ryan and Mia."

She was distracted, and I knew why. She was making Grandad Tommy's favourite—shepherd's pie. They used to make it together, Mum mashing the potatoes, Tommy stirring the diced lamb into the sauce. She'd add some salt and he'd add a little more. She'd drag the tines of a fork over the top of the potatoes, scoring them, and he'd go back over it himself before it went in the oven.

Would it taste the same, now that he wasn't here?

"Did you give it enough salt?" I asked.

"I put extra in. For Grandad."

"When will it be ready?" I asked.

"Forty minutes," she said.

And as I turned to go up to my room, I sent Jun a text message. *Callum told me your father's here. You can talk to me.*

In the living room, Mick said, "Have a look at this."

I stuck my head around the door and he waved the remote at the TV. When I came into the room, he was watching a nature documentary that showed a cheetah tearing a gazelle to shreds. A voiceover said that, in some areas, humans were a bigger threat than animals.

"Amazing," Mick said.

"Yeah," I said with polite finality.

But he clicked a button on the remote, scanning back through the programme. "Just watch how fast he takes it down. Just a single swipe of his paw and a snap of his mouth."

"I'm all right, thanks," I said. I looked at my phone. No reply from Jun. But I stood there, watching the TV screen because Mick wanted me to. The cheetah chased the gazelle. Pounced. And then it was feeding.

"You wouldn't like to be the gazelle, would you?" Mick asked, and I actually wasn't sure. Gazelles don't have fathers that want to ship them off to a new country to fix something that isn't broken.

I sent another text. *Jun, please.*

No reply.

Mick paused the documentary, a vivid close-up of teeth

and flesh. "What's wrong with you?"

"Nothing," I said.

"Pull the other one."

"It's nothing," I told him. And I went upstairs.

In my room, I closed the door and started a video call, staring at myself on the screen, waiting for Jun to pick up.

It rang.

And rang.

And then it went dead. Like a gazelle.

A few minutes later, Mick knocked on my bedroom door.

"I'm getting changed," I said, even though I wasn't.

"If there's something wrong, you can let me know," he said, through the wood. I watched the shadow of his feet under the door.

"I'm all right, Mick. You can go back to your show."

There was silence. Then, "Owen?"

"Yeah?" I asked. I pressed my forehead against the door but I didn't open it.

Mick said, "Whatever it is, it's not the end of the world."

I snorted, a short, sharp laugh that was meaner than it needed to be. Mick didn't say anything more. The shadow of his feet hovered for a second longer, and then he walked away. I heard him on the stairs. Heard Mum ask him what's up, and Mick said, "Nothing, love. It's all good."

I breathed. Checked my phone. Hit redial on the video call, knowing he wouldn't answer. Knowing it but doing it anyway.

I wanted to eat dinner in my bedroom but Mum wouldn't let me. So I said I wasn't hungry and Mick said, "Come and eat with us. No questions. No third degree. But you need to eat."

So I sat at the table, with a plate of shepherd's pie and green beans, pushing my fork through the food but not really eating it.

Mum said, "Why did you buy so much black paint?"

"Art project," I said, my voice husky and dry. I took a sip of water.

The evening sun had backed over the yard and speared through the kitchen window to throw light on Grandad Tommy's cacti. The mammillaria was beginning to flower—I only knew their names because he'd labelled them. And I'm glad they were cacti, because I'm not sure if anyone had been watering them since Tommy died.

When somebody dies, other things die too.

After dinner, Mum turned to the fridge to take out a store-bought cheesecake, and Mick rapped his knuckles on my arm to get my attention. He mouthed, "You're okay?"

I nodded, glanced at Mum. We were sharing a secret, he and I, and I'm not sure why. "I'm fine," I whispered.

And Mick smiled. "Looks delicious," he said, when Mum had plated up the cheesecake.

He was on my side and he didn't even know what the issue was. Forget Ryan—if I needed somebody to throat-punch anyone, Mick was the man for the job.

He winked at me before I went upstairs, and I smiled, trying to look normal.

I cleared the desk in my room and spread out some paper, then I took one of the bottles of paint and looked around my room. I needed to fill the suitcase with things, but I wasn't sure what.

The first thing I painted black was an action figure that had stood on my bookshelves, like a guardian of knowledge, since Grandad Tommy bought it for me when I was nine. It was Goku, with moveable limbs and spiky hair, and the orange paint on his Gi was chipped and wearing off. I used to play with it, but not any more.

I coated it in the black acrylic paint and stood him on the paper to dry. Then I poured some of the paint into a large bowl and scrunched one of my T-shirts into a ball, pushing it into the paint to soak it up. It was the T-shirt I'd worn to the hospital last year when Tommy was having a lump removed from his arm that everybody had assured me wasn't cancerous but ought to be cut off anyway. When they patched him up, I sat beside him in the backseat of Mick's car on the way home and a speck of blood had leaked through his bandage onto my T-shirt sleeve. Mum tried to get the spot out at the time, but it wouldn't shift and I hadn't worn it since.

I left it in a ball beside Goku to dry and stiffen.

I had to wash my hands then, scrubbing to get the black off, and I thought maybe I could coat myself in the paint and become a part of the art project, too. Something else I had to carry on my own since Grandad Tommy passed away.

Back in my room, I couldn't take the silence any longer. I put some music on—K-pop, because why the hell not?—and cranked the volume up. The smell of acrylic paint filled me, and I opened the window to let some evening air in.

The sun was going down, the houses opposite lit from behind, and I watched a pair of birds chase after each other through the empty sky.

I picked up my phone, black paint stains under my

fingernails, and sat it down again without even checking if he'd messaged me. He hadn't. I knew he hadn't.

Outside, the air was cool but not cold. It had been warm all day, and night was only just beginning.

Maybe I should coat my phone in black paint and be done with it.

But I picked it up again. And I sent him a message.

I'm going to the park. If you like me, even just a little bit, you'll meet me there. I'll wait all night if I have to. Please don't ignore me.

I went downstairs, grabbed a light jacket, and quietly slipped out of the house without Mum or Mick hearing me leave.

And with every step I took, my longing came with me.

CHAPTER 28

The park gates were open. I wasn't sure if they would be, and I didn't know what I'd do if they'd been locked. Scaled the wall? Gone home?

I entered the park just before nine-thirty, and apart from one lone jogger, I didn't see anybody else near the entrance. There were a couple of teenagers further along the path, heading towards the bandstand where they were probably going to drink or smoke weed, so I skirted around the treeline to avoid them.

There were ducks in the duck pond for the first time in ages, and I wished I had brought some bread or something to scatter for them. When I sat on the bench opposite the water, they watched me, hopeful, but when I didn't throw food their way, they turned their backs on me. I was used to that now.

If you don't have what somebody wants, they'll discard you with ease.

I looked around. The sky was pink in the west, thin clouds stacked up like Tetris blocks, and in the east it was dark grey. Above me, there were two stars, separated by the shift in colour of the night sky. Grandad Tommy would have named each of those colours, from the pink horizon, through the blues overhead, to the grey at the far side. And the stars flickered like candleflames that were almost extinguished.

I wish I may, I wish I might.

A wood pigeon warbled, unseen in the trees, and a swarm of evening midges fought above the water's edge.

Something splashed in the pond—a duck or a frog—and in the silence that followed, I heard the quiet whisper of crickets that stopped, collectively, as if they were listening out for something, before shredding their music again.

What was I doing here?

I looked along the path. Nobody was coming. The darkness among the trees was getting thicker, and the blood in my veins was pumping harder. I'd never been here so late. Why couldn't I have said I'd meet him at a café or a busy, well-lit area of town? The streetlamps along the park's path were giving off very little light, enough to reveal the gravel beneath them and nothing more.

The pink sky was turning red and purple, like a dirty bruise, and the clouds were masking more of its colour. The light would be gone soon.

And I was all alone.

I checked my phone, partly to give the bench some warm light from its glow, partly to see if Jun had replied.

He hadn't.

A duck came out of the water, stood on the sloping bank, and preened itself, a black shape against the dark grass. And when I shifted my weight, twisting my hips, the duck flapped its wings and went back into the water.

Something crunched.

My shoulder muscles tightened with shock. And when I looked, somebody was coming along the path, dark under the trees, lacking colour as he passed under the lamps. But it was Jun.

I knew it was him.

He came to the bench. He stared at me for a second, signing nothing, not even blinking, and then he sat on the edge of the bench, furthest from me. There was a gap between us, wider than the three feet that space allowed.

I shifted on the bench, leaning forward, staring at the dark water. I didn't look at him. If I did, I'd—what? Laugh? Cry? Maybe both.

The kids at the bandstand, far out of view, were suddenly noisy, laughing at their own antics, before the silence settled over us again. And I realised: how do you start a conversation in the dark?

Jun moved his hands. And against my will, I had to look at him.

I came, he signed.

Thank you, I told him.

The crickets were silent now and the midges were invisible as the darkness crept across the park. I moved my feet, letting the sound of the gravel fill my head where my words were no longer forming.

We sat that way, in the failing light, not looking at each other, not interacting. We were two strangers, sharing a bench and nothing more. I could smell him, that same cologne he always wore, the smell of something sweeter underneath—a scent I could only define as Jun, like a combination of other smells, a multitude of them, that made up the shape of him. The imprint.

He folded his hands together in his lap and waited.

I leaned back. My own hands were clasped, like my body was praying even if my mind wasn't. And I cleared my throat. He was here; he came. Now what?

Jun signed something again, and in his movement, my mouth broke free. "You should have told me," I said. I wasn't signing now. I said, "You didn't have to disappear. If you'd told me, I'd have understood."

Jun signed, and I looked up.

It's dark, he told me. He took his phone out, turned the flashlight on, and sat it on the bench between us. Darkness causes silence for the Deaf.

I opened my mouth to repeat myself, but the words I had already said were out there now, unseen, unheard. Instead, I said, "I missed you."

Sorry, Jun said.

"When did your dad get here?" I asked, my voice a whisper.

Father, he corrected—a different sign, harsher than Dad. *Last Monday*, he signed.

I nodded. I met his eyes now, in the dark, the light splashing up from his phone, elongating his features. It made him look older, like his brother.

I said, "Woo-sung? He seems pleasant." The way he'd

spoken to Jun in Korean, with what I guessed was KSL, and the way he'd given me the once-over before walking away, I got the sense he was more like Jun's father than their mother.

Jun's smile was short-lived. *He's my brother*, he signed. *Family*, he added.

"Family is everything," I said, and I wasn't sure I meant it as a compliment. But Jun nodded.

A moth danced around the glow of his flashlight and I swatted it away.

I stood up. Turned away from him. And then I spun back to face him. "You lied to me."

No, he signed.

Yes, I replied. "Or at least you didn't tell me the truth. Which is the same as lying."

His eyes turned to the gravel under our feet, and I moved my hand for his attention. I needed him to look at me. I needed him to see me.

"I had to hear it from Callum," I said, signing only the important words, because my hands were shaking. "If I hadn't seen you outside the bookshop, would you have just disappeared?"

No.

"So you were going to show your face, just to say goodbye?"

No, he signed again. *It's not like that*. He looked at me, and his eyes pulled at my weight, unbalancing me. So I sat.

I studied Jun's face, the eyes that Mr Madden once called sad when he'd seen my portraits of him. The straight nose that cut off like a square above his full, red lips. High cheekbones. Skin that I wanted to taste, wanted to press my voice against.

I almost reached out to take his hand, but I stopped myself, in case he'd pull away from me.

And into the dark, I said, "Why didn't you tell me the truth?"

Jun didn't answer at once. He watched my face, turned to stare at the water, and I know he was thinking about how best to talk to me. He signed something—not to me but to the pond, and then he reached for his phone.

When he picked it up, I used the flashlight on mine to replace it. Even if he was going to type, I still needed to see his face.

I was scared, he typed.

"Why?"

I didn't want to make you sad.

"But you did anyway," I said.

I'm sorry I'm sorry I'm sorry, he typed.

I shook my head. "Don't say sorry. Just tell me what's going on."

Jun paused. Took a breath. Then he typed, *You don't know him. He's… strict. You don't say no to my father. I never could, before. Mum couldn't either. Coming here was our escape. Their divorce was one-sided—maybe divorce always is. And now he's here, making demands. He waited until Woo-sung had finished military service and they both came, united.*

"He wants you to go back to Korea," I said.

No, Jun signed. He typed, *He doesn't want it, he demands it.*

"He has no right."

Try telling him that, Jun said.

I shuffled closer on the bench, shrinking the space between us. I said, "I will. I'll tell him."

Jun closed his eyes, shook his head. When he looked at me again, his eyes were wet. *Cute*, he signed.

"What?"

You.

"No," I said. But he nodded his head.

He typed, *I don't want to go.*

I said, "I don't want you to go, either."

And then I took the phone out of his hands, sat it on the bench beside mine, and closed the gap between us again. I took his hands. I said, "Don't go."

Jun couldn't sign anything because I'd locked my fingers around his hands, couldn't type because his phone was on the bench. So he nodded.

And I kissed him.

Jun pulled his hands out of mine, wrapped his arms around my neck, and pulled me into him, our knees clashing, my hip smarting on the bench. I held the back of his head as we kissed, fingers in his hair, and his back arched when I touched him there, refusing to let go, leaning into him as if we could be one.

When the kiss broke, I pressed my cheek against his. I wasn't ready to break away from him. Not yet.

Jun drew something on my back. Not a word this time. A heart.

And I squeezed him tighter. "Don't go," I said, knowing he couldn't hear me, couldn't feel it. "Don't leave me."

Jun pressed his lips against my ear, and he made a humming noise that came from deep within him. It wasn't a word, but it said everything. Wasn't a declaration, but still a way forward.

I held his shoulders, pulling back from him so I could look at his face. And I said, "What are we going to do?"

Jun shook his head. He didn't know. He tapped my thigh, and I brought one leg up onto the bench, stretching it out so he could sit between my legs and lean his back into me. He lifted his phone again, and the glow splashed around us, opening the world beyond our lips.

He typed, *Woo-sung is on father's side. Mum has been trying her hardest to show them that I don't need "fixed". But father is stubborn.*

I draped my arms around his neck and kissed the back of his head before resting my chin on his shoulder, watching as he typed. And instead of asking him to turn his head so he could lipread my words, I took his phone and added below his sentence: *Why can't he see the truth?*

Jun shrugged against me, took his phone back. *He thinks deaf = broken.*

I typed, *You're not.*

He said, *I know.* And then he typed, *Meningitis wasn't in my father's plan. It wasn't in mine, either, but it is what it is. I'm me because of it, but he can't see that.*

He tilted his head towards me and I kissed him again, gentle this time, but no less passionate. Then I said, "He should have faith in you."

Faith, Jun signed. Then he typed, *You don't have to believe in anything in order to believe in humans.*

I reached out to his phone, opened the emoji drawer and tapped the love heart.

And he added three more below it.

Then he sat up and I lowered my foot to the ground. I

took his hand and we faced the dark pond. The sun was gone now, but we shared our own light.

I said, "We should do something."

What? he asked.

"I don't know. Something to prove to him that hearing won't change who you are."

There's nothing, he typed. *I'm out of options.*

"I refuse to believe that. There's always an option." I touched his cheek, kissed his forehead, and pulled him into me. "I'll think of something," I said. "Even if I have to kidnap you."

Jun smiled, a tentative pull of his lips. *You don't need to steal me*, he typed. *You already have my heart.*

CHAPTER 29

I woke before my alarm. It was the first day of exams and my nerves had kept me awake most of the night. I'd spent two hours on a video call with Jun last night, not talking, just studying, and every so often he'd hold up his textbook and point to a word, then he'd sign it for me in ISL. History. Famine. High King.

And I asked him to sign words like eloquent and zoology and wave-particle.

His mum came into his room before midnight and signed, *Bedtime. Both of you.*

And I said, "Good night, Eileen." I waited until she'd left his room and Jun picked his phone up from its stand on his desk, then I said, "See you in the morning?"

He nodded, and made one half of a heart with his fingers.

I formed the other half with mine.

And I lay in bed with yellow highlighter ink on my fingertips and a row of objects drying in the corner of my room, painted black and ready for my art project. I had to hand it in next week. But for now, I had to worry about exams.

In the morning, I was showered and dressed even before Mick came downstairs, drinking tea in the kitchen, sitting in Grandad Tommy's chair at the table.

"Oh," Mick said, and I think he was more surprised about the seat I'd chosen than being dressed for school already.

I said, "I'm taking Tommy's luck with me."

Mick nudged my shoulder. "Good idea. Not that you'll need it."

I got the bus into town and Jun was already sitting at a window table of McDoogan's Café, studying the laminated menu. He grinned when I waved at him through the window, and when I went inside, he stood up to hug me.

He was gorgeous in his school uniform, dark green jumper with a blazer over the top, tie in a pristine Windsor knot, and a smile that made me want to put him in my schoolbag and take him with me.

"Will you still make it to school on time from here?" I asked.

He nodded. We chose McDoogan's because it was as close to both schools as we could find. He signed, *First exam?*

"English Lit," I said. "Then physics this afternoon."

He pulled a face. He had history this morning and then nothing until Wednesday.

We ordered breakfast, and I watched Jun stir three packets of sugar into his tea. He had told me, after our late-night excursion to the park, that his father had rented an apartment near Jun's place, and he was expected to eat dinner with him and Woo-sung almost every evening.

And if it wasn't for his father's desire to restore his marriage as well as Jun's hearing, they'd have already boarded a plane to South Korea.

"Small mercies," I'd said. "Fingers crossed your mum holds out long enough for him to give up."

He won't give up, Jun had told me. *He doesn't lose.*

"He will," I said, taking Jun's hand. "This time."

We ate breakfast—scrambled eggs and toast—in silence, watching each other, bumping knees together under the table, and then Jun typed, *We should come here every morning.*

"Are the eggs that good?"

He smiled. Said, *Not the eggs. The company.*

I pushed my shoe against his under the table. "Even tomorrow?" I asked. "When you have no reason to get out of bed?"

I can think of a reason, he said.

Me? I signed, feigning bashfulness.

But he rolled his eyes. *Eggs*, he signed.

I laughed and touched his hand.

And then somebody pounded on the window beside us. Ryan and Mia.

He pushed the door open and stuck his head in. "You're going to be late," he said.

We paid and stood on the street, everybody hugging and wishing each other good luck. And then Jun and Mia went in one direction—their schools were west of here—and Ryan slapped my back.

"You'll see him again," he said as I stared at Jun's back.

But every time he walked away from me, I wasn't sure if I ever would.

At the top of the street, they stopped and looked back. Mia gave Ryan a two-armed wave and Ryan blew her a kiss. Jun lifted one hand, reserved beside Mia's excitement, and I mimicked him, feeding back the wave he gave me. A wave that said, Good luck. That said, You've got Shakespeare by the balls. And even from this distance, I saw his fingers curl into one half of a heart.

And Ryan said, "Well?"

"Well what?"

"Are we going to stand here, pining after them, or are we going to go and kick some exam butt?"

"How do you kick an exam in the butt?" I asked. I lowered my arm and Jun and Mia disappeared around the corner.

Ryan said, "With centrifugal force."

"That makes no sense," I said, turning from him and walking away from the café.

"It's exam day," Ryan said. "Nobody told me I had to make sense."

It felt stupid to be carrying a half-empty schoolbag with nothing but my cram-notes and a pencil case. Stupid to be worrying about essay structure and quotations when I'd just been holding somebody that I wasn't sure I'd get to keep.

I wondered what Mia was saying to him as they walked towards their schools. Would she wish him luck before going their separate ways? Would she tell him her secrets? Ryan's secrets?

We walked up the hill and I said, "How do you know if

you're in love?"

Ryan said, "Give me your phone."

"Why?"

"I'm not going to text anyone, I swear." I handed it over and he scrolled through my YouTube history. Clips of Shakespeare plays and physics lectures, interspersed with music videos, K-pop and western pop as well as the occasional power ballad, the kind Mum would often play after a few glasses of wine on a Friday night. "Yeah," he said, passing my phone back. "You're in love."

"Shut up," I told him. But my cheeks were burning.

At school, the front gate was swarmed with students exchanging notes and looking terrified. The older kids, the eighteen-year-olds who were taking their final Leaving Cert exams, weren't in uniform, wearing jeans and T-shirts instead. But that was a small comfort when the rest of your life hung on the next two weeks.

Ryan dragged me into a hug and thumped my back. "You got this."

"I don't, but thanks," I said. I didn't need to encourage him or wish him luck. Ryan would ace his exams; he always did. But I said, "Go kick some exams in the butt," and he danced away from me.

Inside, the exam rooms were already set up, single desks in long rows with candidate numbers Sellotaped to them, scrap paper booklets stacked neatly.

I found my seat, watched the clock as the room filled up, and exam papers were distributed. And I clicked my pen on. Off again. On again.

The invigilator said, "You may begin."

I turned over the paper and wrote my name.

When I scanned the essay questions, I was given two options to choose from, and I picked the one that felt most like story-writing instead of the one that seemed much more objective, because objectivity went out the window the second I sat down. "Imagine you are Horatio. Write an account of your interactions with Hamlet, paying particular attention to your background and narrative story."

I thought about it. Horatio was Hamlet's closest friend and confidant, offering stability and rationality. I tried to put it into words that made sense. Was I Ryan's Horatio? Was he mine? Maybe we were both Horatio at times, Hamlet at other times. Weren't we all?

Maybe Horatio used to fancy Hamlet, a long time ago, until a cute Korean boy came along and casually stuffed some butterflies into his stomach. But I didn't write that bit in my essay. I just thought it.

When I finished writing, I moved on to the next section. *Of Mice and Men*. Poor old Lennie.

"Loneliness is an inescapable part of the characters' lives in Steinbeck's novella. To what extent do you agree or disagree?"

I bullshitted my answer, because Steinbeck bored me. Honestly, by the time I'd finished answering it and closed my paper, I couldn't even tell you what I'd written.

And when I sat with Ryan in the canteen at lunch time, eating lukewarm pizza slices and chips—carb-loading—he had loosened his tie and looked exhausted. Being in a higher set had its drawbacks.

We didn't discuss our answers, because doing so would only drag the mood down, but Ryan said, "I should probably just flunk out now and join my dad at the docks."

"You're overthinking it," I told him. "You'll ace your exams and forget why you were worried."

"How much money do rent boys make?"

"Probably more than dockworkers," I conceded.

Jun had messaged me after his history exam, saying he thought he'd done all right. I replied saying, *When you become a historian, you can write a book and become rich. Then you can support me for the rest of my days.*

Deal, he replied. And for today, we didn't acknowledge the threat of his departure that loomed over us.

I handed Ryan my physics notes and said, "Quiz me."

Ryan said, "If you don't know this stuff by now, you'll never know it."

And I stuffed myself full of pizza because that was easier than panicking.

Back in the exam hall, I took my seat, scribbled my pen against some scrap paper to check the ink still flowed, and I felt my stomach full of pizza, weighing me down.

"Begin," the invigilator said, a different man from this morning, gruffer of voice and far more vigilant (is that where the name came from?). He walked along the aisles, hands behind his back, and his head spun as if he was prowling for cheats.

Somebody coughed. Somebody else responded.

Chairs creaked under pressure and when the boy in front of me sneezed, I whispered, "Bless you."

"Silence," the invigilator said from the far end of the room.

Physics. I was never going to use any of this outside of school. Would it even matter if I flunked the exam and joined

Ryan at the docks?

I read the first question. "The Doppler Effect explains why the sound of a passing ambulance changes pitch as it moves past a stationary observer. In your own words, reflect on how this phenomenon demonstrates that sound perception is relative, not absolute."

My brain sparked, cogs whirring, and all I could imagine was standing on a street corner, listening to an ambulance blaring past, with Jun inside it, his face pressed against the dark glass of the rear window. I don't remember who Doppler was, but his Effect was crazy.

I knew what it meant: sound changes depending on where you are. If you're standing still, it rises and falls as something speeds past. If you're moving with it, you hear something different. It's the same siren—but we all hear it differently.

I tapped my pen against the blank page. And suddenly I wasn't thinking about ambulances. I was thinking only about Jun.

Everyone—his father included—thought that he couldn't hear. But that wasn't exactly true. I'd already seen it in action at the Cedar Hill construction site, when he'd stomped his feet in the concrete culvert to *hear* the vibrations. What if Jun didn't hear less than others—just differently?

The Doppler Effect wasn't about silence, it was about change. About position. It was about how sound changed depending on where you were. Sound was a wave, right? A vibration. And that was art.

Art.

On my paper, I wrote about the source. The direction. The movement. And the space in between. I underlined those words—*the space in between*—without meaning to. Because that's where Jun and I were. In between words.

My pen scratched across the page, answering what I had to, but my mind was already somewhere else. It was in the quiet, in the dark.

In the art of silence.

When the invigilator called time, I stood, dropping my pen into the pencil case. And I weaved through the tables, down the corridor, and out into the sunlight where I blinked, looked around, knowing I was in a hurry but wanting to make sure Ryan was okay after his exam.

His tie was completely undone now, draped around his neck like a dead snake.

"How'd it go?" I asked.

He shrugged. "You?"

"Yeah," I said. "I have to go."

"Where?"

"I have the answer," I told him, already walking towards the school gate.

"The answer to what?"

"Everything," I said. And then I ran for the bus. I sent Jun a text. *Where are you?*

I'm at home. Why? he said.

I'm coming over, I told him. *I know what we have to do.*

What? he asked.

But my brain was too busy to reply until I could see him in person.

CHAPTER 30

I rang the doorbell with one hand and knocked on the door with the other.

There was a light inside that flashed when the doorbell was pushed, and when Jun opened the door, I stumbled into the small hallway and kicked my shoes off. I said, "I know what we have to do."

Jun made a motion with his hands, trying to get me to calm down, but my excitement was bubbling out of my throat. He put his fingers against my mouth, the index finger of his other hand to his lips.

And then he pushed me forward.

In the small living room, Eileen sat on the armchair. I was going to wave, to say hello, but opposite her, on the couch where Jun and I had once sat like strangers, I saw Woo-sung and an older man. Jun's father. Teacups in hand. Scowls on faces.

My excitement went off the boil and the bubbles stopped.

It was weird, seeing Jun's father in a suit—blazer and all—but with no shoes. Just a pair of diamond-patterned argyle socks beneath his trousers. I looked, and in the hallway were two pairs of unfamiliar shoes.

Homework, Jun signed to his mum. And he pushed me down the hall to the stairs.

Eileen said something in Korean to her ex-husband and I heard him grunt as Jun forced me up the stairs. In his room, he closed the door, and when I leaned in to kiss him, he pulled away from me.

When I looked shocked, my mouth hanging open, Jun said sorry, and he drew me into a quick hug. Then he got his phone. *Be quiet*, he typed.

I paced his room, in the short space between his bed and his desk, and I told him about my physics exam. About the Doppler Effect. About how sound is different depending on perspective.

He looked at me like I was insane.

Downstairs, somebody coughed, and it reminded me that if I could hear them, they could hear me.

I lowered my voice. "So, we have to show him."

Show him what? he asked.

"That you can hear—just not the same way he does."

How? he signed.

I stepped into his space. Put my hands on his face. I tilted his head, pressed my lips against his cheek, and hummed, loud enough for him to feel it.

What? he signed, while I was still against him. So I did it again. Louder. Intense vibrations.

Jun extracted himself from my arms. He looked at his bedroom door, then at the window. And then he typed, *If you do that to my father, he'll probably strangle you.*

"We'll strangle him first," I said. "With art."

Jun's face contorted into confusion and I laughed.

"We'll put on an exhibition. We'll show him what it's like."

He raised an eyebrow, not quite there yet, his brain not in the same vicinity as mine.

"We'll show everybody," I said, "that they can still hear without ears."

And then he got it. A smile warped across his face, and he slapped my chest as if he was punctuating the point. Then he raised his phone again. Typed. Showed me.

Hear without ear is just H.

I laughed. "And H is always silent," I told him.

I don't know how your brain works, he typed, *but I love it.*

And I hugged him tight, because he'd said the L word, even if it was directed at my brain and not my whole being.

Go now, he signed, trying to pull the smile off his face.

I whispered, "Why are they here?"

To talk, he said. *You should go now.*

I nodded. "I need you to come with me tomorrow evening."

Where?

"Just be ready at four-thirty. I'll pick you up." I kissed him, followed him downstairs, stood in the doorway of the living room and signed, *Thanks for the homework help.* Then I signed goodbye to Eileen and slipped my shoes back on. And when the door clicked closed behind me, I was still smiling. Mr Lee's presence couldn't dampen my mood. In fact, seeing him at last only filled me with resolve.

We'd show him.

We had to.

I formulated my thoughts—designs, ideas—all the way home.

That night, even though I had a maths exam in the morning, I opened my sketchbook to the shaded page, staring at the scrawls of pencil lead across it. It wasn't just darkness anymore. There was light in between. In the scratches, in the cracks. And that's where ideas were formed.

My maths exam was horrendous. Expanding cubic brackets and quadratic sequences. Scatter graphs and histograms. And when it was over, I closed my paper. I'd had to sharpen my pencil twice, and I scooped the butterfly-shards of wafer-thin pencil shavings into my pencil case so I could dispose of them later.

And that afternoon, I changed into a pair of loose-fit denim jeans and an oversized T-shirt with a slogan that reminded me it was either time to eat or time to sleep. And I asked Mick to drive me to my ISL class, the last one before summer break. "But can we pick up Jun on the way?"

Mick said, "I don't think a sign-language expert needs to go to a sign-language class, do you?"

And I said, "It's a refresher course." I smiled.

Mick didn't buy it, but he drove me to Jun's house anyway. When we arrived, I sent him a message, letting him know I was outside—I didn't want to risk bumping into his father again—and Jun came out two minutes later.

He stood on the drive, hesitating before he got in the back seat, signed hello to Mick, and asked me, *Where are we going?*

I just grinned and turned to face the front.

When we pulled up at the community centre, I jumped out of the car and opened the door for Jun. I offered him my hand, like I was helping a prince out of a carriage, and he took it, standing in the car park with me as Mick drove away.

Why are we here? he asked.

I-S-L class, I told him. He shook his head, but I nodded and wrapped my arm around his waist. I said, "Don't panic. I have an idea."

And he came with me, willingly, through the doors and down the corridor to room 1C where the ring of chairs we usually sat in were grouped haphazardly, as if the final class of the season meant even the chairs had dressed down for the occasion.

When Jun saw Ella, I felt his shoulders relax, and she bounced over to us with more energy than a leprechaun on steroids. She hugged him, kissed his cheek, and signed, *What are you doing here?*

He shrugged. Pointed at me as if that explained it.

I held my hands up, defensively. "I might need your help," I said.

"Why don't I like that look on your face?" she asked.

And Jun signed, *Me, too.*

When Sean arrived, he sat his briefcase under the board at the front of the room and signed hello, and when he saw Jun in the seat between Ella and me, he signed, *A last minute newbie?*

I touched Jun's arm and fingerspelled his name with my

free hand. Then I explained, "He's my boyfriend. He's not here to take part in the class. I hope you don't mind. But I did want to talk to you about something after class."

When I spoke, Ella gasped. She put her hand to her mouth and I looked at her. "What?" I asked.

Between us, Jun was staring at me, his mouth open, eyes wide.

"What?" I asked again.

Jun signed, *Boy*. And then, *friend*.

And in the heat that followed, Ella said, "He's gone redder than Santa Claus on his summer holiday."

"I have not," I said. And I looked at Jun. *Sorry*, I signed.

But he signed again. *Boy. Friend.* ISL had formal signs for partner, wife, husband. But not boyfriend or girlfriend. Nothing that rolled off the fingers easily.

Boy friend, I signed.

And he smiled.

"Well," Sean said. "Now that that's out of the way, what did you want to ask me?" I hinted at my idea, and he said, "Let's get everybody going, first." He opened his briefcase, pulled out a pack of flashcards, and said, "Seeing as it's the final class before summer, I thought we could do something fun. No more groups of twos or threes, just one big class game of charades. Because charades is just informal sign language, only now you guys know better." He took the cards out of their pack and shuffled them, then asked, "Who'd like to go first?"

Ella pounced out of her seat and took the cards. She turned the top one over to read it and then she signed, *Oh no. A tough one.*

But before long, even Jun was getting involved.

I sat in the corner of the room, near the open window, and Sean dragged a chair over to join me. "I get it now," he said.

"Get what?"

"Why you chose to learn."

I glanced at Jun. Then I said, "I messed up. We hadn't discussed the boyfriend word yet."

Jun was at the front of the class now, studying one of the cards before attempting to sign it for the group, and Sean said, "It doesn't look like you messed up to me. What can I help you with?"

I leaned forward and Sean copied me, turning ourselves into co-conspirators. I tried to tell him about the Doppler Effect, sound waves and perspective, but Sean wasn't getting it. So in the end, I said, "I want to put on an exhibit. Art. Sound. I need someone to know that Jun being Deaf isn't wrong. It's just different."

"Someone?" Sean asked.

I nodded. "Somebody important."

"I see," he said. But I'm not sure he did. He watched Jun and Ella high five as he took his seat again and somebody else took to the floor, then he said, "I'm still not sure how I can help."

"I need a venue," I said. "Do you know the name of whoever is in charge of the centre? If I can speak to them, maybe I can—"

"What?" Sean laughed. "Blind them with science?" He reached into his jacket pocket and got his phone. "You keep your Doppler Effect to yourself," he said. "Let me call Jim. I can't promise anything—I don't know what the summer plans are for the main hall—but give me ten minutes. I'll see what I can do."

Sean stepped out of the room and I rejoined the group, flopping into the chair beside Jun and trying to pay attention to Sharon who was mimicking a bus or a train, I couldn't tell. But I kept my eyes on the door instead, watching Sean pace past the small window as he held his phone to his ear.

When he came back in, he said, "I've left him a message. I'm sure he'll get back to me when he can."

The joy in my chest subsided, dampening down into my stomach. We were getting somewhere, but not fast enough.

When we'd finished the game of charades, we broke off into smaller groups and Sean had somehow managed to get his hands on the key for the vending machine in the hallway, so we sat with cold cans of soft drinks and talked about our summer plans, strictly in sign language. It seemed like everybody wanted to test their signing skills on Jun, and this time, they weren't talking to him because he was different, but because they were.

He was smiling, replying to somebody, while somebody else was trying to attract his attention, and as I watched him, I told Ella about my plan to stage something big, something audible, even if not with sound.

"His dad's a real piece of work, is he?" she asked.

"Father," I corrected. "And, yeah, I guess he is. He wants his wife back. And he wants Jun to hear."

Ella nodded. I could tell she was thinking about something deeply, and I prodded her to say it. "Just devil's advocate," she said. "But don't you want him to hear your voice?"

I shook my head. "He can already hear me. That's my

whole point."

And Ella grinned. She put her hand on my arm, like the connection made it even more personal. She said, "Good. So, where do we start?"

"You'll help?"

"Damn right, I will."

Before the end of class—not that we were learning anything new, just practicing repetition and making friends with classmates that had so far only been background noise in my life—Sean got a callback from Jim, and he stepped out of the room to take it.

Ella crossed her fingers, and Jun gripped my hand, and when class ended, Sean was still on the phone. Everybody hugged each other, said they'd see us again after summer when the class started up again, and some people exchanged phone numbers with others.

A custodian came up the corridor with a mop bucket on wheels, and Sean waved at us as everyone left. He pressed the phone against his chest and said, "Good luck everyone. Have a great summer. Owen, can you stick around?"

I nodded, told him we'd wait outside, and he went back to his phone call, pacing outside room 1C as the cleaning guy dragged the mop across the floor and into the room.

Ella stood with us for a few minutes until Paulie arrived, but instead of getting into his car and leaving, she waved him over to us. He smoked a cigarette while she told him the plan and he said, "Sounds awesome. I'm good with a hammer if you need anything nailed together."

"Come on, Romeo," Ella told him. "Take me home and maybe I'll let you use your hammer on me."

Paulie stubbed his cigarette butt under his shoe and smiled. "She means she's getting nailed."

When they were gone, Jun let out the laughter he'd been containing.

And then I sat on the wall, feet dangling, and Jun stood between my legs, pressing his back against me with my arms wrapped around his shoulders. I laid my hand flat against his chest, feeling the rhythm of his heart, watching the traffic roll by, and he turned his head to kiss my cheek.

Boy friend, he signed.

Boy friend, I replied.

He leaned deeper into me and breathed heavily. When he looked behind us at the community centre building with its stark red-brick façade, he signed, *Scared*.

Why? I asked.

And he shrugged.

A few minutes later, Sean came out of the community centre, carrying his briefcase and the large cardboard box of noise-cancelling headphones he'd collected from us earlier.

"Boys," he said.

I couldn't read his face.

He said, "I asked Jim about allowing you the use of the main hall. I told him it was for a very worthy cause."

"But?" I asked, pre-empting him.

"But he wouldn't agree." He sat the box on the wall beside us. "Apparently," he said, "renting out the main hall for something as important as your idea, just wasn't enough."

I narrowed my eyes. "What are you saying?"

"He wouldn't give you the main hall—on its own. He's giving you the hall and three of the side rooms, too. If you need them."

I jumped off the wall, startling Jun, and I pulled Sean into a hug. "You had me for a second," I said.

Sean laughed. "You can use the hall to prep, and then exhibit at the start of July before the Teenie Tots ballet class takes over the space. There are some rules, of course, and I promised to come along and keep an eye on things, but you're basically sorted."

"July," I said. "We don't have long."

Jun looked in the cardboard box where the flaps hadn't been closed right. He pointed at them. *What are these?* he asked.

Sean opened the box.

"Perfect," I said. "We can use them. Can't we?"

And Sean closed the box again. He said, "If you break them…"

"I know," I said. "You break 'em, you buy 'em."

CHAPTER 31

Mick helped me carry the crate of blackened objects down from my bedroom and out to Mum's car. "I still don't know what it means," he said.

"You don't have to," I told him. "You're not the one judging it."

He looked inside the plastic crate as I strapped it into the backseat of the car. "It looks," he said, trying to find a polite way to say whatever was on his mind, "like death in a box."

I smiled. "It kind of is, I guess."

"And that's art?"

"It is now," I said. I slipped into the front passenger seat and tooted the horn to hurry Mum up. And when she came down the driveway, Mick kissed her and held the driver's door open.

"Good luck," he said. "Mind your speed limit. And don't destroy whatever that is in the back seat."

He closed the door and Mum lowered the window for final goodbyes. Mick was one of those Irishmen that would stand at the end of the drive, waving while you drove away, even after you were gone. Mum said, "You'll be late for work."

And I said, "I'll be late for my exam, never mind work. Can we go already?"

She pulled out of the driveway and turned up the street, and the objects in the plastic crate rattled.

I had my French exam this morning, and the judging of our art pieces in the afternoon. And as long as Mum got me to school on time, I'd have thirty minutes to finalise my art piece before *l'examen de français*. The painted suitcase was in the art room, waiting for me with the blacked-out cards of emotions.

I sped through the school doors, nodded at some of the boys from my class, dropped my bag off at my locker and then carried the crate down to the art department.

"We're getting set up in the staff room," Mr Madden said. "I was about to disqualify you for failing to show up." He was joking—I could tell by the smile that split his beard—but it wasn't funny.

I dumped all my items out of the crate and onto a desk. The T-shirt I'd worn when Grandad Tommy's non-cancerous lump was removed. The Goku figurine. One of my old sketchbooks from a few years ago, filled with childish drawings of Transformers and Ryan's face and three pages of an apple study, sectioned and cross-sectioned. I painted every page black, cover and spine too.

I pulled the paint-spattered dust sheet off the top of the suitcase and rearranged the cards that stuck out of it at different angles. Then I placed each item inside—a Christmas card that Grandad Tommy had given me when I was seven. I'd pinned it to the wall of my bedroom and it had remained there ever since. Until now.

A controller from my old PS4; I tried to teach him how to use it once, but after ten minutes he gave up.

And, last night, I pulled a dozen strawberries from his strawberry bush in the greenhouse. They'd ripened just as June had ripened too, and I coated their skin in black paint, brushing over the tiny seeds, making them look the least appetising thing in the world. I piled them in a corner of the old suitcase, stacking other items around them.

Sugar packets because he was a sweet old man, all painted black.

A canvas on a wooden mount—just a small one, postcard sized. The black paint I'd layered over it had dried and cracked, but instead of giving it a second coat, I allowed Tommy's artwork to bleed through the darkness, just as he bled into mine.

A rusty old key, painted black like the night, as if it was thick with soot. It was for Tommy's old shed, a wooden monstrosity that he'd replaced three years ago with a sleek, corrugated structure at the bottom of the garden. And even though the old shed was gone, the key still hung from a hook in the laundry room, like maybe one day it would come in useful.

Maybe today.

A ticket stub for the Santa Train, an old steam engine that rode the line from Dublin to Drogheda, where Santa would hand out gifts to little kids. Grandad Tommy took me every year and we'd marvel at the clean white smoke that chugged out of the engine, click-clacking our mouths in time with the wheels on the tracks.

"Ready?" Mr Madden asked.

"Hold on," I said, adding the finishing touches, and then I carefully picked up the suitcase, its lid propped open with black wire, and carried it to the staff room behind him. All the halls and larger classrooms were being used for exams, so our art pieces weren't on public display—which was actually a relief.

In the room, I sat the case on a table near the corner, and I ran back to my locker, got the small glass bowl I'd brought from home, and dropped some ten-cent coins into it—not as a donation jar but for the judges to use. I took it back to the staff room, sat it beside my artwork, and then Blu-Tacked the interactive instructions to the table: *Scratch me*. That was it. That was all I wrote. And then, to demonstrate, I used a coin to scrape the black coating off one of the cards like a lottery scratchcard. I didn't know which was which. But it felt like fate when I'd revealed the word underneath.

Sadness.

"Owen," Mr Madden said. "Don't you have an exam to get to?"

"*L'art est plus important que le français,*" I told him, in my awful French accent.

I conjugated verbs in my head as I found the room where my exam was being held, and when the invigilator said, "Begin," the next two hours went by slower than butter could walk. I jumped when an end-of-class bell sounded, even though nobody was in class any more, and I wrote about the misadventures of Stefan and Marcel from our workbook in what I hoped was passable French. *C'est la vie.*

After the exam, I sat on the grass outside the main building and video-called Jun, but the sun shone on my screen so much that it was difficult to make out his signs. So I blew him a kiss and said I'd see him later, and he wished me luck while the judging was going on inside.

At three p.m., Mr Madden rounded the class up, and we followed him back to the staff room where a dozen teachers were gathered. "Whatever happens," he said in the corridor, before opening the door, "you've all done amazingly. This competition was just for fun. First place or tenth, it won't affect your overall grades." And then he opened the door.

The awards had already been granted. Four rosettes—first to third, plus an honourable mention—were pinned to the tables around the room. I went straight to my art piece.

Second place.

I should have been happy, but I wasn't. Most of the cards had been scratched, black shards of paint-dust on the table, revealing words like joy, pain, anger, love.

I turned. Looked for the first-place rosette.

Jared. Of course. He stood beside his sculpture with a shit-eating grin on his face, and the principal, Mrs O'Connor, shook his hand.

"Wow," somebody said.

"What is it?" someone else asked.

Jared came to me once Mrs O'Connor stepped away from him. "Sorry," he said.

I nodded. Shook his hand. Squeezed a little too hard.

And then I looked at his piece. It was a wire frame, an oak leaf, large and wide, perfectly balanced on the very edge of a mobile phone, also formed out of the wire—like the balancing bird trick. You could have tapped the leaf and made it collapse, it looked so fragile.

Somebody blew on it and the oak leaf rocked, swayed, balanced, and returned to its natural pose. I looked at the table to remind me which topic he'd chosen: Nature vs Nurture.

"Very clever," I said. The oak leaf signified nature while the mobile phone, with its wide buttons and an Instagram icon fashioned from the wire, was human-driven nurture.

And I wish I'd thought of it.

"Told you you'd come in second," he said.

I nodded. It was one thing to come first, it was another to gloat about it.

I left the staff room before he could say anything else, and I messaged Jun, telling him the outcome of the awards. *I'm sorry*, he replied. *I was sure you'd come first.*

I got the bus into town and walked the rest of the way to the community centre where everyone had gathered in the main hall. Ryan was halfway up a ladder, helping Sean screw timber braces to the walls while Mia dragged taped floor markings across the linoleum like she was laying the foundations for something sacred.

"Second place?" Ryan called to me as I entered.

"Jun told you?"

He shrugged. "He said it in a positive way, if that helps."

"Thanks," I said. It didn't.

"What about French?" Ryan asked.

"Stefan and Marcel kiss on their boat trip in Paris, don't

they?" I asked.

"Only in your dreams, mate."

"Dammit," I laughed. I loosened my school tie and slipped it out of the collar. It didn't feel real, being done with exams, and I was still deflated from coming second. I dropped my schoolbag and kicked it into the corner of the room under a table that Sean had turned to as Ryan came off the ladder. Our plans were laid out on sheets of graph paper.

We'd section the main hall into smaller rooms, one leading into another, so that visitors had to follow a set path—like Ikea but with organised emotion—and Paulie had managed to secure a load of plywood boards that we could use to erect the temporary walls. He was in the centre of the room, arguing with Ella about what height the walls should be.

I looked at the plans. We'd start with a quiet room, forcing sensory deprivation, asking visitors to put on the noise-cancelling headphones and experience the silence before they moved on. Sean and Paulie had driven to a hardware store to pick up ten litre drums of black paint—as if I wasn't already done with black paint—for the walls.

"Where's Jun?" I asked, and there was a clatter as Ryan accidentally knocked the ladder over. I'm just glad he wasn't on top of it when it fell.

"I nearly killed myself," he said.

And Mia said, "Watch what you're doing or *I'll* kill you." Then she kissed him.

Cute, Sean signed.

Gross, I told him.

Ella pointed at the store room at the end of the hall. "Lover boy is in there," she said.

I followed the sounds of quiet scratching, walking across the patches of light from the windows that would eventually be covered to create darkness for the exhibition, and Jun was sitting in the store room on top of a stack of gym mats like he was the king of the junkyard. He was trimming a piece of wood with a sharp knife, and he smiled when I ducked under a half-finished archway made of PVC and black-out fabric, and stepped in front of him.

I climbed onto the mats beside him and stared through the store room doors at the activity of our friends, dust motes dancing around their heads in the slanting daylight, and I closed my eyes.

Jun tapped my knee.

Second place is good, he signed.

I nodded. I wanted to forget about my project now. We'd be allowed into school on Monday to pick up our art pieces, and I had no idea what I'd do with mine. I'd turned everything black, darkened the history of my soul, and I'm not sure if the paint would wash off. If I even wanted it to.

What did Michaelangelo or Damien Hirst do with their sculptures when they were no longer needed?

I said, "The winner's art was clever. He deserved to win."

He signed, *Yours had more heart.*

And I smiled. He hadn't seen Jared's balancing piece, but I appreciated his words. I wrapped my arms around him and he put down the wooden block and the knife, out of harm's reach. I kissed him, soft at first, then deeper, letting my body fold into him, and he shuffled on the gym mats, laying down so I could lie behind him and drape my arm over his side.

Together, we watched the others building walls and

dipping paint rollers into trays, and although I felt guilty, needed to get up and help, I didn't want to move. I slipped my hand under the loose hem of Jun's sweatshirt and felt the heat of his stomach on my fingertips, where the cold of my hand made him clench his muscles. My finger dipped into the indentation of his navel and he rolled his head back against me.

I had to get up. We were getting far too comfortable together. Far too close. I pulled my hand away from his warm flesh and kissed his cheek.

And when I sat up, Ryan said, "You should charge for shows like that. You'd make a fortune."

"Shut up," I laughed, and Jun covered my face with his hands. Then I gripped his stomach and said, "This is as close as you'll get to having a fit body."

Ryan flexed his muscles with a grunt and Mia slapped his stomach with the flat of her hand. "In your dreams," she said.

Jun sat up and touched my cheek. There was no reason for it, I just think he needed to touch me sometimes as much as I needed to feel him against me.

I kissed him and he signed, *What if it doesn't work?* His expression had clouded, eyes blinking at me.

I thought about Jared's balancing act, how close it looked to collapse.

"It will work," I told him.

What if I can't convince my father to come? he asked.

I took his hands and said, "You will. We have no choice. He has to come."

And he nodded. But I could see in his eyes that he didn't believe it.

We stayed like that for a few minutes longer, knees brushing together on the gym mats, fingers twined, watching our friends build a world out of plywood and stubborn hope.

But then I stood, helped Jun to his feet, and said, "We've got this. Come on. We have a war to win."

And we went into battle in the middle of the hall, raising walls, pinning fabric, sweeping floors, surrounded by our soldiers—Sean sketching modifications to the plans on paper, Paulie and Ryan carrying a wooden beam to the far wall, Mia painting while Ella danced in a circle with a stretch of black voile. Even Callum was there, somewhere. I couldn't see him, but I heard him whistling a tune that he made up, sharp and nonsensical.

We would win. I believed it, even if Jun didn't.

Or, at least, I did. Until he sent me a message at ten p.m. that night.

Emergency, he said. *Meet me at the park.*

And as I pulled my shoes on, I was already stepping on my heart.

CHAPTER 32

I wasn't scared of the park this time. I was scared of what Jun would say.

I sat on the bench, staring across the dark pond, hearing but not seeing the splash of ducks, and I twisted my hands together with worry. I didn't know what his emergency was, but I knew it wouldn't be good. Nobody said emergency and then gave you cake, even if they should, just to soften the blow of the real emergency.

I rolled my foot over the gravel. Curled my fingers around the intricate iron armrest, grimacing when I touched what I thought—or hoped—was gum. And when Jun arrived, he came along the path with a slow drag of his feet.

I stood up. Waved. And then went to meet him because he was taking too long to get to me. "What's wrong?" I asked.

He signed something, but I couldn't make it out in the dark. I slid my phone out of my pocket and turned the flashlight on. Jun signed again.

"I don't know what that means," I said. He'd signed the word *don't*, and then something else.

He took my phone. Typed. *Don't freak out.*

When I looked at his words, I turned the flashlight back to his face. "That's freaking me out," I told him.

Jun pointed at the bench and I followed him there. When he sat, he took something from his pocket, turned it over twice, and then looked at me. He held it out.

"What is it?" I asked. But I could see what it was. An airline packet. Inside, was a ticket. Business class. Dublin Airport to Incheon International, which I had to assume was in Korea. "No," I said.

Yes, he signed.

His name was on the ticket, written in English. Jun-ho Lee.

I moved the flashlight, read the date. Third of July—the day after our exhibition opening.

"This is a joke," I said.

Jun shook his head. When I looked at him, his eyes were wide, light reflecting in his pupils, and his eyelids were red, as if he was exhausted.

I put the ticket back in its paper folder—tearing it up wouldn't make a difference—and I took his hands. "You can't go."

He didn't respond. What could he say?

So I hugged him, the airline packet still in my hand, the feel of his breath on my neck. I put my fingers on his back, drew a heart there, the way he'd done to me on this same bench. And his arms pulled tighter around me.

When he let go, I kissed him, lightly, because even if there was passion in my fingertips, it couldn't be on my lips. Not while I held his plane ticket. Not if he was leaving me.

Jun faced the pond, dragged a hand through his hair, and then made one sign.

Father.

I nodded. He didn't need to say anything else. His father had come to make demands, like a reaper, and now he was collecting.

I touched his leg to get his attention. "What about your mum?"

He shrugged. Took out his phone at last. Typed, *She tried. But I think he realises he won't win her back. So if he takes me, maybe she'll follow.*

"He can't just take you," I said.

He will, Jun typed. Then he added, *Mum says if I have the cochlear consultation, I can still say no.* He looked at me, then cleared the screen. He typed something new, but didn't show me at first. He stood up, rolled his shoulders, then handed me the phone.

If I go, I won't have a choice.

I leapt off the bench. "I won't let that happen," I said. "You're not going. You can't."

How? he signed, and I knew he meant how do we stop this and how do I stand up to my father and how can we live without each other.

"We still have the exhibit," I told him.

For one day, he signed.

I took his hands again. "That's all we need. He'll come. He'll see what this means to you. And he won't force you to go."

Jun leaned into me. Then he signed, *You don't know him.*

I held his face. And I said, "He doesn't know me."

My chest was tight as I walked home. Jun was kicking around inside my heart and his father was about to rip him out of my grasp. There was no way I would let that happen. Not without a fight.

So I sat at my desk, while other kids who'd finished their exams and the school year were having parties and drinking beer and making out. I spread the graph paper in front of me, looking over our plans for the exhibition, and I moved some things around. This wasn't going to be an exhibit of different items, like the disparate display of art pieces in the school staff room. There was unity here, cohesion. We were telling a story—not just Jun's but everyone who had ever been told what was best for them when the outcome would be wrong. This was no longer about Jun's Deafness but about his place in the world.

A world that we would make understand.

Because nothing else mattered now. Only Jun and his happiness.

Only love.

I rolled into bed at three a.m., long after Mum and Mick had fallen asleep, my eyes stinging from tiredness under the light of the lamp on my desk. I don't think I slept much, tossing and turning, kicking the duvet off and then pulling it back over me. And in the morning, I returned to my desk, and then dragged my ass to the community centre where I pulled the nails out of a plywood wall, hauling the wood on my own to its new spot near the front, struggling to hold it in place while I nailed it to the supporting strut. By lunchtime, when the others arrived, I was soaked in sweat.

"Go home," Ryan said. "You need a shower."

A few days later, Mum said, "I'm going to the cemetery. Do you want to come?"

"No," I said. But then, "Yes. I will." My eyes were going fuzzy from staring at too many sheets of graph paper. Callum had driven by at first light and picked up Ryan. I'd waved at them from my window. They were driving over to Tullamore where Callum had managed to wrangle some profession-al-grade audio speakers from a college friend of his.

I changed my shirt, because the one I was wearing had been covered in paint, and when we got in the car, Mum made a stop at the local florist for a fresh bouquet of flowers.

The cemetery, when we arrived, was quiet. A single bird said something and got no reply.

I saluted St Michael as we passed him and smiled at Grandad Tommy's headstone. The thin paintbrush I'd left there before was gone, carried away by the wind or an animal, and I thought maybe I should bring one of the items from my blackened suitcase to replace it with.

Mum stooped and brushed away the dead petals of last week's flowers that had collected at the base of the stone, and then she pulled the old bouquet out of the holder, replacing it with the fresh ones. She handed the dead bunch to me and I held it in my hands, like the memory of a child that was no longer there.

"Hi, Dad," she said. "Hi, Mum."

She kissed her fingertips and pressed them against the cold stone. Then she stood up and we stared at their names in silence. I knew she was praying.

I closed my eyes. Praying wasn't something I did often, but today I did. Not to God, but to Tommy. If you're up there, I prayed, keep an eye on Jun, please. I don't need your help now, he does.

Tommy didn't answer me. And I don't know if that meant he wasn't there, or if he was already leaping into action without a word.

"Tommy Two must have been here," Mum said.

"How can you tell?"

She pointed. I hadn't seen it when we arrived, but beside the headstone was an unopened bottle of beer, lying on the grass, Tommy Two's favourite brand. I imagined him sitting on the ground, sharing a bottle with Grandad, telling him drunken stories or maybe singing. Grandad Tommy loved a singalong. Most Irishmen do.

"We should open it," I said. "Pour it onto the grass and leave the empty bottle for Tommy Two to find. Like Grandad Tommy drank it."

She laughed. "That'd scare him." Then her smile softened, turning in at the edges.

I said, "Jun might be leaving."

She looked at me.

"His dad wants him to go back to Korea," I said. I didn't tell her he was demanding it, that he'd already bought the ticket, but I think she heard the finality in my voice.

She said, "What does Jun want?"

"Thank you," I said. When she questioned me with a look,

I said, "You've asked the one thing his father hasn't."

Mum took the bouquet of dead flowers from me and cradled them. She said, "I don't know a lot about Korea, but I know the kids study from morning to night. Not like here where you do a few hours and are home by four. Maybe his dad just wants what's best for him."

"It's not about studying," I said. "It's about his hearing." I looked at her. "His dad thinks he's broken."

"I'm sure he doesn't think that."

"He does," I said. "And I don't know what to do."

"Your art show," she said.

I corrected her. "It's not an art show. It's an exhibition."

"It means a lot to you," she said. "And if it means that much, you'll put all your effort into it. Blood, sweat and tears, Owen. You can't win without all three."

"I got a splinter yesterday," I told her.

"See? You're halfway there. Mick would say the work is never done until you finish bleeding."

"Mick faints at the sight of blood," I laughed. And as we walked back to the car, I said, "He's good for you."

She touched my back. "I know," she said. "But it's nice that you see it too."

"I don't think I've said it before, but I'm glad you have him. I'm glad he's in our lives."

Mum said, "You say it every day. When you eat the food he cooks, or help him in the garage, or when you laugh at his lame jokes. You think I don't see it but I do. Mick lights up our house. And we need that. Both of us."

"He completes your circuit," I said.

She shook her head. "He completes *our* circuit." She

unlocked the car, put the dead flowers in the back seat. "You'll have that too," she said. "One day."

"I have Jun," I told her.

And Mum nodded. "You do. I don't know what the future holds for you, Owen, but I know you'll continue to make the right choices. Whether Jun leaves or stays, I know you have Mick's strength in you."

She started the car. But she let the engine idle.

"You're destined for great things," she said. "You just have to keep your heart open."

CHAPTER 33

The community hall had changed.

The loose boards were gone. The clutter. The sense of temporary mess. In their place were fabric-wrapped partitions, soft lights strung in organic patterns, and shapes that invited touch without explanation. There were textures on the walls—velvet, woodgrain, woven canvas, sandpaper, fur. It was a space to be felt, not understood.

And in the centre, after the expressive art pieces of emotion on the walls, Sean was backing into a corner, Callum pushing a large speaker from the rear, and they stopped long enough to connect it to the power lines that were taped to the ground where they couldn't be tripped over.

The speaker popped to life and a dull sound rolled out of it, rumbling under my feet like the softest earthquake.

"Push it flush against the wall," I said. "It needs to be as invisible as possible."

Callum tore some black electrical tape from a roll and covered the speaker's power light, and the black case against the black wall fitted into the darkness.

I turned, went back to the front, near the entrance, and helped Ryan align a freestanding frame to the guide markings on the floor. He grunted, wiped his forehead with his sleeve, and said, "Take a break. You've been at this all week."

"I'll take a break when it's done," I said.

"Owen."

"Ryan," I mocked.

He took my elbows, staring at me with those tender eyes that Mia must have fallen in love with by now. Eyes that I'd been looking at my whole life but never really saw. Eyes that now told me how proud he was. He said, "When did you last eat?"

I shrugged.

"Somebody get me a packet of cheese and onion crisps, stat!" he called.

"We're going for dinner tomorrow," I told him.

But he said, "You can't eat once a week. I don't want your mum coming down on me like a tonne of bricks. I know what she's like when she's angry. You remember the last time you didn't eat?"

"Don't go there," I said, but I knew what he was driving at. "I'm not refusing to eat. I've just been too busy." I'd thought he'd forgotten about that period of my life. I'd told him about it one night, in the safety of my bedroom, back when kids could have sleepovers and it wasn't considered to be inappropriate. Why do boys stop doing that? I'd love to have a sleepover now—snacks and horror movies and late-night laughter.

Why does being a grownup mean no longer having fun?

Ella threw a packet of crisps at Ryan and he snatched them in mid-air.

"Here," he said.

And to prove I wasn't slipping into ancient ways, I tore the bag open, pulled out a fistful of crisps, and stuffed them into my mouth. And while I chomped on them, I said, "Happy now?" Crisp crumbs flew everywhere.

"Not until you swallow," he told me.

When I'd swallowed, I grinned. "That's what he said."

Paulie and Mia passed us, carrying a crate of musty old books that I could smell even though the lid was closed. Mia said, "Don't just stand there. We've got work to do."

"Less than two days," Ryan said, clapping his hands, spurring everyone on like a fast-food manager.

Tomorrow, we would make our final preparations, and we'd open the exhibition the next day. And on Tuesday, the day after that, Jun would be leaving. Or he wouldn't. And only time would tell.

I looked for him. He was crouched a few metres away, taping down a strip of LED lighting wire with firm, repetitive pressure. He'd started at the front of the hall two days ago, while we worked around him, and laid the groundwork for the visitors' path.

"Who's looking after the videos?" Sean asked as I went to Jun and got to my knees beside him.

"I am," Ella said. "I'll be able to finish them tonight. Are the TVs connected?"

And somewhere across the hall, hidden by a wall or a dozen walls, Paulie shouted, "I need a longer extension cable."

Jun kept his head down, pulling plastic from the roll of lights and sticking them down.

I tapped his leg. "How's it going?"

He didn't look up, just peeled another strip of tape. Stuck it down. Peeled another.

I waited.

And finally, Jun lifted his head. I couldn't read his expression. Then, rolling sticky-tape off his fingers, he signed, *What's the point if he doesn't come?*

I'd said it before, but I had to say it again. "He will."

Jun's hands hesitated. Then he signed, *But the plane tickets.*

"I know," I said.

I've already packed, he signed.

He looked at the floor. And so did I. He'd mentioned the other day about packing. Just in case. We could be hopeful, he'd said, but he still had to face reality. If his father didn't come around to the idea of letting him stay, letting him make his own decisions, then he'd be dragged onto a plane with or without luggage. *And I'd like to keep my fluffy pyjamas*, he'd joked. I'd pinched him at the time, because I wasn't in the mood for jokes. But at least he was capable of being humorously honest. That was more than I could do.

I touched his chin, made him look at me as the LED lights ghosted across his skin. He was tired. I could see it in his eyes. We all were.

But I said, "You didn't build this for him. Not entirely. You did it for you. For us."

Jun shook his head.

I leaned in, pressed my forehead to his. Then I said, "He'll come. He'll see sense."

And Jun nodded, once. *Yes*, he signed. And he turned back to his strip of lights.

On Sunday, we gathered at the community centre at nine a.m., and Sean was already there. There was a woman with him, his wife, it turned out, and while he was walking from boxed-off room to room across the hall, calling out if each of the TVs were working, she was standing in the corner where the laptop had been set up. "Running diagnostics," she told us. "You must be Owen."

I smiled.

"You've done an amazing job," she said. "Honestly. You should be really proud."

"I didn't do it," I told her. "We all did." Then I added, "I'll be proud if it works."

I don't think she knew the weight those words carried, but she nodded and tapped something on the laptop. "Virus free," she said. "I've swapped out the RAM for a bigger card, so you shouldn't have any issues. But I'll be on standby in the morning, in case any of the tech fails."

"It could fail?" I asked, panicked. If the tech failed, everything failed.

"No," she said. "Don't worry. We'll make sure it doesn't."

We worked through the day, and Sean's wife left at noon, coming back forty minutes later with sandwiches and drinks cans. We sat in a circle on the floor, eating in silence, and Ryan lay on his back with his head on Mia's lap as she fed him some crisps.

"He's like an emperor," Paulie said. "Does she peel your grapes for you, too?"

"His grapes are perfectly fine as they are," she told Paulie. And for the first time in years, I saw Ryan blush.

By late evening, Jun and I did a final walkthrough of the hall, following the strips of guiding lights on the floor from room to room.

Is it enough? he asked me.

I took his hand. It had to be enough.

And then Sean said, "Who's going in the lead car so we don't get lost?"

I squeezed Jun's hand and then raised my other one. We'd lead the way.

Sean's wife had gone home in the afternoon, after showing us photos of their two-year-old who'd been with her granny all morning, so when we gathered around the large table at Dalbit Restaurant, it felt like a family, like a close-knit group of exhausted siblings.

Ella and Paulie, Callum and Sean, Ryan and Mia.

Me and Jun.

I held his hand under the table as drinks were poured, and Jun and I had a beer. "That's a very brown-looking Fanta," Sean said with a wink.

I kissed the beer foam from Jun's lips and everybody groaned. But we weren't the only couple at the table. Ella was leaning into Paulie, who'd wrapped his arm around her neck, and Mia's head was on Ryan's shoulder.

Callum held his hand out to Sean and said, "We can be gay for the night if you want."

And Sean took his hand, kissed the back of it, and said,

"Tempting, but I'll have to decline."

"Spoilsport," Callum said, and I hadn't admitted it yet, but he was kind of all right.

They all were.

"I thought this was an Asian restaurant," Ryan said, flicking his fingers over the cutlery. "Where are the chopsticks?"

"Oh," I smiled, and I skimmed my hand along the lip of the table to find the secret drawer.

The owner came back with plates of food, and everyone fell upon their dishes with unchecked enthusiasm. Chopsticks clicked together, lips smacked. Ryan moaned with every mouthful.

And Jun picked at his rice with tiny bites, as if he'd practiced picking up three grains at a time.

I squeezed his leg and he smiled at me, but it was barely there, hidden under the threat of a plane ride none of us wanted him to take.

"You okay?" I whispered, knowing it wasn't all that long ago that people were asking me the same question when Grandad Tommy had passed away.

Jun nodded and brought his chopsticks to my mouth so I could taste his food. He was doing it just to shut me up.

"I can't believe all the hard work is done," Ella said. Then she signed to Jun, *Because we love you.*

Jun looked at her, then the others. And he signed, *I love you too.*

Callum put his hand to his heart.

And Paulie said, "Who needs weed when you've got this, right here?"

"Tomorrow will rock," Mia said. She put her hand in the

centre of the table and Ryan's hand went on top of hers.

Callum joined them, then Ella and Paulie. Sean nodded, put his hand in too, and I smiled. There was a pain in my chest that wasn't from the spices, but I added my hand to the pile.

And I looked at Jun.

He blushed. *Friends*, he signed. And he put his hand on top of mine.

Boy friend, I signed with my free hand. And everyone laughed.

When we'd finished eating, the restaurant owner took our plates away and returned with dessert, but we were so full of spicy meat and rice and noodles that we barely picked at it. Ryan said, "Wrap it up, I'll take it home with me."

Callum burped, said, "Better out than in," and Ella wafted the air in front of her face.

"You're disgusting," she said.

And Paulie's belch was louder.

We all chipped in for the meal, covering the food and the tip—which Jun said wasn't a thing in Korea—and when we gathered on the street outside, Sean offered us a lift home.

But Jun took my hand and signed, *Can we walk?*

I nodded. It was a long way, but I didn't care.

We walked slow, letting the night wrap around us. And Jun kept his hand in mine the whole time, speaking to me with his fingers, with the warmth of his presence.

We stopped on the bridge that overlooked the river, watching the streetlamps dazzle in its surface. A bird slipped by overhead and there was no traffic to speak of. A tugboat was moored further up the bank, bobbing on the swell.

And I pointed, not at the boat but at everything. I said, "This is what silence feels like to me."

Quiet, he signed, the word hanging between us.

I nodded.

Jun put his hand on his chest, his other on mine. Held them there. Then he turned and signed, *Silence is a heartbeat*.

I didn't have anything to add to that. So I leaned into him on the bridge and kissed his temple. We'd open the doors of the community centre in the morning, and the future would change, one way or another. We had no control over it now.

Whatever was coming, was already on its way.

Jun signed, *If I have to leave*, and then he paused as a truck rolled by, kicking up smoke behind it that clung to us long after it was gone. In the quiet that followed, Jun said, *I'll video call you. Every day. Until I can come back.*

I faced him and said, "You make it sound like it's already over, but it isn't."

I'm being real, he signed.

And I said, "Nothing's real until it happens. Come on. Let's go back to mine so we can make out."

CHAPTER 34

I breathed. Paced. Breathed.

"Can you stop that?" Ella asked.

I shook my head and paced back the other way.

The community hall felt tiny this morning, like somebody had come in overnight and squeezed it, wrapping everything in a tight knot around me. The old air-conditioning unit hummed, but if it was spitting out cool air, I couldn't feel it. Outside, the sun was blazing—one of those mornings when you step out of the shower and immediately need another one.

"It's too hot," I said, swiping at the damp hair that clung to my forehead.

Ella took a clip from her hair, pale green and coated with glitter, and pushed my fringe out of my face, pinning it on top. "There," she said. "You look like a princess."

Perched on the welcome table with his legs crossed, Ryan grinned. "I've always seen him as more of a queen."

"Funny," I said, deadpan.

"Either way, it's royalty," Ella smirked. She kissed my cheek, then wiped her lipstick smear away with her thumb.

I jabbed the buttons on the AC, desperate for air.

"Leave it," Ella said, "before you blow us all up."

"What time is it?" I asked.

Everybody pulled their phones out. "Ten fifty-two," Callum said. "Eight minutes."

"We should have opened at nine," Ryan moaned.

I ignored him and looked for Jun. "Where is he?" I asked.

"He was here a second ago," Ella said. "Is he outside, handing out flyers with the others?"

I was surprised we had any flyers left, we'd been handing them out all weekend.

I cut through the welcome area and into the first of the quiet rooms. Jun stood in the corner, reading and rereading the sheet of paper in his hands. We were going to do an opening speech that Sean would record and throw up on the screens to loop through the rest of the day.

When I came to him, he looked up. His smile was nervous and shaky like my knees.

"He'll come," I whispered.

Jun pushed my chest, making me stumble back. It had become our joke over the last week. I'd say, "He'll come," and Jun would knock me, like I was a stuck record saying the same thing over and over again.

But the more I said it, the less I believed it.

You look amazing, I signed. He'd swapped out his oversized sweaters and hoodies for a slim-fitting brown button-down shirt and narrow chinos.

He touched his collar, making sure it was straight, and signed, *You too*.

"Guys," Ella said, her voice high with energy.

"Holy shit," Ryan swore.

I turned at the sound of their panic, and I signed to Jun that something was up. We raced into the welcome space.

"There's a queue," Ryan said, his face mashed against the frosted glass of the wide window.

"No way," I said.

"There's a literal queue of people."

I turned to Jun. Grinned. *People*, I signed. *Lots of people*.

"Two minutes," Callum said, as Sean, Mia and Paulie slipped in through the side door.

Ryan turned. "Does anyone want to puke? No? Just me?"

"Have you seen it?" Mia's face was glowing. "There's got to be thirty people out there. Maybe more."

Father? Jun signed.

I translated for him, and Mia hesitated, glancing at Jun. "I didn't see any Korean-looking men out there." Then she added, "Sorry."

I pulled Jun into a tight hug. "We're open all day," I told him. "He'll come." And this time, he didn't push me.

"One minute."

Sean clapped my shoulder. "Places, everybody. Let's give them a show to remember."

And Callum said, "Ten. Nine. Eight."

But Jun signed. *Open it.*

"You don't want the countdown?"

Open it, he signed again.

And I faked a smile while Callum and Ryan pulled the doors wide. "Come on in," they said. "There's plenty of space. The first tour will begin in a minute."

Jun's hand slipped into mine, our palms sweaty, fingers tingling. *Show time*, I signed.

And he gave me a single, steady nod.

We stood by the welcome desk where Ryan and Mia had printed out an enormous banner across multiple pages, taping them together to stretch across the front of the table. It said, in English and Korean, *THE SOUND OF YOU*. And in smaller print underneath, *Hearing without Ears: An Exploration*.

We watched as visitors crowded into the narrow space, people I'd never met and people I knew. Mum and Mick. Jun's mum, Eileen. Ryan's mum. All of these people who should be at work but had chosen to be here, to support us. I signed to Mum and Mick, *Thank you*, and I knew they understood.

To Eileen, Jun signed, *Father?*

She shook her head, her eyes hooded. *Maybe later*, she signed back. She'd already told him about the exhibition, and Jun had given him one of our flyers days ago.

"Guys?" Sean said, quietly. He stood behind the video camera, its red light already glowing.

I cleared my throat, glanced at Jun for his nod, and then turned to the gathered crowd. I didn't speak until Jun signed. This wasn't like a Sunday morning news show with a tiny signing box in the corner. This was a signed speech, with spoken word in the corner.

Jun glanced at the sheet of paper once, then sat it on the lectern in front of us. He tugged his collar, smoothed his shirt, and raised his hands.

And as he signed, I found my voice alongside him.

"Welcome," we said, my words carrying through the mic, "to The Sound of You. We made this exhibition with care. Not just with our hands, but with who we are. This is not about sound. Or speech. Or even silence. It's about presence. About how we move through a world that doesn't always know how to meet us where we are."

We paused, letting the moment settle.

"We hope it speaks to you. Not here—" we tapped our heads, "but here." We pressed our hands to our hearts. "Because listening is a reaction, not an action. Listening and hearing are connected, but they are not the same. Today, you will learn that you can hear without sound."

As a member of the Deaf community, Jun signed, and I watched him as I translated it instead of looking at the crowd, *I want to share with you my experience. This is how I hear. This is how I understand the world. This is… The Sound of You.*

The applause rose through the air, soft and insistent, and only then did I feel the cool breeze shifting in through the open doors.

"This way," Ryan said, unhooking the rope barrier at the archway leading into the first room. "Single file. Please take a pair of headphones. They'll reduce the noise as we guide you through."

We split the visitors into groups of six, and on the wall in the first room, the monitor showed members of my ISL class. Sean had managed to contact them after our final session.

Individually, they signed to the camera, subtitles underneath, but no spoken word. *I'm learning to sign for my daughter, who was born with congenital deafness*, Sharon said. *I'm learning for my sister's new husband*, Graham said. *I'm learning ISL so that my son will have somebody to talk to when he's older*, Debbie said. At the end of the video, there was a class shot of everybody, waving and signing, *Thank you for coming*.

In the narrow corridor between rooms, where we'd lined the walls with strips of textured fabric, woodgrain, ridged plastic and a fine sandpaper, I put my own noise-cancelling headphones on and followed the first group. They touched the tactile walls, some hesitantly, some with closed eyes. The lights were low and white, the dim corridor feeling cooler than the foyer, and I let the outside world fall away. *Touch and hear with your fingers*, printed signs said, in English and Korean hangeul.

As we passed under an arch into the second room, the walls were decorated with photographs of me, Jun, Ryan and everybody else, pulling faces, showing emotions. Enlarged and black-and-white. None of them were labelled.

A large sign on the wall read, *People speak with their faces every day. No words needed. Can you hear the emotions presented here?*

A kid pointed. "Anger," she said, her voice faint outside my headphones. And again. "He's crying, so he's sad."

"Shush," her mother told her, and she looked at me apologetically. I smiled.

We studied the large photos for a few minutes, soaking in the visible emotions, and then we moved on.

In the next passageway, we'd strung hundreds of threadlike

strands from the ceiling, each with a tiny bell that didn't ring. We had to brush through them to get past, bells moving in silent suspension, drifting over shoulders and against necks, and I noticed some widened eyes and careful smiles.

I'm not sure if anybody detected it yet, but under my feet, I could feel the soft vibrations of the speakers further in, pulsing beneath us like a heartbeat.

We moved into the next room, smaller and low-lit, where the air shifted as soon as we crossed the threshold. A wall was lined with old books and a soft breeze from hidden fans carried their smells—dry paper and timeworn leather—then scents of cut grass, faint vanilla, and something sharper, like rain on pavement.

There were no instructions on the wall this time, just a single line printed on the doorframe as we entered.

Memory has no sound.

The visitors slowed. A woman lifted her head, eyes half-closed, her mouth parting as if she could taste the memory that bloomed beneath the scent. A man's shoulders dropped, the tension slipping away as his nose caught the smell of something familiar.

For the next few minutes, nobody moved. We stood there, letting the air remind us of things we'd forgotten, things we needed to remember.

Memories that were never buried deep.

The next room was empty, except for one TV screen. Black walls drove everyone's attention to the monitor, where an exposed human heart from some medical footage beat without sound. Ella had superimposed a mute-volume icon in the corner. The low thrumming was heavier here, enough that the vibrations were just starting to flood under our feet.

A sign below the monitor, small enough that you had to lean in to read it, said, *You can't hear the heart beating. But can you feel it?*

The silent vibrations pulsed.

Somebody touched the screen, as if they could feel the beat with their fingertips.

I saw Jun behind us, leading the second wave of guests, and I nodded at him. He flattened his lips, too nervous to smile.

Further along the path, someone had paused to watch a projection against the wall. It showed a close-up video of Jun's hands signing slowly—no translation provided. The signs were looped. Repeated. First in ISL, then in KSL. I didn't need any captions. I knew the words.

This is who I am. You don't need to hear me to know me.

In the next room, with the pulsing underfoot getting heavier, louder almost, the lights faded entirely.

Darkness.

Silence.

There was nothing to see here. No signs. No images. Just a space to be. To exist.

At the far end of the room, on the way out, a small placard, lit by a tiny wall light, read, *This is what it feels like when I'm alone in a hearing world.*

And from the visitors, there was also silence. No coughing or shuffling of feet. They stood there, in the quiet, in the emptiness, looking at each other. Holding their breath.

In the dark, I imagined Jun's hand in mine. Nothing would be empty as long as he was here.

A woman near me, in her forties, brushed her fingertips over the small sign on the wall, then pressed them to her chest as if testing her own heartbeat.

We moved on. The corridor was warm. Steady. Wordless. On the wall, a plaster-cast pair of hands jutted out of the dark, stark white against the black. The hands were forming the word *Family* in ISL, but nobody would know that. There was no sign. People touched the sculpted hands when we passed.

As we entered the final room, a sign by the door said, simply, *Hear with your body*.

And as we went in, the speakers were ramped up. Heavy bass, no volume. Thrumming all around us.

Spotlights overhead cast round pools on the floor, and the visitors stood in them, starring in their own production, as the vibrations from the hidden speakers set hairs on end. Some of them raised their arms, watching the hair stand to attention.

I stood under one of the spotlights with them, and I closed my eyes. The pulsing thrum from the invisible speakers drove through me, echoing inside my chest, rattling up my legs and creating that weightless feeling in my stomach that you get at the top of a rollercoaster.

Beat after beat. Wave after wave.

We pulsed together, in time, each of us in our own world, as the hammering vibrations changed. It wasn't thumping us now, it washed over us like music, like a million bass guitars thrumming out a noiseless concert.

We floated on the wave pattern, and as the intensity decreased, signifying our time to move on, the woman who'd touched the placard earlier, pulled me into her arms. And she held me for the longest time.

When she let go, she signed, *Thank you. I will tell all my friends. You get me.*

No, I sighed. *Thank you.*

In the final corridor that led us back to the main entrance, a row of screens lined one wall, benches along the other. The monitors showed Jun, smiling and signing. There were subtitles now so that people could listen to him.

Being Deaf doesn't mean not hearing. It means hearing differently. Every day, I read your body language, your expressions, your uniqueness. You also hear without your ears. We're not so different, you and me. As you leave, please hand your headphones in. And walk through the rest of your day—hearing with your heart. Thank you for listening.

At the door that led us back into the welcome area, a sign read, *"It takes a great man to be a good listener." — Calvin Coolidge.*

Beyond the door, Callum stood with a donation jar. We hadn't planned that, and when I narrowed my eyes at him, he signed, *To cover Sean's time. And for pizza.*

I grinned. And as the first group left, I heard them say, "Wow. Amazing. It's so good."

On the other side of the cordon, the press of people moved forward, eager to enter the first room.

When Jun came through the door behind me, one of his group members was crying. She put her hand on his back, smiling through her tears, before leaving quietly.

Jun hesitated, ducking his head like he was unsure what to do with her reaction.

And then he came to my side, embarrassed.

I pulled him into my arms. "It's amazing," I said. "I can still feel it in my chest."

Jun nodded, solemnly, holding onto me.

Then he looked around, eyes sweeping the room, flickering to the doorway.

But there was still no sign of his father.

CHAPTER 35

People came. People went. And I don't know if they were leaving better off than when they entered.

We took turns, leading small groups silently through the exhibition, and the steady flow of visitors trickled into the lunchtime rush. We broke off from tour-guide duty in threes so that we could catch our breath and eat something.

I sat in the side room where Sean had held our ISL classes, and watched as Ryan munched on a triple-decker sandwich, and Jun peeled the top slice of bread from his, picking at the contents with small bites.

I wanted to say something, but words weren't forming in my brain.

Ryan smiled. Nodded. Nudged Jun's arm and made a happy face. He was always happy when he was eating.

Jun dropped a slice of chicken into his mouth in response.

And I brought my attention back to my own sandwich. Not that I was hungry. I was too nervous. The closer we got to six p.m., the closer Jun's departure came. If his dad didn't show up—and let's face it, why the hell would he?—Jun would be on the three o'clock plane out of Dublin tomorrow.

Mum and Mick had hugged me after they walked through the exhibit, telling me how wonderful it was, how wonderful I was. But it didn't mean anything. They said Tommy Two would stop by after work if he could get out on time, and they said Grandad Tommy was with me, watching over my shoulder.

But it would amount to nothing if Jun's father didn't come. And I was already planning on handcuffing myself to the airplane tomorrow. Or throwing paint on the runway. Anything to stop the flight from taking off.

When I looked up, Jun was staring at me, a tiny dot of mayo on the edge of his lip. I picked up a napkin, wiped it from him, and crushed the napkin in my hand like my hopes.

Eat, Jun signed.

I glanced at Ryan. Had he said something? Had he told my ancient secrets? But Ryan was oblivious.

So I picked up my sandwich and bit into it.

And then Mia, Ella and Sean came in. "I'm starving," Ella said. "Hop to it, guys, there's still a queue out there."

Jun looked at her, hopeful, but she shook her head and he lowered his gaze, wrapping what was left of his sandwich in its paper. He stood up, dusted his hands, and reached down to help me up.

I'd never seen Ryan so quiet, and when we left the room, I

let Jun walk ahead, touching Ryan's arm. "You all right?"

"Shouldn't I be asking you that?"

"Probably. But I'm asking you," I said.

He nodded. "Mia told me she loves me last night. After the restaurant."

"Woah," I said. "Do you feel the same?"

"Of course," Ryan told me. "I mean, look at her. But it made me realise—if she was leaving tomorrow, if I had done all this to stop it, would it be enough? Would it make a difference?"

I filled my lungs before speaking. "And? Would it?"

"Yes," he said. "Maybe not to her dad, if he was forcing her to go. Maybe not to anybody else. But to her. She'd know it, wouldn't she? Why I did this. Why we all did this." He looked along the corridor to the entrance area where Jun was handing sets of headphones to a group of young girls who looked bored.

He said, "Jun knows it too. That's what I'm getting at. Whatever happens, he knows you love him. Even if you haven't said it. Even if you never will, because I know how chicken-shit you are."

"I'm not," I said, flustered. Because I was.

And I followed him down the corridor to lead the next group of guests through our silent exhibition, where I hoped they could hear everything that I heard.

Everything I wished.

The day rolled on, group after group, and the donation jar filled up with notes—fives and tens and the occasional twenty.

By late afternoon, the hall had settled into a quiet hum.

Fewer voices now, just the quiet scrape of chairs in the welcome area, the drag of footsteps, and the occasional clink of coins in Callum's jar. Outside, the light had lost its focus, stretching through the frosted windows, painting wide gold stripes on the floor.

I leaned against the welcome desk, rolling a coin between my fingers. My legs ached. Shoulders ached. Brain ached. But in a way that said we'd done good, had built something living.

Ryan wandered over with two cans of Fanta that he'd scavenged from the back room, pressing one into my hand. I cracked it open, the fizz making a sound that was loud in the hush of the almost-empty hall.

"What time is it?" I whispered.

"Almost ten to six." He looked at his can. It was warm. "A beer would be good. Vodka would be better."

I nodded, absently, barely aware of his words.

Across the empty space, Jun sat on one of the low benches near the headphone-return rack. Ella came through the door, leading the stragglers out of the exhibit, and she nudged Callum's donation jar closer to them on the table.

"Thanks for coming," she said, signing it too.

Jun looked calm, but I knew better. His foot tapped against the leg of the bench in a restless rhythm, his eyes downcast. I'm not sure when he'd stopped looking at the door. An hour ago? Two?

I sipped my warm drink, put it on the welcome desk, and wandered over, sinking down onto the bench beside him. For a while, we didn't sign, didn't look at each other. I closed my eyes and listened to the sounds that were only whispers—the air-conditioner's quiet hum, the shuffle of Mia straightening out the flyers on the welcome table, Paulie teasing Ella near the coat rack.

Jun let out a slow breath and tilted his head against my shoulder. I pressed my cheek into his hair, feeling the soft tickle of it under my jaw.

"Do you think we'll remember this?" I murmured against his scalp. Jun looked up and I repeated myself so he could lipread.

Always, he signed.

And maybe that was all we needed. Maybe that was all we were allowed.

I looked at Sean, who was fidgeting with the laptop behind the desk. He held up three fingers, telling me how many minutes were left before we had to close the doors, before everything we worked for would end. For good.

I didn't say, "He'll come," now, because we had as much time as we had luck. None.

I looked at the door. Callum stood outside, in the shadows where the sun no longer reached, smoking a cigarette. He caught me looking and he shrugged.

"I'm sorry," Sean said quietly. "We're only licenced until six. It's time to lock up."

"Just another minute," I said, my voice raw.

But Jun stood up. *It's okay*, he signed. *Close the doors*.

I got to my feet. My throat was tight. Tears prickled behind my eyes but I refused to let them out.

I said, "Jun."

He looked at me. Shook his head.

And I pulled him into my arms. He buried his face in my neck and I felt his hands clasp at my back, holding me tight.

Callum stubbed the cigarette under his foot, and he pulled the doors closed as he came inside.

They shut, loud in the quiet silence of our breath.

Ella came to us. "I'm sorry," she whispered, touching Jun's back.

And I felt him rock against me, crying, slick tears on my skin.

"It's okay," I said, my lips against his face. "It's okay."

Ryan hugged us. And Ella came in too. Then Sean, Mia, Paulie, Callum.

"We did what we could," Sean said. "I'm sorry it wasn't enough."

I couldn't speak. Jun pressed himself against me, surrounded by our friends, people that would remember us forever, and I felt his hot breath on my neck, his silent tears on my cheek. And somebody else was crying too. I couldn't tell who.

Maybe it was me.

And in the soft quiet of our embrace, somebody knocked on the door.

"Is it him?" I asked.

Callum said, "It'll be stragglers. I'll get rid of them."

Our group hug broke. Callum opened the door and I pulled Jun even tighter, clenching my eyes, listening to Callum's voice say, "Sorry, we're closed."

And then Mick's voice. "I think you might want to open up."

CHAPTER 36

I turned. "Mick?"

"It's me, son," he said, through the half-opened door.

Callum eased it wide so I could see. "Let him in," I said. "Why are you here?"

Mick faced me, his shirt sleeves rolled up, car keys in hand. He said, "I know it's late. Do you have time for one more tour?"

I narrowed my eyes. He'd already been through earlier, he didn't need to see the exhibition again.

But he looked at Jun. Signed, *J-U-N*. And then he curled his fingers, beckoning us to the door.

On the street outside, Mum was standing by the rear door of Mick's car. She opened it, and Eileen stepped out.

Jun signed, *Mum?*

Woo-sung got out behind her. He stood tall, towering over his mother. He said something in Korean, signed it in KSL, and Jun gripped my hand.

The far door of Mick's car opened. Lee Sang-hwan, Jun's father, got out. He closed the door, but he stood on the road as if he couldn't bring himself to step onto the pavement.

Mum said, "Please. Let's go inside."

"Guys," Sean said, looking at his watch.

And Callum shook his head. "It's only five to six, Sean. Isn't that right?"

Sean eyed me, then his watch, and looked at Callum. He nodded. "Yeah. Five fifty-five. My watch must be fast. We have time for one more tour."

I couldn't breathe. Mr Lee was almost as tall as Woo-sung, dressed in a dark grey suit, white shirt, no tie. His face was long, with a sharp nose and hair brushed to the side. He didn't speak.

When he came around the car, Jun bowed from the waist. He stayed like that for a count of three before rising. His father didn't return the bow.

"Come in," Sean said, and he closed the doors behind them.

Mr Lee looked around, reading the sign on the welcome desk that had been written in English and Korean. He picked up one of the flyers, turning it around in his hands, as Jun moved quietly to the headphone rack.

I couldn't help myself.

I curled my fists, digging my fingernails into my palms for strength, and stepped in front of the man in his pristine business suit. I said, "Mr Lee."

He looked at me.

"You have to understand. We did all this for you. To show you that Jun isn't broken. Whatever you think, he hears more than most, just not the way you do. Don't take him away. Please."

Mr Lee stared at me. I'm not sure if he understood. Or wanted to. After a moment, he said something in Korean, sharp as a slap, then turned away.

Nobody translated it for me. Maybe it was better that way.

When Jun approached, he held out a pair of headphones, and Mr Lee looked before accepting them. He took them in his hand but didn't put them on, and Jun offered a second pair to his brother.

Woo-sung kept his hands in the pockets of his bomber jacket, rocking on his feet like he didn't know how to stand still. He was fresh out of military service and you could see the hard lines on his face, like he was still carrying a K2 rifle in his mind.

Jun glanced at me, just for a second, and then he gestured at the door, slow and open-palmed, allowing his father and brother to step through before him.

I stayed behind with everyone else. I wanted to follow, to be there with him—for him—but this was Jun's fight now. I had nothing left to do.

I watched as Mr Lee studied the monitor, seeing the people from my ISL class. And then they moved on. They paused in the tactile corridor, but they didn't touch the walls. And then Jun motioned for them to follow.

They disappeared out of sight.

"Why didn't we put cameras inside?" Ryan asked.

His words broke me from my trance, watching Jun get swallowed by the darkness, followed by his father, and I turned to Mick and Mum. "How?" I asked. It was the only word I could manage.

"We just couldn't sit around at home," Mum said. "And Mick knew where Jun's mum lived, so we got in the car."

Eileen stepped up beside my mum. She said, "When they knocked on my door, I didn't know what to think. But together, we managed to convince him to come." She softened her voice then, and said, "Don't get your hopes up, Owen. He's here. But he might not change his mind."

I wanted to say, "You could end this. You could tell him you won't allow your son to travel back to Korea. Demand it." But I didn't know her circumstances. Didn't know what kind of man Mr Lee was. Or how they came to be where they were.

I only knew that Jun was here. And I needed him to stay.

"Are they taking forever?" Mia asked.

"It's only been a minute," Sean said.

And then somebody came back down the corridor. Out through the in door. Woo-sung.

He stopped. Looked at Eileen. Looked at me. Didn't say anything.

He pushed out through the exit and left.

"Woo-sung," Eileen called after him. She gripped my shoulders. "Go to Jun." Then she went after her eldest son.

I turned, looking down the long corridor, into the darkness. I hesitated, my feet glued to the floor.

"Go," Mick urged.

And I raced through the quiet in search of Jun.

I found them in the scent room, just beyond the corridor of silent, hanging bells. The old books lined one wall, faint fans stirring soft wisps of memories between them.

Jun faced his father. They were speaking in KSL. Arguing, I thought. Sharp gestures. Clipped motions.

"Jun?" I said, voice quiet, not wanting to break into their moment.

"Silence," Mr Lee commanded, the word heavily accented. He didn't look at me.

Jun signed something. Twice.

The air shifted again, from cut grass to coffee and then something floral and soft.

Mr Lee turned from Jun. He stared at me. Looked at his son.

He lifted his hand. Pointed. At me.

Jun signed again. I caught none of it, the shapes strange and unfamiliar, KSL's rhythm unlike the ISL I knew.

The scent looped back to old books, musty and thick. Mr Lee lowered his gaze, staring at his shoes, and I stood there, waiting, watching, fists clenched at my sides.

Jun made a small motion with his hand, beckoning. Come. He turned and walked on without looking back.

And in the stillness, Mr Lee lingered.

"Please," I said, my voice cracking in the quiet.

He opened his mouth, but no words came. Then he followed Jun into the next room, the beating heart on the TV screen. The dull vibrations underfoot.

And in the corridor beyond, Jun kept walking.

As we followed, Mr Lee paused, watching the projection—Jun's hands as they looped and repeated, *This is who*

I am. You don't need to hear me to know me. I knew he'd recognised the signs, but his face gave nothing away.

We moved on.

In the darkened room, Jun stopped in the middle, hands clasped at his waist, and he closed his eyes, shoulders rising with each soft breath.

Mr Lee rolled his neck and exhaled sharply. The darkness was thick, cutting into us. Swimming in the soup of its isolation. And even without covering my ears, there was little to hear. Mr Lee's hand, still holding the noise-cancelling headphones, rose at last as he pulled them over his head.

And we stood there. Quiet. Alone. Together.

We moved into the corridor, and Mr Lee reached up, touched the plaster-cast sculpture of Jun's hands. Slowly, carefully, he slotted his fingers into the space between them, plaster dust falling to the floor like fine snow.

In the final room, the vibrations were ramped up.

Jun signed nothing. He didn't stand under one of the spotlights, didn't lift his chin.

But Mr Lee did.

He scanned the darkened space, eyes searching for the source of the pulsing bass. Then, with a shake of his head, he closed his eyes and, under the soft glow of the spotlight, I watched him breathe.

The vibrations pushed against him. Pulsed. Washed through the room.

It came in waves, filling him with sensation, with atmosphere.

With noiseless sound.

And when the lights shifted, the pulse receding, Mr Lee

didn't move.

Overhead, the stark white spotlights softened into a cool blue. The experience was over. For the final time.

Jun signed something. Short. Sparce. Maybe it was *Father*. Maybe it was *Dad*.

Mr Lee reached up and slid the headphones off.

And he stepped into the corridor beyond, where the row of monitors showed Jun's smiling face, signing his closing message: *Spend the rest of your day listening with your heart.*

When we followed him, Mr Lee cleared his throat.

I looked at Jun.

He nodded once. Didn't smile. But the look in his eyes told me what he needed. To be alone with his father.

So I stepped back, down the corridor and through the exit. And the door whispered shut behind me.

Mum was the first to reach my side when I came through the door, her arms pulling me into a hug.

"Where's Eileen and Woo-sung?" I asked.

"Outside," she said. "Talking."

I nodded.

"Jun?" she asked.

"Inside," I said. "Talking."

Ryan let out a heavy breath. "How is he?"

"Jun? Or his father? Either way, I'm not sure," I said.

Ella hugged me, then folded herself into Paulie's arms, her face buried against his chest. He kissed the top of her head.

"Now what?" Mia asked.

I shrugged. "We wait."

Sean powered down the interior speakers, and when the quiet hum of the pulse room faded, the emptiness that followed seemed even louder.

Mick squeezed my shoulder.

Ryan fist-bumped me.

Callum, counting the banknotes from the donation jar, snapped the lid closed and said, "We need a pizza party."

I laughed, quiet and tired.

"Yeah," Sean said. "We deserve it."

I watched the door, waiting for Jun to come through it, maybe with his father's arm around his shoulders, both of them smiling, maybe even laughing. But the door stayed closed.

Behind me, Ryan said, "No pineapple. I draw the line at pineapple on pizza."

"You're a heathen," Callum said. "What's wrong with pineapple?"

"It's the devil's food."

I drifted towards the front, peering through the main door, propped open a few inches with a wedge-shaped wooden doorstop. Eileen and Woo-sung sat on the kerbside bench, under the fading daylight. They weren't holding hands, weren't even looking at each other, but I saw Eileen's lips move. And Woo-sung nodded.

Then, behind me, the interior door opened.

Mr Lee came through, headphones still in his hand.

He looked at each of us. Then he eased his arm forward, offering me the headphones.

I took them.

And he bowed. Not from the waist, not as deep as Jun had bowed to him, but a lingering bow of the head.

Respectful.

Necessary.

He didn't speak. He stepped outside into the soft evening light, and stood beside Mick's car.

I turned back to the interior door. It had swung closed again, and Jun hadn't come through it.

I didn't need to be told this time. I pulled the door open and stepped into the corridor. Seven Juns greeted me on the wall, the row of monitors looping through his farewell speech.

And one Jun stood near the end, hands at his sides, face unreadable.

I walked to him.

"Jun?"

He inhaled, chest rising, and he held it for a minute.

Then he signed, *I can stay.*

I didn't react. Not at first. Jun wasn't smiling, and because of that, my brain took longer to register the sign.

He said it again. Slowly.

And at last, I dragged him into a hug.

He fell against me, weak with relief.

And before we kissed, I felt the soft whisper of his smile against my lips.

CHAPTER 37

The door behind us cracked open. When I turned my head, Ryan and Mia were peering through the narrow gap.

"It's okay," I whispered, and they pushed the door wide.

They hovered at the end of the corridor until Ryan said, "Well?"

Jun kept his face against my neck. I felt his heart hammering on my chest.

I nodded. "We did it."

Jun's shoulders shook. But when I tilted his face to me, he wasn't crying. He was laughing, full of nervous energy.

Ryan whooped. Mia let out a scream. And suddenly we were surrounded by everybody, Mum and Mick included, while Jun's looping signs played on the monitors above us.

"Oh my God," they said.

"Fantastic news," they said.

"Jesus H. Christ," Ryan laughed. "I nearly peed myself."

Mia smacked his arm. "I told you to bring a change of undies." Then she hugged him.

At the end of the corridor, Callum shouted, "Pizza!" like he'd won the World Cup.

We laughed. And because we couldn't stay at the community centre any longer—we'd already outstayed our welcome—Mum said, "Everybody back to ours."

That's how I found myself on the couch, sitting beside Jun, gripping his hand so tight that I don't think I could have let go if I'd wanted to.

Mick had driven Eileen, Woo-sung and Mr Lee home. Before they left, Woo-sung spoke with Jun. I didn't know what they were saying, but before turning away, Woo-sung slipped his hands back into his pockets and dipped his head, drawing a close to their conversation.

Jun made one final motion with his hands, and when they were gone, I asked, "What was that sign? What'd you say at the end?"

He thought for a minute, then fingerspelled it in ISL. *H-Y-U-N-G.*

Brother.

He took my hand without waiting for me to search for his, and I gave his fingers a squeeze.

That night, Mum's kitchen filled with people, with friends. I stood near the sink, watching Jun at the table, sitting in Grandad Tommy's chair, signing something to Ella. I couldn't stop smiling, even when Mum nudged my shoulder with hers, mug of tea in hand, and said, "He looks comfortable there."

I kept my eyes on Jun. "Yeah."

On the wall behind him, there was a photograph. Grandad Tommy and me when I was three or four, sitting on his lap, laughing at whatever silly thing he'd said, one of his famous jokes.

Mum leaned in again. "You should invite him to dinner on Friday."

I didn't answer her. I was too busy watching Jun, his face bright with laughter. Right then, I was just grateful we would have a Friday together at all.

When people started to leave, after the sun had gone down, Jun and I stood on the doorstep, my arm tight around his waist, exchanging hugs and handshakes.

Sean said, "Now you have a reason to keep learning ISL. No excuses. I'll see you after the summer break."

"I wouldn't miss it," I said.

Ella hugged us both, kissing our cheeks. "I haven't cried this much in all my life. I love you guys."

Paulie clapped our backs, and Callum pulled Jun into a hug, then turned to me, scowled, and hugged me with a grin.

Ryan and Mia were the last to leave. We stood with them in the garden, four friends, two couples, not needing any words. Mia kissed me, then Jun.

When they were on the other side of the garden gate, Ryan stopped her.

"Wait," he said, hand on the latch. "Aren't we supposed to run the exhibition for two more days?"

"Shit," I said. I hadn't been thinking past today, past Mr Lee.

"I'll call the others," Ryan said. "Mia, hand me the bat

phone."

We watched them walk up the street.

When we were alone, Jun signed, *You're coming with me tomorrow?*

"Try and stop me," I said. "They can handle the exhibition without us."

The kitchen smelled like stone-baked pizza when we went back inside. Mum and Mick had tidied up, tossing the empty boxes, and they were sitting at the kitchen table. Mum had her mug of tea; Mick nursed a bottle of beer and was shuffling a deck of cards.

"You want in?" he asked.

I gave Jun a questioning look.

Isn't it late? he signed.

When I translated, Mick grinned. "You don't have school tomorrow. Why don't you stay over?"

"On the sofa," Mum added, the smallest hint of a smile on her lips.

And I blushed.

We sat at the table. "What are we playing?"

"Hearts," Mick said, dealing us in. "Do you know how to play?" He gave us a quick rundown of the rules, and I translated what I could, stumbling over words like "clubs" and "ace".

When I finished, Jun lifted his cards, glanced at them, and signed, *If I win, you have to kiss me on my special place.*

"What?" Mum asked, leaning forward, smile widening. "What'd he say?"

I looked at my cards, cheeks glowing like a campfire.

And Mick chuckled. "Something rude, by the look of it."

I didn't look up for the rest of the game, but out of the

corner of my eye, I saw Jun's shoulders shaking with his silent laugh.

In the morning, we ate breakfast together, and Mick drove Jun home. The house was quiet without him, even though he wasn't noisy.

I sat on the sofa where he'd laid his head the night before, and I worried at the corner tassel on a scatter cushion until, at eleven a.m., Mick said, "It's time."

He drove me to Jun's house and Mr Lee and Woo-sung were already there with their suitcases in the garden, slotting them into the boot of Eileen's car.

As I passed, Woo-sung said, "You. Help."

I narrowed my eyes, ready for a fight. But he cracked his face into a smile. It was huge and fake, but he was trying. I lifted the heavy end of his suitcase and helped to wedge it into the car.

And on the way to the airport, Eileen driving, Mr Lee in the front, Woo-sung, Jun and I squeezed into the back, with Jun in the middle. He dropped his hand between our legs so he could hold mine.

His fingers were warm, but they were loose, as if he was ready to let go at any second.

"Radio?" Eileen asked as we hit the motorway.

"No," Mr Lee said.

She turned it on anyway, and I looked through the window instead of meeting her eyes in the rearview mirror.

She reversed into a bay in the short-stay carpark, and I trailed behind them with Jun as we crossed the busy walkway and into the terminal, one hand in mine, the other in his pocket. He'd barely said anything since this morning.

I squeezed his fingers. Signed, *You all right?*

He blinked at me but didn't answer, and then we waited while Mr Lee and Woo-sung checked their bags in at the desk.

Jun pulled something from his pocket—his own ticket— and a sudden panic flooded through my veins. The breath caught in my chest like a stab wound. But he raised it in both hands, holding it out to his father.

Mr Lee took it. Considered it. Crumpled it.

Sorry, Jun signed in ISL. Then he said something in KSL—the same word, I figured.

Mr Lee scratched the two-day-old stubble on his cheeks and turned from him, scanning the departure screen for his flight.

IX703 DUB-ICN 15:00. PROCEED TO GATE 407.

Eileen drew Woo-sung into her arms and held him for the longest time. "Come visit soon," she said.

In English, he told her, "When Jun-ho comes to forfeit military service."

I'd almost forgotten. One day, when Jun turned eighteen, he'd have to go back to Korea anyway. He'd be exempt from mandatory service, but foreign medical records wouldn't be enough. He'd need to fly there for a consultation. But we'd worry about that when the time came.

Jun and I stepped back to let Woo-sung and Eileen have their goodbyes. I gripped his hand, watching the slow-moving queue of people going through security. Then I noticed Mr Lee watching us.

"Jun-ho," Woo-sung said.

Jun slipped his hand out of mine so he could go to his

brother, and I'd never felt so lonely in my life, standing there, watching them talk in Korean sign language.

Mr Lee raised his hand, twitched a finger at me, telling me to come to him. But my feet wouldn't move, so he stepped closer.

He put his hands in his trouser pockets, his suit jacket bunching around his arms.

When he spoke, his words were clipped. "You have great influence over my son."

I looked at Jun who was sharing a group hug with Eileen and Woo-sung. And to Mr Lee, I said, "No. We influence each other."

He stared, for longer than I'd like, and then he nodded.

He turned from me, picked up his carry-on bag, and spoke briefly with Jun. I'm going to have to learn Korean just to understand these secret conversations.

Before they got in the queue to pass through security, Mr Lee stood close to Eileen. While he talked, she folded her arms. She nodded a few times, shook her head, and then watched as he entered the queue without shaking her hand or hugging her.

Jun waved. Bowed.

And ten minutes later, they passed beyond the security gate and out of sight, while the queue continued to snake behind them.

Eileen touched her face, then her neck. She smiled at me and tugged Jun into a quiet embrace. And when she released him, she said, "Let's go home."

I nodded.

We walked back through the busy terminal to the exit,

and Jun pressed his body against me while Eileen pushed her carparking ticket into the payment machine. I felt his hands on my back, smoothing across my shoulder blades, and his lips brushed quietly over my skin. He hummed against my cheek where I felt his vibrations. And I wanted to hold him forever.

But Eileen said, "Ready?"

He pulled out of my embrace, and when we stood outside the terminal in the crosswind, an airplane rose into the sky behind us.

Jun closed his eyes, spread his hands at his sides, and he stood there, feeling the airport. Hearing it inside him.

Eileen nodded. Turned from us.

I slipped my hand into Jun's, standing beside him. I closed my eyes and thought about Grandad Tommy. About how he used to say artists don't see with their eyes—they see with their hearts. This was the same. Jun and I, we were hearing with something else. Something deep.

I felt the burr of the planes. The rattle of suitcase wheels on the concrete. The pull of the air as the automatic doors opened and closed behind us. The exhaust fumes on my legs from a travel coach. The drum of a million feet. A breath of wind.

And I felt Jun beside me.

Solid.

Whole.

Mine.

We didn't speak. There was no need.

The silence was all we had. It was everything we needed.

Find Simon Online

simondoylebooks.com